COLD FIRE

OTHER WORKS BY DUSTIN STEVENS

Quarterback
Be My Eyes
Scars and Stars
Catastrophic
21 Hours
Ohana
Twelve
Liberation Day
Just a Game
Ink
Four
Motive

The Zoo Crew Novels

Tracer
Dead Peasants
The Zoo Crew

COLD FIRE

A THRILLER

DUSTIN STEVENS

THOMAS & MERCER

Text copyright © 2014, 2015 by Dustin Stevens
All rights reserved.

Published by Thomas & Mercer, Seattle

www.apub.com

Amazon, the Amazon logo, and Thomas & Mercer are trademarks of Amazon.com, Inc., or its affiliates.

ISBN-13: 9781477830062
ISBN-10: 1477830065

Cover design by David Drummond

Library of Congress Control Number: 2014958623

Printed in the United States of America

For my parents.

It is better to conquer yourself than to win a thousand battles. Then the victory is yours. It cannot be taken from you, not by angels or by demons, heaven or hell.

—*Buddha*

PART I

Every time I closed my eyes, it was the same damn dream.

After six weeks on the road, slogging through some of the worst shit this world had to offer, I just wanted to be home. Sleep in a bed with an actual mattress. Eat food that wasn't prepackaged or freeze-dried. Hold something close to me that didn't have a firing pin and a full magazine.

The thoughts filled my head as I drove southeast out of San Diego, the late-day sun just a sliver above the horizon behind me. It threw the shadow of my beat-up pickup out onto the blacktop in front of my tires, an ominous black cloak preceding my arrival.

My mood was upbeat, jovial even. I had long since shed my sport coat and tie, rolling the sleeves of my dress shirt to the elbows. I leaned forward and blasted the radio as I tore down a desolate stretch of California highway, "Free Bird" piping in through the speakers. Throat stripped raw from weeks in the desert sand, I tapped out a drum solo with my thumbs against the black leather of the steering wheel, playing along to the beat.

The first thing that hit me was the smell.

There is simply no logical explanation for how that happened. I should have seen the glow against the darkening evening sky, or at least the smoke rising up in charcoal curlicues, but I didn't.

Instead I noticed the scent. The undeniable, acrid aroma of smoke dancing across the breeze. Even with my reduced sense of smell, it was unmistakable.

My first thought was somebody was having a barbecue, squeezing in a few more moments of summer before the calendar turned to November and the desert chill settled in for the year. The thought lingered for almost a mile before my mind pieced together where I was, too far from anywhere for a simple cookout to be detected.

Right then, in that moment, the first tiny spark of doubt ignited in the back of my mind. I had no reason to believe anything was wrong, no evidence that a single whiff was about to turn my world upside down, but somehow I knew.

Whether that was the case at the time, or it was the reconstruction my mind created after replaying the scene for five long years, there was no way of knowing.

Reaching out, I switched off the radio and took up my cell phone from the cup holder on the middle console. I flipped it open and pressed the first speed dial. The line cut straight to voice mail, and the automated voice told me the person I was trying to reach was unavailable.

I snapped the phone shut before the automaton had a chance to finish, and I leaned on the gas a little harder. That tiny spark in the back of my mind grew into an ember as I drove, the moisture fleeing my mouth, the taste of desperation settling in.

My aging rig passed over eighty-five miles an hour as a battered green roadside sign flew by on the right shoulder. I'd seen it enough times to know it was informing me that Tecate, California, was two miles away, the United States–Mexican border crossing a mile farther than that.

None of that mattered, though. I wasn't going as far as either one.

The smell grew stronger as I drove. It was laced with the smell of charred meat that bordered on roasted pork. The aroma flitted across my nostrils, disappearing just as fast while I sped forward into the encroaching night.

Behind me, the last bit of the sun slid beneath the horizon, the tiny orange arc disappearing from my rearview mirror. The world around me grew darker, the shadow of my truck less pronounced on the road, as the first stars peeked out overhead.

It wasn't until that moment that I noticed the glow.

It began as just a small orange orb, rising no more than a few inches above the earth. Not until the last bit of sun was gone did it grow strong enough to draw my attention, pulling my gaze south.

My stomach constricted itself into a tight ball, and my right foot nudged farther down toward the floorboard. The V-6 engine whined in protest as the truck pushed on toward a hundred. I kept my attention aimed out the right side of my windshield.

I had never been a religious man. I had nothing against God, or Buddha, or Allah, or any other being that might be out there. I'd just never given the time or energy to figure out what any of them were all about, and without that I didn't see the point in casting my lot with them.

In that moment, though, feeling my palms grow sweaty, having the air pulled out of my lungs, I prayed. I prayed long and hard. I pushed the words out with every ounce of sincerity I could muster, calling on every higher being I'd ever heard of.

I asked all of them to please not let me be right. To make me look like the biggest, most paranoid fool that had ever walked the earth for even thinking such a thing.

To not make my family pay for the sins of my past.

And every damn time, as if my mind, or all those higher beings I called on, or some unknown cosmic force I had yet to even consider, wanted to remind me of what had happened, of what I had said, the things I had promised, that was when I woke up.

Why that was, I had long since stopped trying to figure out, my body no longer able to take the exhaustion that came with it. If there was some overarching story, some life lesson, that it was meant to impart, I guess it was lost on me, because after five years, there was still only one thing I could think every morning when I woke up, the sheets wet beneath me with sweat, my heartbeat racing.

Lot of damn good it did me.

Chapter One

"You folks have a nice trip back," I said, pushing the tailgate on their SUV closed. The bulging pile of gear crammed into the rear space resisted a bit against the door as it went, and the latch only caught halfway.

"And maybe come a little earlier next year, before it gets too cold," I added with a smile, releasing the gate and slamming it shut once more. This time the myriad of bags and coolers inside were no match, the articles jostling about as the rear hatch locked into place.

"We'll do that," the driver said, an affable man in his late forties who had insisted all week that I call him JP. Why a man his age would insist on going by that instead of some variation of his given Jon Paul I had no idea, but it wasn't my place to judge.

The family had paid top dollar and gotten along reasonably well on our five-day excursion, which was about the best I could have asked for. By late in the trip they did start to complain a fair bit about the weather, but I'd anticipated that when they booked it.

People from Florida just aren't cut out for Yellowstone in October.

"Thank you again for everything," JP said, pausing by the driver's-side door. His family, a wife and two kids, were already stowed inside, no doubt holding their hands up to the vents blasting warm air as fast as the registers would allow.

"Thank you," I said, raising my hand in farewell. "I appreciate your business."

JP returned the gesture, nodded once for emphasis, and climbed inside. I could hear the fan on the heater whirring as it pushed heat through the car. Everyone hunkered low in their winter gear. It was a scenario I'd seen a hundred times before. They'd be as far north as Bozeman before any of them realized they were riding in a sauna.

I waited until their taillights disappeared from view before turning and surveying the building that housed my business. The fact that it was still standing and in one piece was a good sign, something I learned long ago not to take for granted.

A single story tall and constructed of flat-front pine boards, the entire structure was painted dark brown, the door and windows trimmed out in forest green. A rough-hewn wooden sign stretched across most of the roof, the same dark brown color inlaid with green letters.

HAWK'S EYE VIEWS:
WEST YELLOWSTONE'S FAVORITE PRIVATE GUIDE

Slightly less than modest, perhaps, but in a market as saturated as Yellowstone in the summer, being humble didn't pay the bills.

Gravel crunched beneath my feet as I walked across the front lot and up the three stairs leading to the door. A small bell hanging from the ceiling jangled as I stepped in, and a rush of warm air hit me in the face.

"Just a minute," a familiar voice called from the back.

The entire front part of the building was one open room. A waist-high wooden counter ran most of the way across it, framed by doorways on either end. To the left was the restroom, a simple affair with a toilet and sink. On the right was my office, taking up the rear half of the building.

The smell of fresh coffee drew my attention toward the wall, leading me to a half-full pot still sitting on the burner. Grabbing a Styrofoam cup from the stack, I filled it with straight black, guzzled down half of it, then refilled it.

"Take your time, Kaylan," I said, returning the pot to its place. I wasn't sure what she was doing back in my office, but after three years together, I trusted her enough not to care.

The floorboards creaked beneath my weight as I crossed over to the front counter and leaned against it, taking another swig of coffee. The brew was black as motor oil and tasted much the same, exactly the way we both took it.

"Hey, Hawk," Kaylan said, bustling out of the side door, a pencil stuck behind her ear. A bundle of messy curls was piled atop her head, and the sleeves of her green sweater were bunched up to her elbows. Even in boots she came no more than a few inches above five feet tall, her body graced with just a couple of extra pounds. She pulled the door shut behind her as she went, and it closed against the wooden jamb with a bang.

"Hey, Kay," I said, "what's going on?"

"How'd it go with the Olsons?" Kay asked, ignoring my question. She tossed the pencil down on the desk and settled heavily into her chair, letting out an audible sigh as she went.

"It was good," I said, which was mostly the truth.

"Two kids, disinterested mother, father trying way too hard for the perfect vacation," Kaylan said, rattling off the list as she had done an infinite number of times before. "Had all the makings of a disaster on your hands."

"Oh, I know it. I believe I even said that to you as we were leaving."

One side of Kaylan's mouth curled up at being caught parroting my own words back to me, though we both let it slide.

"So?" she pressed.

I finished off the last of my coffee and crossed over to the pot to pour myself another. "It really was okay. The kids were pretty into it, got along much better than most adolescent boy-girl pairings. The parents, too. The only thing that tripped them up was the cold."

"Ahh," Kaylan said, rocking her head back. "I actually thought about that last night when it got down in the low thirties."

I made my way back to the counter and tilted my head an inch to the side, feigning flattery. "Aw, you were worried about me?"

"You? God, no," Kaylan said, letting out a snort. "I was concerned for them, being from Orlando and all."

"Right," I said, swirling the dark liquid in my cup and taking another drink. She was absolutely correct, and we both knew it. After five years on the job, cold just wasn't something that got to me anymore. "How's the year-end stuff coming along?"

Kaylan raised her eyebrows at me and said, "Well, I don't think we're quite there yet, Boss."

I cast a glance at the West Yellowstone National Bank calendar hanging on the wall, red X's crossing out everything up to the twenty-fourth of the month. "What do you mean not quite there yet? Next week is Halloween. And like you said, it's getting damn cold at night."

"Hey, not my doing," Kaylan said, raising her hands by her side before hooking a thumb at the wall behind her. "Talk to the crazy lady in your office right now about it."

I opened my mouth to respond, but stopped just as quickly and looked at her. Taking on the Olsons at such a late date was pretty rare, exceedingly so in a year where winter seemed poised to arrive at any moment.

"There's someone in there now?" I asked, letting my surprise show on my face, in my voice.

"Why do you think the door's shut?" she asked.

"I don't know," I said. "Thought maybe you needed to give your boyfriend a chance to escape through the window."

Kaylan's head rolled back an inch in a smirk as she stared at me. "If that was you trying to ask if I'm single, the answer is yes."

Despite her being just six years younger than me, I often failed to see Kaylan as anything other than a kid. While her twenty-eight to my thirty-four didn't seem like much in terms of years, we were much further apart than that in life experience.

"What's she want?" I asked, pushing right past Kaylan's statement. She stared at me a long moment, knowing full well what I'd done, before shaking her head. "A guide, of course. Something about her brother went camping and hasn't checked in for a few days."

A look somewhere between a grimace and a sneer crossed my face as I pushed myself away from the counter. "You tell her we're done for the year?"

"I did."

"And?" I asked, finishing the coffee in my cup and dropping it into the trash can at my feet.

"And she made a very compelling offer," Kaylan said.

"Doesn't matter," I replied. "The Olsons were the last run of the season. It's been a good year, but I'll be glad to get off my feet for a while."

"That may be," Kaylan said, dipping the top of her head in agreement, "but I figured I would at least give you the right to refuse her."

My brow furrowed as I walked slowly around the front of the desk, my fingertips dragging along behind me. "Meaning?"

"Just trust me," Kaylan said, twisting the base of her chair to track my movement. "You're going to at least want to hear this one out."

Chapter Two

Kaylan and I had a running joke: The only way we would ever take a client before May 15 or after October 15 was if they made us an offer so ridiculous we would be fools to refuse it.

I don't know why, but for some reason that came to mind as I pushed through the closed door into my office. She hadn't said those exact words, hadn't given any true indication that was what she meant, but I couldn't shake the feeling that was what I was about to encounter.

Three steps inside I realized I was wrong.

Standing behind my desk was a woman I was quite certain I had never seen before, the kind of woman I doubt anybody in West Yellowstone had ever seen before.

She seemed to be no more than four or five inches shorter than me, which made her at least five-ten. Long hair hung past her shoulders, and her hands were shoved into the pockets of jeans that hugged shapely legs. A black leather jacket and matching knee-high boots completed the look.

On first impression, she could have been anything from a biker chick to a supermodel.

"Can I help you?" I asked, shrugging the coat off my shoulders. I caught it alongside my waist and tossed it on the freestanding rack in the corner, the brown fabric of my coat blending in with the wood of the coatrack.

At the sound of my voice, she turned away from the bookshelf she'd been studying intently. She gave me a quick once-over, her gaze traveling to the floor and back in a fraction of a second before an oversized smile stretched across her face.

Perfect teeth, framed by full lips and a pert nose. The only thing at all that seemed out of place on her was a thin scar above her left eye.

"Hello," she said, circling out away from my desk and extending a hand in front of her. From just a single word I could detect a hint of an accent, and despite her appearance it was definitely nothing from the Western Hemisphere, more along the lines of the old Eastern Bloc.

Bulgaria. Albania, maybe.

"Good afternoon," I said, reciprocating the handshake, her grip firm within mine. "Hawk."

Her brow furrowed in confusion a moment as I released the handshake. "My name. Please, call me Hawk."

"And I am Lita," she replied. The English was smooth coming out, though again I could tell by her word choice and sentence formation it was not her first language.

She pointed to a certificate hanging on the wall and said, "I thought your name was Jeremiah? Jeremiah Tate?"

I smiled and walked around my desk, pulling out the faded brown leather chair from behind it. "Please, sit," I said, extending a hand to a matching seat across from me.

She did so, the chair wheezing as she settled down into it.

"My full name is Jeremiah Hawkens Tate," I said. "My father was a big *Jeremiah Johnson* fan. But everybody has always just called me Hawk."

The top of Lita's head rocked back slightly in understanding. "And here I thought this was a nickname you'd received based on your expertise as a guide."

"Well, it doesn't hurt, that's for sure," I said, offering her a small smirk. "Anything to get folks in the door, right?"

Once more Lita flashed the oversized smile at me, a jack-o'-lantern grin that seemed to stretch from one ear to the other. "It got me, so there you go."

"So what can I do for you, Lita?" I asked, leaning back and lacing my fingers across my stomach. The springs on my chair moaned just slightly as I reclined, my weight shifting into a comfortable position.

The smile vanished with the question. Lita cast a quick glance back to the bookshelf she'd been studying when I walked in, her top teeth sliding out over her bottom lip. "I would like to hire you for two, maybe three days."

"I'm very sorry—" I began, already poised to launch into my standard denial speech.

"It's my brother," she pushed out, a look of concern crossing her features. "He came up here to go camping a week ago, and we haven't heard a word from him in four days."

I paused a moment, my mind switching gears from the prefabricated talk I had on tap. Every year there were a few stragglers that came and tried to make one last run, seasonal hazards be damned.

The first season I had caved and made the trip.

Never again.

"When were you expecting him back?" I asked.

"Not for a few more days," Lita said, glancing down at her hands folded in her lap. "But he knew he was supposed to call every day and let us know he was okay."

I held a hand up to stop her. For the briefest of moments I had thought maybe she had a legit concern, but it had passed just as fast.

"You have to realize, Yellowstone Park is over 3,500 square miles, almost all of it considered backcountry. No phone reception, no Internet access, nothing. Just because he hasn't checked in for a few days doesn't mean anything." A lot of the people I worked with didn't realize just how remote the park was. They were used to living in big cities, where pitching a tent in the backyard or having less than three bars of cell service was considered roughing it.

"But he made sure to call frequently the first part of his trip," Lita pressed, shaking her head from side to side, her hair brushing the tops of her shoulders. "And then, nothing. He's a careful man, would never worry our mother like that. Something must be wrong."

I remained motionless and drew in a deep breath through my nose. This wasn't the first worried relative to ever cross my doorstep, and the odds were it wouldn't be the last. Most of the time they weren't actually looking for my services, but for someone to tell them everything was OK.

"Like I said, there aren't that many places in the park with reception. My guess is he's just camping somewhere off the grid and didn't want to hike out every day to make a call."

Again Lita shook her head. "But he had a satellite phone. He could have made the call from anywhere."

I stared back at her a long moment before raising my chair to vertical and twisting it to the side. Unlacing my fingers, I dug through the desk drawer on my left and extracted a map of Yellowstone, spreading it atop the desk.

"Do you know where he was going?"

Lita dug into her coat pocket and removed a single piece of folded white paper from it. A series of numbers were scribbled out on it in black ink, four different sets written one below the other.

"The last coordinates he gave me were 44.2678°N, 110.4889°W," she said, reading from the sheet. "Do you know where this is?"

After five years of making a living scouring the park, I knew the coordinates for every major landmark from memory. Still, these were foreign even to me.

Running a hand down along the side of the map I found the latitude she'd given me, then passed a finger along it until I'd found the corresponding longitude.

"Huh," I said, leaning back and studying the outcome.

"What?" Lita asked, looking from me to the map and back again.

"Heart Lake," I said. "If he's down there, it's no wonder you're not hearing much out of him."

"Why? Is this a bad area?" Lita asked, concern rising in her voice.

The corners of my mouth curled up at the question, a small snort sliding from my nose. "Well, there is no such thing as a *bad area* here, at least not as you might be used to it. This isn't Southeast D.C. or East LA or anything.

"I'm just surprised is all. Heart Lake is pretty well off the beaten path, a good thirty-five miles from Old Faithful, the closest tourist attraction by far."

Across from me Lita lowered her gaze back to the map. I could see her tracing out the route as she stared at it, starting at Old Faithful and working her way down from there.

"So why do people go there?" she asked.

"For the most part? Because they don't want to be found," I replied. "See that road there? That's US 287, the only road through that entire part of the park. There are a couple of smaller dirt roads that are open in the summertime, but this time of year? The only way to get to Heart Lake is park along the highway and hoof it in."

Lita's eyes grew a touch bigger as she glanced from me to the map again. "You mean walk? How far is it?"

"More like hike," I corrected. "And given that the coordinates he gave you are on the back side of the lake, probably ten miles or more. All backcountry."

Things weren't really as bad as I was making them out to be; it was just that the thought of leading an obvious city girl on a twenty-mile round-trip through dense forest was less than appealing. I still hadn't unpacked the truck from the Olson trip. There was no way I was about to hold her hand on an unnecessary rescue mission.

"So when can we go?" she asked, snapping her head back up from the map and leaning back in her chair.

"Excuse me?" I said, my eyes widening in surprise.

"To Heart Lake," Lita pressed. "When can we go?"

I reached out and pulled the map toward me, folding it slowly to buy myself a second. I waited until it was all put away before looking at her and saying, "Look, I can respect the concern you have for your brother. I really can. But if he is down at Heart Lake, it's because he wanted to be left alone. I'm sure everything is fine."

Lita stared at me a long moment, the concern in her face receding to a hard visage. "I'm glad you can feel that way, but I simply can't. If something has happened to him and I don't go help, I will never be able to look at myself in the mirror again."

A feeling of dread started to roil within me. Most of the time, simple logic was enough to assuage these people. Every once in a while, though, somebody took things personally, got a little ugly.

This had all the earmarks of turning into the latter.

"Look, Lita—"

"I can pay you," she spat, cutting me off before I had a chance to protest any further. "Twenty thousand, cash."

The feeling of dread evaporated, replaced by shock. Twenty grand was almost ten times my going rate for a trip of this length. I kept my face completely impassive as I stared back at her, forcing air in and out through my nose.

"Really, this isn't about money," I said. "This late in the season, at that elevation—"

"Fifty," Lita said, inserting herself again before I could finish.

Fifty thousand dollars was in the neighborhood of what I had made in June and July combined. That kind of money would keep me in the black for years to come. Put a new roof on my winter cabin. Maybe even ensure that I wasn't still doing this at the age of seventy.

A dozen questions entered my mind at once, ranging from how she had that kind of cash on hand to did she realize she could get the guys down the road to do it for a quarter of that?

Still, I let every one of them pass.

"Meet me here tomorrow morning at seven."

Lita nodded in understanding and left without another word, leaving me seated behind my desk, trying to process what had just taken place. A moment later Kaylan popped her head into the room, a smug smile on her face.

"So, what happened?" she asked.

"Ridiculous showed up," I replied, drawing a knowing grin from her as she disappeared back the way she'd come.

Chapter Three

The engine of my pickup ticked in the silence of the morning as I spread a map across the front hood. A slight tendril of steam could be seen rising from the grille into the cold air, the mist disintegrating within a few inches as it rose.

"Okay," I said, pointing a finger at the western edge of the image. "As you can see, the roads of the park are laid out in a basic figure eight. We started over here in West Yellowstone at the midpoint and came down around the bottom half. When we got past Old Faithful we headed due south about twenty miles to here."

I marked the position on the map for her with one hand and pointed to a wooden sign with yellow letters affixed to a fence in front of us. "And now we are here, at the Red Mountain trailhead."

"Mhmm," Lita said, giving me a nod. So far on the morning she had said about fifteen words total, most of them two syllables or less. She wasn't quite surly, but the strain of the situation was clearly wearing on her.

She seemed worried, on the verge of desperation.

I'd been there myself, so I let it slide. It's amazing what the thought of losing a loved one can do to somebody's psyche.

"We have two choices," I said, swapping out the larger road map for a small topographical. Folded back to display the area we were in, it was gridded with various lines marking out river flows and changes in elevations. Striped across it in bright red were the various trails that covered the region, traversing it in a misshapen pattern like veins on a forearm.

"We can follow the northern route, which is about twelve miles in total. It's pretty flat, follows that dirt road over there most of the way."

I gestured with my chin toward a two-track path that extended away from the parking lot, a metal gate across it announcing the road was closed for the season.

"The southern route is a bit more tricky," I said, outlining the other option. "It goes up and over Mount Sheridan, but is only about eight, eight and a half, miles total."

"Let's take the southern route," Lita said, her voice firm.

I glanced up from the map and gave her a quick once-over. She had traded out the leather jacket and boots for a black down parka and hiking treads, both of which looked like she'd removed the tags from them that morning. A knit cap covered most of her hair, and insulated mittens swung from straps at the cuffs of her coat.

Her attire didn't worry me.

What did was the single duffel bag she had tossed over a shoulder. No larger than something I would have taken to the gym in a different life, it couldn't have held more than a change of clothes and some dried food. Maybe a bottle of water.

Nothing near what would be needed to ascend a mountain in late October.

I glanced over at Lita before turning my back to the truck and staring off into the distance. "Maybe you're not properly appreciating what we're looking at, given how close we are to it, but Mount Sheridan is a ten-thousand-foot peak. Even from where we're now standing, that's an elevation change of six grand and a temperature drop of probably twenty degrees."

Lita stared up at the mountain a moment before shifting her attention back to me. Her face was void of emotion as she looked over, her eyes revealing nothing. "So?"

"Don't let the eight-mile part fool you—it will take most of the day," I said, incredulity sifting into my voice. "And the gear I brought is best suited for a night at six thousand feet, not at elevation."

My argument seemed to have little effect on her. "I've walked farther than sixteen miles in a day before. Two years ago I ran a marathon in under four hours."

"I don't doubt that," I said, raising my eyebrows, fighting to keep my voice under control, "but I bet you did it at sea level in seventy-five-degree weather, didn't you?"

She looked at me a long moment before turning away, confirming I was right. She stood stock still before sniffing the air and taking two steps away from the truck.

"My brother will have supplies where he is. I will stay in his tent tonight. And we're surrounded by water. It will be fine."

Lightbulbs flashed bright warning signs inside my head as I stood and looked at her standing away from the truck, refusing to glance my direction. I had no reason to believe she was anything other than a concerned sister determined to reach her brother, but I couldn't shake the feeling that something wasn't quite right.

The woman I had met yesterday had faded, taking with her a great deal of the warmth and compassion that had persuaded me to take the job. In their place was a steely resolve, the kind of resolute determination that could get us both killed.

As if reading my mind, she turned her head to face me. "Please, Hawk, I've come a long way to find my brother. I have to make it the last eight miles."

For whatever reason, I couldn't tell her no.

I remember what I had once been like when I was on a mission, determined to find someone I'd long thought missing. No amount of hiking, no mountain, no lack of drinking water would stand in my way.

If this woman needed to find her brother, I would help her.

"Okay," I said, folding up the map and stowing it in my pocket. I hefted the pack to one shoulder and slid my other arm through the strap, cinching it into place across my chest. In total I had enough gear for three days, the sum weight of it just over twenty-five pounds.

Seeing her so ill equipped already had me wishing I'd brought more.

"But no drinking the water along the way. Every drop in this park is sulfuric. The last thing I want is to have to carry you out of here."

Chapter Four

Two hours passed in almost total silence, no words shared between us save the occasional direction from me, the grunt of response from Lita. For her part, she did an excellent job of keeping up. At thirty-four years old and a full-time guide, I was used to the elevation and strenuous nature of hiking. There was probably no way I could run a marathon or hop on a treadmill and pound out miles at an 8.0 clip, but I knew I could walk up and down hills in the park all day long.

Because of that, I was always careful with the pace I kept. Most folks, even the ones who worked out on a regular basis, were in no way prepared for the task of trekking in the backcountry. The inclines were too steep, the air too thin, the loads too heavy to ever re-create and prepare for.

Despite that, Lita stayed three steps behind me the entire way. Each time I suggested a shortcut through rough terrain she jumped at the opportunity, always intent on getting there as fast as we could. Behind me I could hear her breath coming in even draws, never rising to the point of panting.

"Where did you say you were from?" I asked, picking my way over a felled log slashing across the trail before us. Little more than a footpath used by game, it was just wide enough for my boots. The ground was packed hard beneath them.

A long moment passed as Lita scrambled over the tree behind me, her mittens still swinging free by her sides. "Mexico," she replied.

"Mexico? Really?" I asked, keeping my tone light and even. Nothing about her accent said Mexican to me. Even the way she spoke English, formed her sentences, didn't remind me of someone with a Spanish-speaking background.

Ahead of me I could see the precipice of Mount Sheridan was less than a half mile away. After walking in silence all morning I wanted to get her talking, to put her in a better state of mind about what we might find on the other side. Doing that meant ignoring whatever inconsistencies her story contained.

The odds were, my earlier assessment was right. Her brother had just walked off and wanted to be alone for a while.

On the off chance that wasn't the case, I wanted to make sure she was okay before we got there. If not, the sight of whatever we might find could push her into a state of catatonia.

Trying to wrestle her back down the mountain in such a condition was not something I would particularly look forward to.

"No, no," Lita said. "*New* Mexico. The state."

"Ahh," I said, glancing back over my shoulder at her, trying my best to appear engaged. If my memory served, less than 5 percent of the state was non-Mexican immigrants. It still wasn't impossible that she was telling me the truth, but it was growing quite unlikely. "Nice country down that way."

"You've been there?" Lita asked, her tone a bit lighter. I couldn't tell if she cared at all or was just going through the motions, but at the very least she was starting to interact.

"Spent some time there," I said, the answer not the entire truth, but close enough. "Down near the border."

"Hmm," Lita replied. "We are from a little farther north."

Overhead, the first puffs of dark clouds started to appear. Reflexively my stomach clenched at the sight of them, the telltale sign that a winter storm wouldn't be far behind. Set against a background sky the color of milk, they rolled in one after another, dark blobs the shade of lead.

At the sight of them I picked up my pace a half step. The top of Mount Sheridan was just a few hundred yards away.

"What do you guys do down there?" I asked.

"We all work in the family business," Lita said, matching my pace stride for stride. "I run the warehouse. My brother is the bookkeeper."

"Ah," I said again, nodding my head. "Agriculture?"

"Yes," Lita replied. "Green chilies."

I grunted in response as the trail widened out. The angle of ascent diminished before us as we slowed our pace, coming to a stop on the apex of the mountain. From where we stood we had a 360-degree view of the world around us, our bodies being at the highest point for ten miles in any direction.

Spinning on the ball of my foot, I turned back the way we had come. I swept a hand back over my head, pulling away a stocking cap, shaggy hair falling down in front of my eyes.

There was a time I wouldn't have dreamed of letting it get that long. Now, I had no intention of cutting it until spring, when the return of business required me to look semipresentable at all times.

"Wow," Lita said, the first word all morning that sounded sincere. "I now see why you didn't stay in New Mexico."

A wan smile crossed my lips as I stared down at the sprawl of green stretching out from us. Mountainsides carpeted with lush pines, punctuated by the occasional riverbed knifing through it, their waters laced with white fingers from scouring over rocks and tree roots.

"Something like that," I said, sliding the cap back onto my head and turning to face forward.

Up ahead, the back side of Mount Sheridan sloped away toward Heart Lake, a body of water named for the shape it took, nestled down between us and Flat Mountain across the way. I'd been there before when the water flashed bright blue beneath the summer sun, reflecting up into the sky, making it impossible to determine where one started and the other ended.

Today, there was no such trouble. The lake sat silent and cold, the water dark gray as it remained mirror calm, casting an air of foreboding over the entire scene.

Squeezing on the plastic clasp across my chest, I slid my arms from the pack and let it drop to the ground beside me. I unlatched my canteen from the side of it and took a long swig, passing it over to Lita as I extracted my binoculars from the side bin and held them to my eyes.

"The coordinates you gave me were for the lake itself, which is pretty damn big," I said, my face scrunched up behind the lenses of the binoculars. Starting on the north end of the shoreline, I swept the glasses down along the bank, scouring for signs of life.

"So what do we do?" Lita asked, taking one more drink of water before twisting the lid back on. I could hear the sound of metal scraping against metal as she did so. A cold wind at the top of the mountain blew across our bodies.

"Well," I said, keeping my attention aimed on the rocky outcroppings lining the lake. "Most of the area is too rugged for good camping. My guess is he'll set up just off the shore somewhere, where he can have access to water and fishing without being exposed to the wind."

A sharp inhalation rolled out of Lita, the auditory equivalent of a wince. "This lake looks to be fifteen miles across. How are we ever going to find him there?"

Once more I noted her tone, the seeming lack of empathy in her voice. The first several comments I had written off as merely the actions of a worried sibling, but for some reason her candor was beginning to rub me the wrong way, as if the mission was more important than the goal.

I couldn't place how or why, but something seemed a bit off.

"What did you say your brother's name was again?" I asked.

I kept the binoculars pressed to my face, my view trained on the lake below, but I could sense her staring. A quiver of tension passed through the air between us, dropping the temperature a degree or two around me.

"Matthew," she replied quickly. "Are you going to be able to find him or not?"

It was a simple question, one that should not have raised her ire. As a test, she had passed, but just barely. The only thing that made me believe her even a little bit was the fact that she had not hesitated in the slightest at responding with his name.

Halfway down the far bank, a slight smudge caught my attention. Stopping my swing south, I focused in on it, nothing more than a few quick wisps, white against a dark green backdrop.

Smoke.

"Can you find him or not?" Lita repeated, her voice a tad sharper than before. Again I heard the twang of her native accent, definitely ranging from somewhere on the European-Asian border.

I kept my focus on the smoke a moment longer, lowering my aim to the shoreline where a simple blue pup tent was tucked in low between a clump of lodgepole pines. A moment of queasiness passed through me as I stared at it, lowering the binoculars away from my eyes.

There was absolutely no concrete reason for me to feel like this entire thing had been a setup. Nothing more than a conglomeration of bad feelings and inconsistencies.

There were fifty thousand reasons why I should just take her down and get away as fast as I could.

"Relax," I said. "I think I already have."

Chapter Five

Overhead the clouds continued to roll in, the first gray clumps serving as a precursor to angry black thunderheads. Inch by inch they appeared from behind the peak of Flat Mountain, a tangle of multicolored tendrils, all fighting for the upper hand. With them came an uptick in the wind, the temperature plummeting. As we hiked down toward the lake, our breath became visible, little puffs of white vapor extending from our faces.

"I don't like the look of those clouds at all," I said, motioning with the top of my head.

Behind me I could hear Lita grunt a response. "I didn't think a guide would be afraid of a little rain."

I felt my hands clench into fists for a moment, a natural reaction to the unprovoked barb in my direction. I waited a full moment to let the feeling subside, the animosity within me recede, before replying. "This temperature? At this altitude? That's not going to be rain. Not by a long shot."

Our boots crunched as we walked downward, the trail that had been covered in leaves and crusted earth all morning now giving way to gravel as we descended toward the lake. My quads began to burn a bit from walking at such a steep decline, and my toes curled against the front of my boots, gravity forcing them forward.

"He's right over there," Lita said. "We have time to grab him and get out before it hits."

Two things caught my attention. First was the way she said *grab him*. I wasn't sure why, but it caught in the back of my mind, an odd word choice, even for someone who wasn't a native speaker.

Second was her insinuation that we could be on our way before the snows arrived. We would be lucky to get to Matthew's camp before the powder starting swirling. Getting out would be a different game altogether.

A handful of retorts came to mind, each a little more pointed than the one before it. One by one I shoved them back, settling on, "This isn't New Mexico."

If she got my point, she didn't let on, remaining silent as we tramped along.

Underfoot the ground leveled out, depositing us on the bank of Heart Lake. The walking became easier; my feet slid back into their normal positions in my boots, and the pack on my back no longer tried to propel me down the mountain. Gone was any trace of the forest floor. The shoreline was made entirely of gray stone deposited by glaciers centuries before. It scraped beneath us as we went, the sound rippling out across the water.

My watch said it was nearing two o'clock in the afternoon, though it appeared much later than that. The ominous clouds had blotted out almost all sun from the sky, casting a gray pallor over the lake. The world around us was still, void of any wildlife, any sounds of nature.

The only sign of any life at all was the lazy curl of smoke that continued to rise into the air. I could pick up just the slightest hint of it on the breeze as I walked, the clean scent of pine wood burning slowly.

The expanse of the rocky beach allowed Lita to draw even with me, her stride increasing in length, beckoning me to match her pace. Within a hundred yards we were almost jogging over the uneven ground, the tread on my boots clinging to any traction it could find as we went.

"Is there a reason we're running?" I asked as I fought to inflate my lungs with the thin air. Under the weight of my pack and winter hiking gear I could feel my back starting to get warm. My scalp began to itch under my cap, a sure sign of rising body heat.

"He's right there," Lita said. "I have to get to him."

Again her word choice struck me as odd, though I didn't press it. My attention was aimed at the impending storm above, on reaching the campsite and getting my tent up before the snow started to fly.

We came up on the camp from the northwest, rounding the top loop of the heart-shaped lake and coming down toward the center. For almost a quarter mile the shoreline wrapped us out of sight from the camp, the smell of smoke our only reminder that it was still just up ahead.

The moment the tent disappeared from sight Lita picked up her pace again, pushing us as fast as the terrain would allow. Her mouth drew back into a tight line, and the skin around her eyes pinched by the temples, obvious signs of strain.

Sensing me studying her through sideways glances, she looked over at me and made a show of slowing a half step. She forced a lopsided smile onto her face and said, "Sorry. Just excited."

"Ahh," I said, nodding as if I believed her, already counting down in my head the minutes until I could be free of her and on my way again.

Together we rounded one last bend in the trail, coming out on a narrow sliver of beach just forty yards from our destination. On our left, dense forest pushed down off the mountainside, forcing us close to the water. On the right, the water lapped up at our feet, spurred on by the wind howling across the water, staining the rocks dark gray.

"There it is," I muttered, picking my way through the stone field. Beside me I could hear an audible sniff from Lita, a sharp inhalation of air through her nose, but nothing more.

The camp was made on a rocky outcropping rising three or four feet above the trail. Formed from a single piece of limestone laid flat on its side, the stone created a makeshift shelf that protruded out over the water below.

As campsites went, it was an excellent choice. It was elevated from, but still easily accessible to, the water. Dense forestation nudged right up beside it, providing cover and firewood.

The trail ended abruptly at the side of the shelf and disappeared beneath it, no doubt continuing on the opposite side. I walked to the edge and placed my palms flat atop it, hoisting myself up onto my knees and scrambling to a standing position. By the time I made it up Lita was already there and waiting for me, a look on her face that bordered on contempt as she watched me regain my balance.

"Where is he?" she asked.

"Not sure," I said, taking a look around. On the back end of the shelf was a small campsite, a two-person dome tent staked down into the earth at its center. Constructed of blue nylon, it looked like it was just a week out of the box, bright white lines anchoring it to the ground.

To the left of it was a foldout chair made of the same blue nylon and a fishing rod with a spin reel leaned against it. A coffee pot and two pans were on the ground nearby, each made from polished steel.

All of the items looked to be brand new and barely used, the results of a five-hundred-dollar trip to REI on the way into the park.

In front of the arrangement was the campfire we'd first spotted at the top of Mount Sheridan, the logs on it no more than half burned.

"Somebody's been here recently," I said, looking away from the fire and checking the storm as it gathered steam above us. "And there's a good chance it was your brother."

My last words drew Lita's stare, her gaze snapping over at me in a quick movement. "Why do you say that?"

I matched the look, waiting a long moment before nodding to the fire. "The wood on there is still burning strong. It's been added recently."

"And what makes you think that this is Matthew's camp?"

"Same reason," I said. "The wood is arranged in a log cabin formation. Anybody who's ever spent time in the woods knows a teepee fire burns hotter and longer."

"Hardly convincing evidence," Lita said, dismissing the statement as fast as I had said it.

"Every bit of this equipment is brand-new," I added.

Lita pursed her lips, considering the information. "Still means nothing. Maybe we should take a look inside the tent to make sure."

It was my turn to snap a surprised look at Lita, my eyes bulging a bit. "Um, no. If this isn't his spread, there's no way we're going poking through some random camper's site. That's a good way to get yourself shot out here."

Though void of humor, the comment brought a smirk to Lita's face.

"Here, let's try this the old-fashioned way," I said, raising a hand to my mouth.

"Matthew!" I called, extending the word out a full ten seconds in length. "Hey, you here?"

The smirk slid from Lita's face as my voice carried into the cold air, reverberating off the mountainside and echoing across the water. Her eyes grew larger and her lips curled back into a snarl, incredulity on her face.

"What are you doing?" she demanded. "I . . . I thought you said that was a good way to get us shot?"

"No," I said, ignoring her glare, keeping my focus on the trees surrounding us. "I said pilfering through someone's camp was a good way to get shot. Announcing our presence is a good way to bring someone into camp so we can talk to them, Matthew or not."

In the distance I heard the faintest sound of a stick snapping, the kind of noise caused by someone stepping down hard on it, breaking it clean in two. I trained my ear toward it, hearing as a second sound emerged, the muffled din of feet scraping through dried leaves.

"I still think we should have waited," Lita said, staring across at me.

"Doesn't matter now," I said with a shrug. "They're on their way down as we speak."

Chapter Six

Our respective attention was aimed in different directions as the owner of the campsite advanced toward us.

I could tell by the rudimentary state of the setup, by the brand-new gear strewn about, that the camp most likely belonged to Matthew. If not him, someone much like him, a neophyte in from a major city, trying their hand at roughing it in the woods for a few days.

There were no signs of a weapon of any kind around. No fresh meat, no boxes of shells, nothing. That didn't mean one wasn't nearby or on their person, but the odds were there wasn't one at all to fear.

Instead, my focus was on the gathering winter storm above us. The clouds seemed to be gathering in the low-pressure dip between the two peaks, swirling into an angry tangle. The wind had continued to pick up to where it was now just short of gale force. Small whitecaps were surfacing on the lake.

The first few flakes of snow started to dart through my field of vision, flung by on the force of the breeze.

Across from me Lita stood with her back to the camp, staring into the water. It was an odd pose for someone expecting her brother, more agitated than hopeful. Once more I reminded myself it was not my place to judge, remembering that every person dealt with family in their own way.

The sound of the person approaching grew louder, thrashing through the forest like a Sasquatch in search of food. I lowered my gaze from the sky overhead toward the trees, already planning my next move. If this wasn't Matthew, we were going to have to find our own place to set up camp, and fast.

Judging by the sky overhead and the white powder gathering in the air, I gave us a half hour, an hour at most, before things started to get nasty.

A flash of yellow caught my attention a few yards up from the camp, and I saw a lone figure coming diagonally down toward it. By the figure's gait and general size, I guessed it to be a male, though it was impossible to tell given the oversized parka that enveloped most of the body.

Lita and I both stood in silence as the figure emerged, a small bundle of firewood in hand. The figure didn't once look up as it wound around the tent and deposited the wood by the fire, the logs ringing out hollow against the limestone.

With its face aimed down at the fire, the figure lowered itself to a kneeling position and grabbed up a stick from the ground, using it as a poker to stoke the coals. Once flames began to lick up into the air, the figure dropped the stick and sat back on its haunches, reaching up with both hands and peeling away the puffy hood shadowing its face.

Dark brown skin came into view, framed by black hair and a heavy beard. A pair of round wire-rimmed glasses were perched on the end of the man's nose, the tip of which was stained red from the cold.

As his face emerged he looked up, seeing us for the first time. Our eyes locked for a moment, recognition clicking with both of us.

Of every person on the planet I had expected to see sitting by a fire on the shore of Heart Lake, this one ranked at the bottom of the list. The sight of his face, after all this time, hit me square in the stomach, driving the air from my lungs. My legs locked themselves in place, my lips parting a fraction of an inch in silence.

The look on the man's face showed his response to be exactly the same as mine. All expression flooded from his features, his eyes wide. "Tate."

"Mateo," I responded, my voice no more than a whisper. It was the first time I'd said the name aloud in years, the taste of it still bitter on my lips.

Something bordering on relief washed over him as he looked at me, the last reaction I expected. "I knew you would—" he began, but stopped himself as his gaze moved to the side, seeing Lita standing beside me.

"Oh Jesus, you're with her?" he exclaimed, any thoughts he had on seeing me vanishing into fear. Pure terror filled his features as he scrambled to his feet, pushing himself back from the fire.

"What do you want?" he said, his voice pleading as he stared at Lita.

His reaction seemed to be exactly what Lita was expecting, a look of amusement spreading across her face. "Hello, Mateo," she said casually, walking forward toward him. "Miss me?"

"What are you doing here?" Mateo said, still pushing himself away, his feet fighting for purchase on the snow-slickened limestone. "What do you want?"

"You already asked that," Lita said, taking two more steps towards him, shifting the duffel bag she was carrying from her shoulder blade. She dropped the strap of it down into her left hand and dug into it with her right, her hand disappearing halfway up the forearm as she searched for what was inside.

In that moment, it all came together.

The late-season trip. The stilted English. The unusual demeanor. All of it.

She was here to murder Mateo. And she wouldn't be leaving any witnesses.

The polished black handle of a Heckler and Koch P7 with a contoured grip emerged, followed by the extended barrel of a noise suppressor. My gaze focused on it a full moment, my feet already carrying me backward, my instincts from a prior life kicking into gear. Without pause Lita raised the gun to shoulder level and fired it at Mateo as his hands and feet still furiously fought to push his body back away from her. Three times she pulled the trigger, oblivious to his cries, a trio of white muzzle flashes erupting between the snowflakes swirling around her.

The first two caught him square in the chest, red splotches growing atop his yellow parka. The third split his glasses in two, cleaving the thin metal frames down the middle and ripping a clean hole through the bridge of his nose. Inside his skull the nine-millimeter parabellum round mushroomed out, sending a plume of blood and brain matter onto the ground behind him.

Rotating at the waist, Lita kept the gun at shoulder level and aimed it at me. Inch by inch I retreated away from her, my hands by my waist, palms facing down.

If it were most anybody else standing across from me, I would have tried to reason with her. I would have told her she didn't have to do this, assured her that I wouldn't say a word. Tried anything to keep her from applying the two pounds of pressure that would send gas-powered projectiles flying my direction, doing to me exactly as they had done to Mateo.

I knew there was no point in even trying with Lita, though. This was a woman who had just spent half a day tromping through the Yellowstone wilderness, then mowed a man down after barely saying so much as hello.

I was a loose end, and people like Lita didn't allow for loose ends.

Despite what my brain knew to be true, my body still acted like there was a chance, calling on the most basic of all primal urges to survive.

Without lifting my feet from the ground I nudged my way backward, closing the gap between me and the edge of the rock face.

Lita watched me retreat away from her, the same look of amusement she'd had on her face before she shot Mateo. Knowing what was about to happen, having just seen her pattern, I did the only thing I could.

"Go to hell," I said, my voice like steel, just loud enough for her to hear me over the sound of the storm.

For one brief moment, the look of amusement faded to one mixed of surprise and something bordering on respect. Just as fast it disappeared, replaced by a fourth and final muzzle flash.

The round slammed into my chest, driving my body back off the edge of the rock shelf. I hung suspended in the air, pain coursing through me, before I splashed back into the water, every nerve ending in my body set ablaze on contact with the frigid water.

Drawing in as much air as I could before going under, I wrapped my arms tight across my chest, letting the weight of my pack pull me to the bottom, the darkness of Heart Lake swallowing me whole.

PART II

Chapter Seven

A pair of double doors opened from the master bedroom onto a sweeping veranda, their curtains swaying in the breeze. The scent of sand and saltwater drifted in with it, filtering through the room, sweeping over Viktor Blok's naked body as he extracted himself from bed and took his feet. Behind him lay the sleeping figure of a local blonde a decade younger, the latest in his conquests since relocating full time to North America.

For a long moment Viktor stood above her, staring down at her sun-kissed skin, the thin cotton sheet outlining her perfect form, and considered diving back in for more. He could still feel the fresh scratches on his back from the previous night, see the smears of blood where he'd lain, the wounds oozing as he slept.

A small quiver ran through him, stimulating his nether regions, but just as fast he shrugged it off. He turned his gaze away from the girl and took up a silk robe from the chair in the corner of the room, wrapping it around himself as he stepped out onto the veranda.

As he emerged from the bedroom, the warmth of the new day's sun hit him full in the face, washing over his body, illuminating his pale skin. He walked in a straight line across the Spanish tile on the floor, its surface smooth against his feet, and came to a stop along the waist-high wall encasing it. He pressed his palms down flat on the stucco finish and leaned forward, the fresh scratches tugging as he stretched his shoulders and back.

"I'm beginning to see why nobody ever returns to Russia after they leave," Viktor said, knowing the comment's target would be there without looking at him.

"Are you referring to the girl, the house, or the weather?" Pavel Vazov asked, his accent thick, his voice a low grumble.

A wan smile crossed Viktor's lips as he finished his stretch and turned to face Pavel. He folded his arms across the silk robe and leaned his backside against the wall, shaking his head.

"Why does one have to separate them?" he asked.

"Because they are not the reason we are here," Pavel said, flint in his voice.

The smile fled from Viktor's face as he looked at his associate. His features grew rigid as he stared across at the man, the folds of skin near his eyes tightening. He set his jaw in a tight clench, feeling his back molars scrape together as he glared.

"I know full well the reason we are here," Viktor said. "And Sergey knows it. That's why he put me in charge, and told you to do everything you can to help me."

Pavel matched the glare a moment, his body poised. "And I have done that."

Viktor remained stiff, examining the man in front of him.

Standing halfway between six and seven feet tall, Pavel was an intimidating presence by any measure. His thick shoulders and neck appeared to have oversized links of coiled chain just beneath the skin, bulging muscles that encased his neck on either side. A thin beard lined his mouth and jaw; bushy eyebrows and a thick head of dark hair made him always seem as if he were brooding, about to explode.

Which, in Viktor's experience, wasn't far from the truth.

Viktor had not wanted his presence on this endeavor. He hadn't
wanted the glowering beast shadowing his every move, inciting fear in
everybody they encountered, no doubt reporting back to Sergey each
night on what happened.

"Any word yet?" Viktor asked, his words clipped.

"No," Pavel said, his features easing just a bit now that the subject
had shifted back to work.

"How long since she last checked in?"

"Nine days," Pavel said, disapproval plain in his tone.

Viktor's eyebrows ticked upward a quarter of an inch at the information. He knew that a bit of radio silence had transpired, but had no
idea it had been well over a week.

"Do we even know if the job is done?"

Pavel met his gaze a long moment before looking away, out over
the waves of the Pacific rolling onto the beach. "No."

Viktor blew a long breath out through his nose and turned back to
face the ocean. He could feel the robe sticking to his back as he moved,
though if it was from sweat or blood he couldn't be sure.

"Do you know where she went?" he asked, pressing his chin into
his shoulder to speak back to Pavel.

"Montana," Pavel said, taking a step forward toward the wall but
maintaining a wide gap between them. "When we last spoke, she had
secured the guide and was heading out in the morning."

"Remind me why we sent her?" Viktor asked, keeping his attention
aimed forward. He already knew the answer to the question before he
asked it, but he wanted to make sure Pavel did as well.

Pavel, sensing the same, took a long pause before replying, "Because
Sergey ordered it."

"Right," Viktor said, nodding as if remembering the way things
had played out, in reality relishing the small victory. "Do we think this
is serious enough to warrant action? Or will she show up again any
moment now?"

Pavel rolled his shoulders one at a time, his massive frame shifting beneath the black T-shirt he wore. He kept his thumbs hooked into the belt loops above his backside and his chest protruded out in front of him.

"This was serious four days ago. By now, it's an emergency."

"Okay," Viktor said, not appreciating the barb tossed in his direction. "Do what you have to. Go find her. Make sure the job is done."

Pavel grunted in response, nodding for added effect. "I will send Yuri. It will be done."

Jutting his thighs out against the wall, Viktor pushed himself away and turned back toward the bedroom. He let the robe fall open on either side of him as he walked. The ocean breeze felt cool against his skin.

"No, you go. Make sure it's finished."

Chapter Eight

I last saw Don Hutchinson four and a half years ago. We had sat in a makeshift office in a double-wide trailer in the California desert. The rickety structure had been made entirely of plywood, and it had shaken every time a stiff breeze blew in off the Pacific.

He had been seated behind a battered metal desk, a hand-me-down from the naval base in San Diego, and an air-conditioner from the same source had been stuck into the window behind him. The aging machine had pushed out a rattle like a smoker's cough over the room as it ran, but the heat outside had been too stifling to even consider turning it off.

If we had been trying to talk to one another we would have had to scream to be heard.

As it had stood, there was nothing more to say. I was done, a fact we had both known for a long time, but neither had said out loud.

The front porch of his new home in Alexandria, Virginia, was bright and open as I sat and waited for him. It was a clear fall evening, and the air was a good fifteen degrees warmer than what I'd left behind in Montana. Tucked away on a swing looking out over his suburban neighborhood, I could hear children at play, saw an older man down the street raking leaves.

Nobody paid me any mind as I sat and waited, forcing my façade to remain serene as my inner workings pulsated at ultrasonic speeds.

My wait turned out to be a little shorter than expected, beginning at five o'clock and ending a few minutes before six thirty. I'd made a point to park my rented green Taurus on the curb so he would see it as he approached, making him aware of my presence without raising any alarms.

The last thing I needed was to anger a ranking DEA official, especially when I was there to solicit his help.

The sun was fast fading from the sky above as a pair of headlights rolled to a stop in front of the house. They paused for a moment along the street, no doubt inspecting the Taurus, possibly even calling in a tag check, before proceeding into the drive. Halfway down the brushed concrete his Chrysler came to a stop, its lights blinking out.

The years and change of address had altered him in the ways that were to be expected. As he emerged from behind the steering wheel, I could see his California tan was gone, as was another inch or two off his hairline. In their stead he had added ten pounds to his midsection; a small paunch strained the bottom buttons of his dress shirt.

"Hawk," he said, standing by the car and assessing me before approaching the front porch. If he was surprised to see me, he didn't show it in the slightest; he kept his voice, his expression, even.

"Hutch," I replied, dipping the top of my head slightly in greeting.

"You're the dumb pilgrim I've been hearing for twenty days and smelling for three."

The corner of my mouth curled up in a smile. Since the first time Hutch had pieced together the origin of my name he'd been quick with a quote from the movie. If not for it being one of my favorites, the practice might have gotten old.

As it was, it was just good to see a familiar face.

The soles of his brown loafers scraped against the concrete steps as he ascended them, his hands shoved in his pockets. He motioned to the small red container on the ground by my feet and asked, "What's in the cooler?"

"We'll get to that."

He walked up without looking at me and took a seat in the Adirondack chair alongside the swing, matching my gaze as we stared out over the darkening neighborhood.

"Tell me everything," he said simply, his voice low and even.

Again I got the impression that he'd been expecting me, waiting to have this very conversation, but in that moment I didn't care. I had things to do, and I needed his help in doing them.

"How much do you know?" I asked, not wanting to rehash any more than necessary.

"Assume I know nothing," Hutch said, his voice the same graveled baritone I remembered.

"She came to see me on October 24, claiming her brother was camping in the park and hadn't checked in in a few days." I leaned forward and rested my forearms on my knees, thinking back to that first encounter just ten days before. "I didn't want to take the job, not that late in the season, not having any time to prepare, but in the end I caved."

"The power of the almighty dollar," Hutch inserted.

"No," I said, shaking my head, "fifty thousand almighty dollars."

A small shrill whistle slid out between his teeth, but he refrained from speaking, signaling for me to continue.

"Every day he'd been calling in on a sat-phone, so she had coordinates for his whereabouts. Her story seemed to check out, so I didn't bother following up on it, just mapped out where he was, and the next morning we went up there.

"Took us a half day to hike in. Her *brother* was holed up on Heart Lake in the backcountry, a good ways off the beaten path. We found his camp easy enough, and within a minute of spotting the guy she pulled a P7 and put three in him. She almost put one in me, too, but I was able to get away."

"Returned fire?" Hutch asked. There was no concern in his voice, no tinge of accusation, simply a follow-up question so he could better understand the story.

"No," I said, shaking my head. "Got damn lucky. Her round smashed into the buckle on my pack. It crushed the thing to bits and left a hell of a bruise on my chest, but it didn't penetrate the skin.

"I used the momentum of the shot to launch myself backward into the lake and let my pack drag me to the bottom where I stayed for a full ninety seconds. I could hear bullets ripping through the water around me, see little streaks of white as they sped by, but I was deep enough that even if they hit me they wouldn't do any harm."

"Damn," Hutch whispered. "Bet that was pleasant."

A nasty, deep-rooted snort rolled out of me, lifting my head a few inches into the air. "About a minute into it I started wishing that bullet had hit flesh. Cold as hell, entire body burning as hypothermia began to set in.

"Once I could take it no more I dragged myself to the water's edge and slid out."

"And she was gone? Just that fast?" Hutch asked.

"Like I said, pure dumb luck. There was a hell of a storm settling over the lake as we hiked in. She had no choice but to get her ass out of there or she was going to be stuck for who knows how long. She waited a minute to make sure I was gone, emptied her clip into the water, then took off."

Hutch nodded, his gaze never moving. In front of us, a sedan rolled by and a young couple walked past, a bulldog on a leash between them, but none of them looked our way.

"Took me two days to ride the storm out," I said. "First night I damn near died of exposure. I built that fire as big as I could get it, put on every piece of clothing the guy had brought with him, even took his bloodstained coat off and used it.

"By the time the storm passed and I was able to hike out, my chest and shoulder were sore as shit from the shot, but everything was in decent working order. On the way out, I found her body. Looked like the elements had gotten to her first, the scavengers not far behind."

Hutch sat a moment in silence, his eyes squinted up a bit in concentration, the way they always had when we worked together. I knew he would remain in that position as long as it took, working out the events in his mind, piecing things together.

"Anything else?"

I took a deep breath, drawing the air in through my mouth and slowly exhaling through my nose. I ran my palms down the front of my thighs, knowing before I even said the words how crazy they were going to sound.

If I hadn't seen it with my own eyes, I wouldn't believe it.

"The man we were looking for was Mateo Perez."

For the first time Hutch took his attention away from the street, snapping his gaze over at me. "Bullshit."

"I knew you'd say that," I said.

I bent down at the waist and lifted the lid on the cooler, sliding it across the wooden planks of the porch so it was just a few inches from his foot. Hutch leaned over and glanced down into it, raising his gaze back to me just as fast.

Inside the cooler were two hands, one stained dark brown with broken nails beginning to yellow, the other pale white, no more than a few days removed from a manicure.

"You could have just brought their fingers, you know," Hutch said, his expression dour.

"I wasn't taking any chances," I replied. "Besides, it's not like they need them anymore."

Hutch nodded once, then reached out and lowered the cooler lid shut. "Come on in. I'll order some food and we'll get to work."

Chapter Nine

The smell of grilled chicken and onions hung throughout the room, its source two oversized sandwiches Hutch had ordered in from somewhere named Benicio's. The name on the box and the heavy-handed application of tomato sauce said the place fancied itself an Italian restaurant, though it tasted more along the lines of cardboard to me.

Still, it was free food. And it wasn't like I'd come across the country for dinner.

I left the last quarter of my sandwich in its box and folded it shut, tossing the scraps into the plastic bag they'd come in. I leaned back in the oversized leather sofa I was sitting on and draped an arm across the back of it, crossing my right leg up onto my opposite thigh.

Throughout dinner, conversation had been light, which was to say nonexistent. Hutch had ordered the food and jumped in the shower, leaving me to my own devices for over twenty minutes. I had no illusions that he was actually cleaning himself that entire time, but I refrained from speculating as to what he might have been up to.

If he had a real problem with me being there, he wouldn't have let me in. As much as I needed his help at the moment, I would have let it go at that.

Now that we were here, though, it was time to get down to it. "Why do I get the impression you're not surprised to see me?" I asked, fixing my gaze on him. He had switched into a pair of track pants and a long-sleeved T-shirt, his hair a puff of fuzz atop his head.

Hutch shrugged and said, "I've been waiting for you to show up here every day for five years now."

While that was probably a true statement, I didn't think it was the entire story. "No, I mean now. Tonight."

A pair of hound-dog eyes fixed on me for a long moment before Hutch lowered his head, nodding in concession. "I've kept a marker out for your name ever since you left. When it came over the wire in connection with two dead bodies in Yellowstone, I paid attention."

The news set me back a half inch, though I did my best to hide it. If Hutch had kept tabs on me all this time, there was no telling who else had as well.

"But not enough to get involved?"

"There was no reason to. The reports didn't list either of the victims, said you were alive and well. I sniffed around a little bit, but all accounts seemed to indicate it was a simple case of Yellowstone claiming two more."

I shoved out a sniff, not at his handling of the situation, but at the media's portrayal of it. "I saw most of Mateo's occipital lobe exit his skull. Trust me, that had nothing to do with Yellowstone."

Hutch nodded in silence, taking a swig of ginger ale from the glass beside him.

Shifting my focus away from him, I did a quick sweep of the room we were sitting in. He had referred to it as the den when suggesting we take our dinner there, though to my eyes it looked more like a cross between a mobile headquarters and a recruiting brochure.

DEA plaques and insignia littered an oversized desk and a pair of matching cherry bookcases. Antique pistols lined multiple shelves, all polished to a gleam, displayed in ornate boxes. Enough electronic equipment covered the desk and two matching side tables to operate Skynet for the foreseeable future, most of it appearing to be brand-new designs since my departure just a few years before.

My career with the DEA had started at the age of twenty-five. I'd earned a joint bachelor's and master's degree from George Washington in criminology and finished a three-year hitch in the Navy with my sights set on law school when the big boys came calling.

They knew exactly what they were doing. They took a young guy like me, full of piss and vinegar, ready to get out into the world and mix it up, and they promised me exactly that. Told me of all the exotic places I'd be working, the international drug rings I would bring down.

I signed on the dotted line after barely reading the papers they put in front of me.

To be fair, they had been mostly right. I did travel the world and I did assist with the apprehension of some major players in the drug trade, but it took a hell of a lot of work. A lot of sleepless nights. A lot of images that were going to be seared onto my brain forever, images that no human being should ever have to carry around with them.

And a loss bigger than anything I ever could have imagined.

"It looks like you've done quite well for yourself here," I said, giving an exaggerated once-over of the room. "Congratulations."

"Thank you," he said, dipping his head in awkward acceptance of the praise.

"I never had you pegged as a bureaucrat," I said, "but it seems to suit you well."

The left side of his mouth twitched upward, sensing the bit of bait I'd laid at his feet. "I'm not, and we both know it. After you left, it was only a few months before Diggs and Martin both bounced, too. Pally still does a little freelance work for me, but without the rest of the team, he really wasn't into it anymore, either."

I nodded once, thinking back to the three other men that had joined Hutch and I to form the most feared Foreign-Deployed Advisory and Support Team the DEA had ever seen.

"You still keep tabs on them, too?" I asked.

"I do."

"Everything okay?"

"It is."

At some point I would have loved to have gotten the full rundown on how everybody was doing, make sure they were safe, but that time was definitely not now.

I leaned forward and rubbed my palms together, casting a glance around the room. "So what's this new Candyland of yours capable of?"

"Not a damn thing with that little present you brought me," Hutch said, nodding toward the kitchen, where the single-sized cooler I'd brought rested. "But any kind of electronic wizardry we could do at the office, we can do from right here."

He spun the chair he was sitting in around and rolled himself over to his desk, shaking a mouse to wake the computer. On cue three different screens sprang to life, the background for each of them emblazoned with the DEA logo.

"Subtle," I muttered, shaking my head at the government's insistence on putting its stamp anywhere it could find enough space to do so. I stood and walked up behind him, extracting a folded piece of paper from my jeans and dropping it down on the keyboard in front of him.

"What have you got?" Hutch said, unfolding the sheet and spreading it out flat.

On the top half of the sheet was a photocopy of a New Mexico driver's license made out to a Lita Haney. Her address was listed as 405 Kovanny Road in a town called Mora. She was listed as five-ten, 128 pounds, and her picture showed two full rows of even white teeth.

"Damn," Hutch said. "She's cute."

"She was," I conceded, "in a hostile sort of way."

The bottom half of the sheet was a copy of her credit card, a Master-Card made out to the same name, set to expire the summer after next.

"You realize these are probably fake, right?" Hutch said, sliding a pair of thick-framed glasses onto the bridge of his nose and bringing up a program from a list of icons on the far left screen. At the click of the cursor, it sprang open, and the entire center screen filled with a sheet customized to have data fed into it.

"I would bet every dollar I have on it, but we have to start some-where," I said.

Hutch grunted in agreement as his head shifted up and down between the printout and the screen. His thick fingers pounded on the keyboard as he input the data, the sound carrying through the quiet house. When he was done he set the program to searching; an over-sized hourglass appeared on the screen, letting us know that things could take a while.

Leaving it to run, Hutch brought up a second program and slid the window over to the far right. Except for the formation of the boxes and some of the text being a little different, the screen looked exactly the same as the first one. In the same painstaking manner Hutch inserted the credit card information and set the program to digging. A fan inside the computer whirred to life as the search commenced.

"Okay," Hutch said, pushing the paper away from him and reclin-ing in his chair. "Now that the red herrings are out of the way, what else have you got?"

While the tone of the question sounded a bit harsh, it wasn't wrong. Everything I'd just fed him could have been done through an unse-cured Yahoo! e-mail. Obviously the hands wouldn't have traveled so well, but I had a couple of other ideas that might take a bit more finesse.

"Fake credit card or not," I said, "the money did hit my account. Any way you can trace it back and find an origin?"

Hutch's eyebrows raised a fraction on his forehead, either from being intrigued at the idea or surprised that I'd thought to bring it up. Either way, he said nothing for a long moment, chewing on the idea.

"Me personally? No. You know how I am with electronics."

"You seemed pretty savvy just now," I said, nodding toward the screens.

"Pure plug and play," Hutch said, twisting his head to the side. "I can get Pally on the phone, though. That sort of thing would be no problem for him."

"Right," I said, nodding at the idea of employing the technical genius who had more than once saved our asses. "And while you're on the phone with him, have him dig around and see if he can figure out where Mateo's car ended up. Odds are it was a rental, but if not, maybe we can get lucky on a VIN number."

Hutch stared off into space a long moment, nodding his head. His eyes glazed over as he sat deep in thought before shaking himself awake. Without a word, he reached for the phone sitting on the desk beside him and pressed the third speed dial.

"Hey, Mike, need a favor . . ."

Chapter Ten

A disgusted look crossed Carlos Juarez's face as he held the remote control a few inches above the arm of his recliner, stabbing it forward at the television. With each movement he pressed the small rubber buttons harder, making the controls disappear down inside the plastic case housing it.

Once he'd jammed the channel change and the volume both up and down, he got disgusted and flung the entire thing across the living room. It exploded against the opposite wall, the outer shell giving way and allowing a myriad of metal components to skitter across the floor.

"To hell with it," he said, pressing his backside deeper into the chair and sitting up a little straighter. "I like the Food Network anyway!"

Carlos folded his arms across his chest and stared intently at the television, watching a young woman he'd never heard of before raving about the benefits of using canned goods, his anger simmering just beneath the surface. His breathing gradually became louder, and his brow was furrowed so low his eyes were nothing more than slits.

"You know the least you guys could have done was get me a remote that works!" he bellowed toward the ceiling. From where he sat he couldn't see the microphones embedded into the fixtures, but he knew without a doubt that they were there, that someone was listening.

They always were.

Carlos stared in hatred toward the ceiling a long moment, waiting for any form of a response before smashing down the leg rest on the chair. He leaned forward and smacked his palms against the padded rests on either side, pausing a moment before doing it again.

"Why did I ever agree to do this? I should just go back. They can't make me stay here," he muttered, shaking his head in disgust.

Halfway through his tirade, a sharp knock on the door sounded out. Three hard bangs in a row, equally spaced, before dying away.

Carlos remained in his chair a long moment, his head twisted to stare at the door behind him, his mouth still hanging open from his outburst. Slowly the corners of it twisted up into a wide grin, revealing both rows of teeth and a tongue wagging back and forth in his mouth.

"Now that's what I'm talking about!" he said, still aiming his voice toward the heavens. "A man needs a remote that works, you bring him a remote that works!"

Carlos stood and glanced down at his attire, taking in the gray boxer shorts and white ribbed tank top he was wearing, both standing in stark contrast to his caramel colored skin.

"Aw, hell with it," he said, sauntering toward the door and snapping it open without checking the peephole to see who was behind it.

"It is about damn time," he said, the grin fading as he saw what stood before him.

It was definitely not somebody bringing him a new remote.

A young Asian man in a brown UPS uniform was rooted in place three feet back from the door, a look mixed of apprehension and surprise on his face. His eyes grew wide as he stared up at Carlos, glancing down at the package in his hands and back up again.

"Excuse me, sir," the young man said, swallowing heavily, a lump traveling the length of his neck as he tried to get it down. "Are you Chris Jansen?"

Confusion clouded Carlos's eyes for a moment, his mind taking a moment to place the name. Just as fast it clicked into place, his head nodding before he even realized it.

"Um, yeah," he said, taking a step forward. "That's me. What's up?"

"Package for you," the young man said, extending a small electronic processor out in front of him, a stylus on a plastic leash hanging down the side of it. "Please sign on the line there, sir."

Carlos snatched the stylus from midair and used it to draw an indiscernible scribble, everything past the first letter C a tangled mess. The delivery man accepted it without so much as a glance, retracting the processor with one hand and extending the package out with the other. "Have a good day, sir."

Using both hands, Carlos accepted the package, noting how light it was immediately. He watched the young man spin on the ball of his foot and disappear down the front walk, not until he was almost gone managing, "Uh, yeah, you too."

The front door slammed against its frame as Carlos swung it shut and slid the deadbolt into place. He balanced the package across his outstretched hands as he turned and made his way back to the living room, the cooking show on the television now a distant memory.

Only a handful of people knew where he was, a hand missing a few fingers at that. Most anybody that had something for him would just call and tell him, or at the very least alert him to keep an eye out. Of those, the number of those who would use the name Chris Jansen was even smaller.

Whatever was in the box, the odds were it wasn't good.

Depositing it on the floor in front of the recliner, Carlos crossed over to the window and peered out. From where he stood he could see nothing but his fenced-in backyard, the grass cut the day before, the bushes trimmed down neat. He went to the front window and did the same thing, seeing a matching pair of maple trees in the yard, a mass of fallen leaves at their base.

Running the front of his hands over his tank top, Carlos stepped back to the recliner and settled down into it. He slid his index finger along the lip of package, freeing the flap from its adhesive, and pulled back the top, peering down at what lay inside.

A single piece of paper.

On it, written in block letters with a black magic marker, were the words, THEY FOUND ME.

Carlos felt his mouth go dry as he turned his face up toward the ceiling and said, "Get me Diaz. Now."

Chapter Eleven

There were only so many ways for a man from the Eastern Bloc to enter the United States without drawing suspicion, even fewer when traveling north from Mexico.

Option A was to get into a car and drive straight to Montana. It included sitting in an interminable line at the Tijuana border crossing, having the car and driver scrutinized closely, and, if they were lucky, making it across the border six to eight hours after starting.

Option B was the airport, though it too posed the problem of going through customs. Beyond that lay the chore of renting a car upon arrival, a task that would leave a paper trail for anybody that might be looking.

Upon getting the word from Viktor, Pavel chose Option C. He called ahead to their contacts in San Diego and had a car posted at the Laguna Beach lot, with the keys stuck in a hideaway in the rear driver's-side tire well. Once that was in order, he caught a ride north on the day's shipment container, using the three-hour ride beneath deck to bank some rest, knowing he would need it soon enough.

There was little doubt that his passports and credit cards would check out if examined closely; they already had on multiple occasions.

The bigger issues were time and visibility, both of which the third route better afforded.

The boat north out of Mexico left at noon sharp, depositing him at the San Diego pier just shy of three o'clock. A twenty-minute cab ride in the thin afternoon traffic took him to Laguna Beach, and just six hours after standing on the veranda with Viktor, he was on his way north.

Folded behind the wheel of a three-year-old Dodge Avenger, he kept the radio off as he stared out at the road ahead, running through every possibility the day could bring him.

Of paramount importance was finding Lita, alive or dead. The name on his passport indicated Pavel was her brother if he needed to show ID to get near a hospital room or identify her body, but beyond that he felt no connection to the woman whatsoever. Though he would never admit as much to Viktor, he too had wondered why Sergey had chosen her for the job. He didn't buy the thinly veiled excuse that a woman would be better suited to gain trust and access in America.

If they had just let him come to begin with, none of this scrambling would be necessary.

The second order of business was to determine if Lita had been successful in eliminating Mateo Perez. Finding him had been a stroke of pure luck, and if he had slipped through their fingers there was no telling when or if he would pop up again.

The third order was the former agent, the Hawk, a loose end from another life, an annoyance that would be eliminated without trouble.

Armed with only a few scattered details of Lita's trip ten days prior, Pavel pieced together what he could about her itinerary from credit card charges made to the company account. A flight from San Diego into Bozeman. Two nights' stay at the Big Sky Plaza Inn. A car rental charge that remained open, the meter running.

A fifty-thousand-dollar expenditure to Hawk's Eye Tours in West Yellowstone.

For fifteen straight hours Pavel sat behind the wheel, his heavy eyebrows knitted into one thick caterpillar across his forehead. He made only five stops the entire way, each time pulling into a Travel Plaza just long enough to fill up the tank, twice grabbing a tall coffee and a PowerBar for the road.

Given the hour time difference between the mountains and the coast, Pavel pulled into West Yellowstone just before eight o'clock in the morning. A thin fog lay over the town as he rolled through; only a handful of people were out in the early-morning light. The automated readout on the Bank of the Rockies sign announced it was thirty-four degrees, a full fifty colder than he'd experienced a day before.

A thin smile crossed Pavel's lips as he stared at the digits, computing the numbers from Fahrenheit to Celsius in his head. His formative years had been spent in the brutal cold, and his body easily adapted to it. He wasn't made for life on the beach—the last year had been an unending torture of sunshine and warmth.

Gripping the wheel in either hand and leaning over it to peer out the windshield, Pavel coasted through town, his gaze darting over every road sign he passed, scanning for the address he'd committed to memory a day before.

In a town like San Diego or Los Angeles, he would have been forced to bring directions with him, running the risk of someone else finding the papers later on. The towns were just too big to navigate blind.

In West Yellowstone, it took him seven minutes to find his intended target.

Hawk's Eye Tours was a single wooden building at the far end of the one main street running through town. To the right of it was a matching wooden cabin with a red-white-and-blue-striped pole above the door. A sign tacked to the front fence stated it was the West Yellowstone Barber Shop. To the left was nothing but thick forest; trees butted up to within a few yards of the building's exterior.

The entire structure looked to have cost less than fifty thousand dollars. What Lita had possibly needed to spend that kind of money on, he couldn't imagine.

Pavel remained behind the wheel for several long minutes, keeping the car angled back toward town so he could see the front door and any morning traffic. Content there was none, he climbed out and crossed over the gravel parking lot, the cold morning air filling his lungs. It was cleaner than he was used to, but the icy temperature of it brought a contented smile to his lips.

Pavel hopped up the three short steps leading to the front door in a quick burst, his body eager for movement after fifteen hours in the Avenger. He walked to the door and knocked on it twice with the back of his hand, even though the posted shop hours in the window said it wouldn't be open until nine. Hearing nothing from within, he pressed the side of his hand to the glass and used it to block any reflection, bringing his face in tight and peering inside.

The office looked like a basic setup, with a small sitting area, a rack of brochures and pamphlets, and a counter running across most of the room. Overhead the lights were still dark, the place giving off the unmistakable vibe that it was void of life.

Blowing out an angry sigh through his nose, Pavel pulled back from the glass and looked in either direction. He turned toward town, walked the length of the front porch, his boots ringing hollow against the wooden floor, and came to a stop in front of a latticed window evenly spaced between the door and the edge of the building.

He turned on the ball of his foot and stared down at the home-made piece of poster board propped up in the corner, with simple black letters on a white background, drawn out in a woman's handwriting:

Thanks for a great season, see you next year!

Pavel balled his hands into fists, thick mallets aching to lash out and strike something. He felt the muscles in his neck and shoulders tighten, running the length of his triceps and down into his forearms. Despite the cold, his body temperature rose, venom welling deep within.

"Dammit," he muttered, hopping off the deck and walking back across the lot.

There were a few other options he had worked out in his mind, but this was by far the easiest. Without knowing where Lita and the guide went, it would be almost impossible for him to determine where to start looking. For all he knew, they could still be in the field, set to return at any time.

Given that the sign in the window said the shop was closed, it seemed unlikely but not completely unfeasible.

Halfway to the car, Pavel slowed his pace. He drew in deep breaths, forcing his mind to compute what he knew, what was available to him. At his disposal he had the last place Lita was known to have gone, a building that at the very least would have records of the trip or an intended location.

He also had going to the authorities and posing as Lita's brother, a less than appealing option, or going into the park and seeing what he could find on his own, which would be even worse.

Casting a glance over his shoulder, he walked to the woods edging up against the parking lot and took a few steps in, making sure he was seen, should anybody be looking. He waited a few moments, pretending to relieve himself in the trees, before again tossing a look back behind him.

Seeing nothing, he circled around through the trees to the far side of the building, a latticed window staring out into the forest, a perfect copy of the ones on either side of the front door. Curling his index finger into a ball, Pavel tapped each of the three bottom panes of glass, listening close for whichever sounded the weakest.

Content that the far right was his preferred target, he shifted himself perpendicular to the building and drew his left arm across his body.

With a mighty exhalation he snapped his torso in a tight arc, his hips twisting, sending his elbow careening into the glass.

The point of his ulnar bone smashed through the glass as if it were tissue paper, and the pane fell away in six jagged shards.

Pavel ran a hand over his skin to make sure there was no blood before snaking his arm up inside and flipping the lock open. The rusted implement resisted for a moment before turning itself free, allowing him to shove the window open. He rested his palms on the outer sill and leaned his head inside, glancing in either direction. After a moment he bent his knees a few inches and vaulted his body through to the waist, moving his hands to the floor and walking himself forward until he was completely inside the room.

The office was warmer than the air outside, though it was obvious the heat was turned down for the winter. Every light was out, shadows stretched across everything, put there by the faintest bit of ambient light drifting in.

Pavel counted to ten, listening for the sound of footsteps, and upon hearing nothing went to work.

The first place he started were the bookshelves, scanning over the volumes there covering every known topic about Yellowstone Park.

Wildlife. Volcanic activity. Hikes, waterfalls, campgrounds.

He hadn't expected to find anything of use, opting to start there to cut away the obvious dead ends first.

Next he went for the desk situated in the middle of the room, leaving the chair in place and moving around behind it, careful not to disturb anything. The top left drawer was filled with maps of every kind, one after another in their own plastic sleeve, each labeled with a particular set of coordinates and a common name. Pavel thumbed through them quickly, none of the names meaning anything to him, and closed the drawer less than a minute after he'd opened it.

The drawer on the left was equally useless, filled with a plastic bag of granola and a couple of chocolate bars. For a moment he thought of his own hunger and considered swiping some fuel for the road, but decided against it, wanting to leave as little of a trail behind as he could.

A broken window could be explained easily enough, especially given how close it was to the forest. An emptied desk would be a little tougher.

Frustration grew within Pavel as he looked around. There was no computer anywhere in the office, no filing cabinets lining the walls. There had to be a system in place for dealing with customers, some way of storing files, he just wasn't seeing it.

Giving up on the office, Pavel went to the door and eased it open, the hinges creaking softly as he peeled it back and peered around it. The front half of the building looked exactly as it had from the front window: everything shrouded in half darkness, the room silent.

Stepping out from the door, Pavel crossed over behind the desk, his eyes alighting on a power cord and an Ethernet cable extended out into the middle of it, connected to nothing. His face curled into an angry sneer, lips pulled back over misshapen teeth, as he tilted his head to the side and swore softly.

As he did so his gaze caught on an item in the trash, an old newspaper rolled up and cast aside. Reaching down he extracted it from the bin and placed it down atop the desk, smoothing it out with his hands.

The anger within Pavel abated as he stared down at the headline stretched across the top of the page. Written in bold block letters, it reported that authorities were still looking for answers in the double murder that had occurred in the park a week earlier.

Pavel nodded in approval. The girl might have gotten herself killed, but she had at least eliminated the primary target first.

The thought was pulled from his head before he had a chance to scan the paper any further, before he was afforded the opportunity to see what happened to the guide.

The alternating pulse of red and blue lights flashed through the front windows, striping across his torso, bathing everything in an unnatural hue. His initial reaction was to reach to the small of his back, grabbing for the USP Compact 9 mm that almost always resided there, before remembering it was tucked away in the middle console of his car.

Outside a pair of shadows crossed in front of the windows, heading for the front door. As he watched them grow closer, a handful of shaky plans passed through Pavel's head, each as unlikely as the one before it.

Faced with no other option, he grabbed up the newspaper from the desk and walked to the front door. He switched the deadbolt down and snapped the door open, catching a pair of middle-aged deputies by complete surprise. Both jumped back a few inches as they stared at him filling the doorway, the paper crumpled between his hands.

Pavel looked at each of them in earnest, doing the best he could to appear sincere, and muttered, "Please, you have to help me. She's my sister."

Chapter Twelve

Despite being kept frozen for the first nine days, and on dry ice the entire time since I'd left Montana, the contents of the cooler were beginning to smell ripe. Not the stale, pungent aroma of milk a week after its expiration date, but the rancid smell of flesh beginning to putrefy.

The tech gave me a look that could melt stone as she lifted the first appendage from within, gripping it gingerly between her thumb and forefinger. Ignoring the thin plastic glove encasing her hand, she had a look on her face that relayed a fear of catching some sort of flesh-eating bacteria just from being in the same room.

Once the specimen was free of the cooler, she flipped the lid on it down, hoping to trap inside what little stench she could. Rotating on the ball of her foot, she dropped the hand down on a sheet of clear glass beside her, the top shelf of a scanner.

"You know, Hutch occasionally alludes to you guys around here," she said, her voice nasal, "but we all just kind of thought it was bullshit. The kind of nostalgia old warhorses feel once they've been confined to a desk job."

My eyebrows tracked a full inch up my forehead as I turned to look at Hutch, a half smile on my face. "There is so much ammunition in that one statement, I don't even know where to begin."

"I do," Hutch responded, his face impassive as he stared at the girl. "You're fired."

A wide smile spread across her face, wide gums standing in exact proportion to her teeth. She shook her head, sending a bright orange ponytail flipping behind her head, eyes twinkling beneath oversized goggles.

"Where did I cross the line?" she asked.

"Old warhorse put out to pasture," Hutch said.

"Claiming our stories were bullshit," I added.

The girl looked at each of us and laughed, again twisting her head. In front of her the scanner kicked to life, a bright fluorescent bulb aiming light toward the ceiling, passing the length of the glass plate and back again. We all stood and watched as it traversed the length of the hand, a digital readout of it appearing on a flat screen on the wall across from us.

"Yeah, well, you both deserve it for putting me through this," she said, sniffing extra loud so we knew exactly what she was getting at.

Above her, the screen took the scan and digitized it, reducing it to nothing more than the identifying prints lining the fingers and palm. Once the background was stripped away it mapped out two dozen individual markers among the myriad of lines, then connected them with iridescent red lines and locked them into place.

Working on a keyboard at the base of the scanner, the girl shifted the network onto a neighboring monitor and set the system to searching. Similar prints flashed by in rapid fashion on the screen.

"How long will this take?" I asked, watching the scans whir by for a moment before shifting my attention back to the girl.

Again her face contorted into a sneer as she lifted the hand away from the plate and dropped it into the cooler. She snapped up an antibacterial wipe and worked to clear the glass, her arm making furious circles, stripping away any remnants of the prior scan.

"Depends," Hutch said, watching the girl work, not bothering to glance my way. "If they're in the system, only a few minutes. If not, we'll have to start digging through Interpol, NSA, whatever we can get our hands on."

I nodded, processing the information. Despite the fancy new equipment they had at their disposal, the databases for fingerprints backing them weren't much different from what we'd had five years before.

"So the longer it runs, the lower the odds," I said, more a statement than a question. I wasn't expecting an answer, didn't take it personally when one wasn't provided.

Instead we both watched as the girl lifted the second hand out of the cooler and plopped it on the glass, the thawing flesh slapping against it with a sickening smack. A few stray droplets of fluid flew out as she did so, sending her retreating back a couple of steps, raising her hands by her side.

"If I never see you again," she said, turning to glare over at me, "I won't be sad."

I considered telling her the feeling was mutual, that I wished nothing more than that this woman claiming to be Lita had never walked into my office. Right now I would be in northern Montana airing out my cabin for the winter, maybe heading down into Glasgow for my big supply run of the season.

Damned sure wouldn't be standing in a lab, smelling the stench of rotting flesh, trying to figure out why the hell this mess had found me after so many years on the sideline.

The girl waited a moment for me to respond before starting the scan, and an image similar to the first one appeared on screen. I could tell just from the much smaller outline and the lighter skin tone it was Lita's, though beyond that the two were indistinguishable.

The driver's license and credit card I had for Lita were both fake; that information came back within an hour. To add insult to injury the address listed on it, Kovanny Road, turned out to be the Russian word for *forged*. The entire thing was complete crap, and she didn't care who knew it.

I'd just been too damn stupid, too blinded by her money, to realize it.

Pally had been all too happy to track the dough and see where it came from, especially after Hutch told him it was a favor for me, even more so once he discovered the origin was most likely Russian. As a first-generation immigrant from Poland, his hatred for the former Soviet Union ran deep, instilled by family members who had spent their lives in constant fear.

If I'd had such an upbringing, I'm sure my ire would have been aimed in that direction as well. As it stood, mine was aimed a little farther south, a little closer to home.

The girl checked to make sure the scan was complete before lifting the hand away, holding it between two fingers, extending her arm as far away from her body as she could manage. Once it was deposited and the top slammed shut she shoved it a few feet across the stainless steel table it sat on, putting space between the cooler and herself.

"I don't care what you guys do with this, just get it the hell out of here," she said, giving her upper body an exaggerated shake. She snatched up the disinfectant wipes and went back to work on the glass, polishing it to a mirrored shine.

"This takes away the stain, but what about the smell?" she grumbled, dropping the wipe into a biohazard container and grabbing another from the box.

Neither one of us answered her, instead focusing on the monitor behind her head.

"I'll be damned," Hutch muttered, his face neutral as he stared at the image on the screen.

The picture had been taken some time ago, before he had a chance to grow out his hair or beard. The broad nose and dark eyes, though, were exactly the way I'd remembered, the same for the pair of wire-rimmed glasses covering his face.

"Mateo Perez," Hutch said, staring at the photo, his body at rapt attention.

"I told you," I muttered, my voice free of gloating, just stating a fact. "The whole back end of his head was gone, but there was no mistaking that face. Not after the amount of time I spent staring at it."

Hutch nodded in agreement. "I don't think any of us will ever forget it."

The girl glanced from the picture to both of us, her hair spinning out away from her head behind her. "Well, I'm glad you guys desecrating my lab did serve some purpose, at least."

"Any luck on the other one yet?" Hutch asked without glancing over at her.

"Not yet," she replied, "but it just started running. It might take a while."

We both grunted in response, lost in our thoughts.

"You guys want me to call if it comes back a hit?" she asked, her voice tinged with hope.

Hutch and I glanced at one another, each of us nodding in unison.

"Please," Hutch said, as we both turned and headed toward the door. Our feet echoed heavily off the tile floor as we went, our pace quick.

"Hey!" the tech yelled at our backs, spinning us both around.

"Don't you two dare leave that thing in here with me," she said, wagging a finger at the cooler. "I don't care what you do with it, but get it out of my lab."

Chapter Thirteen

The black sedan rolled to a stop six inches from the curb, as an overhead light gleamed off the glossy paint job. It idled there a long moment before the ignition was turned off, the engine ticking in the silent desert night. Carlos Juarez sat in the back seat staring out, his hands hanging down between his knees. He ran them once down the front of his khaki chinos, his palms sweaty despite the dry air. It was the first time he'd been back in six months, and just the mere sight of the place brought on a flood of bad memories. They played one after another in his mind on loop, every last image something he could do without ever seeing again.

"She in there?" he asked, motioning toward the front door with his chin.

"She is," the driver said, a thick, bullish man with a head shaved clean. "She's expecting you, and she's none too happy about it."

Carlos nodded, already envisioning the hostile environment he was walking into. Returning wasn't high on his to-do list either, but given what had arrived at his door, he didn't have much choice.

"Yeah, well, the feeling's mutual," Carlos said, letting animosity hang from the words. He threw them out like a challenge, a dare, to see if the driver or his partner riding shotgun would take the bait.

Neither one did. Aside from the few words the driver had just muttered, neither had said a thing since picking him up at the airport a half hour before.

"It's been real, fellas," Carlos said, wrenching open the door and stepping into the night. Behind him he could hear both men chortle at his comment as the realization set in that they were his ride back to the plane.

"So it's like that," he whispered under his breath, coming to a stop in front of the same building he'd voluntarily walked into a few years before. A single story tall, constructed entirely of red brick, it looked like a cross between a school and a DMV.

For an agency trying its best not to be conspicuous, it could not have picked a worse location for its headquarters. The entire place, from the perfectly shaped shrubs to the neatly raked rock beds, screamed bureaucracy.

A plume of stale frigid air passed over Carlos as he stepped through the glass double doors. He paused in the main foyer as they swung closed behind him, the seals clamping shut with an audible sucking sound.

An open hallway extended out straight ahead of him, offices lining it on either side. A wooden receptionist's desk sat off to the left, the seat behind it vacant and the light overhead dim; the person manning it had long since gone home for the night.

"Honey, I'm home," Carlos said, sauntering one foot at a time down the hallway, his unbuttoned dress shirt billowing open over the same ribbed tank top he'd been wearing that morning.

The sound of heels clicking against tile echoed out into the hallway, preceding the arrival of Special Agent in Charge Mia Diaz. She appeared out of an open office door halfway down the hall and stood with arms folded across her chest, frowning back at him.

"So get your ass in here already," she said. "You asked for this meeting, remember?"

She disappeared back into the doorway just as quickly, bringing a smile to Carlos's face. No matter how much they wanted to act like his being here was a pain in the ass, the simple truth was they needed him, and everybody in the building knew it. They could stomp around and piss and moan, but the fact that within hours of demanding the meeting he was on his way to the airport proved how invaluable he really was.

Carlos dragged out the walk as long as he could, pausing every few feet to glance at a poster on the wall, or peek into one of the darkened offices lining the corridor. Deep inside he was scared, or at the very least concerned, about what had arrived on his doorstep. Still, he couldn't let them know that, couldn't give off the impression that he was relying on them.

If that happened, they took back control of the relationship, and that was something he could ill afford.

Swinging through the open doorway, Carlos walked into a conference room almost twenty feet in length. A long, oval table was stretched through the middle of it, and high-backed burgundy leather chairs were spaced about. Almost half of them each contained a man in a suit staring back at him, none of them looking the least bit enthusiastic to be there.

Standing on the right side of the room was Diaz, her arms still folded. She too wore a black pantsuit with a white shirt beneath it, a mess of black curls spilling down onto her shoulders. She stood with her chin drawn back into her neck, accentuating the frown on her face.

"Good evening, lady and gentlemen," Carlos said, raising a hand to his brow and flicking a mock salute. "Trip was good, thanks for asking."

"What the hell do you want, Juarez?" Diaz said, her voice a decibel louder than necessary, no doubt meant to make a point.

Carlos stepped forward and grabbed the back of the closest chair, sliding it out and depositing himself in it. He laced his fingers across his stomach and smiled up at her. "Nice to see you too, Agent Diaz."

Diaz blew a long breath out through her nose and glanced at the ceiling, letting her rage play out plainly across her face. "We all have families and lives to get home to, Juarez. Either start talking or we're out of here."

Carlos knew he was playing it a bit cavalier, but he couldn't give off the vibe of desperation. If he did, he and his cousin were toast.

He raised his hands by his sides as if to signal for a cease-fire and reached into his pants pocket, extracting the single piece of paper he'd received the day before. He left it folded into eighths and tossed it onto the table, one side flat, the other sticking up at an angle.

"What the hell is that?" Diaz asked, jutting her chin toward the paper.

"Open it up and see," Carlos replied. He watched as Diaz flicked her gaze to the closest agent and nodded upward, a quick, curt gesture telling him to take a look.

The man, a thin, wiry guy with blond hair shaved down into a flattop, reached out and took up the paper, unfolding it to its full size. He glanced once down at the words on it before turning it to face the room, rotating it in a half circle so everybody could see it.

THEY FOUND ME.

For a long moment nobody said a word, Carlos panning his gaze around the room, gauging for responses. As best he could tell, there were none, besides a couple of men who seemed to grow a bit more frustrated.

Not the effect he'd been hoping for.

"Who found who?" Diaz said, annoyance in her voice.

Carlos rotated himself in the chair to stare at her. "Mateo. That is the *me* in question there. As for the *they,* I'm pretty certain we all know who that is."

Diaz remained impassive as she stared at him. She didn't outright dismiss what he was saying, but she gave no indication of buying it, either.

"And you know this how?"

"Before we went our separate ways, the three of us—me, Mateo, Cuz—we all agreed that if something happened, we would let the others know. Yesterday, Mateo let me know."

The sound of Diaz's heels clicking again filled the room as she turned away from him, circling the room. "How do you know it was Mateo?"

"Well it damn sure wasn't Cuz, now was it?" Carlos challenged.

The remark earned him an angry glare from Diaz, who held the stare long enough to make her point before breaking eye contact, an unspoken concession that he was right.

"How'd he make contact?"

"That arrived this morning from UPS," Carlos said. "I was sitting around watching some Food Network, learning how to make a nice cheesecake using canned peaches, and this little Asian boy showed up with that letter. Hell of a job you guys did on that one, letting a damn ninja sneak by you."

The frown on Diaz's face grew deeper as she stared at Carlos, her path taking her down around the far end of the table. She looked like she wanted to comment on the statement he'd just made, but to her credit she let it pass.

"How'd he know where to find you?" Diaz asked.

Carlos raised his palms for a moment, letting them slap down loudly against his thighs. "How the hell should I know? Maybe it came from Cuz? Maybe it came from one of your people?"

He knew there was no way his cousin had given Mateo the information. For one thing, his cousin only knew the city Carlos was now located in. For another, despite the fact that Mateo had grown up with them, he still wasn't a Juarez.

There is no way his cousin would have put blood at risk, even for a close friend.

"OK," Diaz said, her focus locked on him, "assuming this is real, which we're not just yet, so you know, but assuming this is real, what's your angle here? Why demand a meeting? Why not just call us and tell us you got a letter in the mail and it has you spooked?"

Carlos made a face at her, an exaggerated expression that relayed his disbelief at her statement. "What do I want? Lady, are you serious?"

There was no visible response at all from Diaz as she stopped her pacing and peered down at him. Both sides remained silent for a long moment before Carlos looked away, breaking into laughter. It started low and ironic, rising in both tenor and hilarity. He pushed out one hoot after another until his body shook, the sound reverberating off the walls.

Throughout the entire outburst, the remainder of the room sat in silence, staring back at him with stony expressions.

Carlos ignored every last one of them until the mirth within him faded.

"I apologize," he said, shaking his head. "I just have to laugh at you government assholes to keep from getting *pissed off.*"

Upon the last two words he drew his voice short, letting them hear his anger, making them feel his burning hatred for the whole situation.

"Look, I get that you guys have to sit here in your little black suits and stare down at me and pretend this is all a big pain in your ass, but this is how it's going to go.

"First, you're getting my ass out of Texas. Actually, let me rephrase that: my ass is never going back to Texas."

More silent stares came back to him, nobody saying a word.

"Second," Carlos said, reaching out and jamming two fingers down into the tabletop, "you guys go find Mateo. Find out where he is, who's chasing him, do whatever you have to. Figure it out.

"And third, I want to see my cousin. Within the next two days."

Carlos leaned back in his chair and placed his hands atop his stomach, his fingers laced. The air had been sucked out of the room as everybody present stared back at him, most of them stewing as if they might explode and hurtle themselves the length of the table at him any moment.

He glanced over each of the men seated around him before settling his attention on Diaz. For all the bravado of having a room full of people so he felt outnumbered, her reaction was the only one that mattered. She stared at him for a full minute, her lips pursed in front of her. Carlos could almost see her mind working as she did so, coming to the same conclusions he had during the preceding hours.

She didn't like it, but she didn't have a choice.

"Is there anything else?" she asked, an edge in her voice.

Carlos stared at her a long moment before nodding his head back against the chair behind him. "Yeah, the next place you send me better have a damn remote that works."

Chapter Fourteen

There was no way for Pavel to know how much time had passed. Judging by the darkness creeping in through the single frosted pane of glass high on the wall above him, he figured it to be sometime early in the evening, though that was just a guess. From where he sat in the holding cell of the West Yellowstone Police Department, there were no clocks of any kind. A deputy had been by midday to bring him a sandwich—three slices of ham and wilted lettuce on a hoagie roll—and some chips, but otherwise he had been left alone.

The entire time, he sat on the metal cot with his back pressed against the block wall behind him, letting the cool feel of it pass through his T-shirt. He kept his hands spread wide, fingers splayed across his thighs, and stared straight ahead, appearing as noncombative as possible. When he had to go to the restroom, he did so. When the food arrived, he ate it. He had little doubt he was being watched by somebody somewhere inside the building, and he needed them to believe he was nothing more than a concerned brother who had taken things a bit too far.

Pavel had considered playing that angle to the hilt, standing along the bars, pleading for anybody listening to let him see Lita. Three different reasons kept him from actually doing so, each one springing to his mind within seconds of him taking a seat inside the cell.

First was the simple fact that his physical dimensions wouldn't allow it. There was nothing to stop him from trying to work that approach, but he was fully aware of how he looked. A man his size, with his general demeanor, would never be believable in that role. He would only be making a mockery of himself, bringing the entire story into question.

Second, there was nobody around to hear it anyway. Pleading only worked if there was a guard sitting at the end of the hall, trying to get work done, tired of hearing the incessant whining. Only then would he have a chance, the guard trading away whatever Pavel wanted for some silence.

Third, and most important, he remembered with great clarity the complainers he'd been forced to endure while incarcerated in St. Petersburg. There was no way he'd lower himself to such a pathetic state.

So instead he sat and waited, his head reclined against the wall, staring at nothing in particular, letting his mind work over what he knew.

Sergey would be expecting a check-in soon, though he still had a day or two before his absence would be cause for alarm. He had been sent on nothing more than a fool's errand, so letting Viktor know what had transpired wasn't necessary.

At some point he would need to check on Lita's and Mateo's deaths, to confirm what the paper told him. While there was no reason to believe the information was incorrect, he needed to be certain.

That left only two ends to tie up before heading back to San Diego. The first was his car, which had almost certainly been impounded. Given the size of the town and the building he now sat in, his best guess was that it was sitting less than fifty yards away from him, keys inside, ready to take him home. There would be the issue of the gun inside, and despite it being registered in California, that could pose a problem.

The other was the guide, Hawk. He'd yet to so much as see a picture of the man, since the article in the paper hadn't mentioned him at all. It didn't appear he had been by his office in a few days, either, so the number of places he could be by now were infinite.

The sound of a door opening at the end of the hall drew Pavel from his thoughts, and he rotated his head toward it. He waited in silence until two men appeared before raising his head and sitting up straighter.

The man on the right was the West Yellowstone sheriff, the man who had booked Pavel earlier in the day. He had sandy-brown hair and a matching moustache. The legs of his tan uniform were rumpled from his sitting for most of the day. He kept his thumbs hooked into the front pockets of his trousers as he walked, his attention aimed at the cell.

Beside him was a man in his late thirties to early forties whom Pavel had never seen before. He had blue-black hair parted severely to the side and a heavy five o'clock shadow. His tie was loosened away from his neck. In his hand he carried a thin green folder.

Both men stood in front of the cell for a long time before either spoke, the sheriff deferring to the man by his side.

"Good evening. I'm Special Agent Andrew Cofey, FBI, assigned to Yellowstone Park. I apologize for the delay in getting here, but I had business on the south end of the park today that kept me away.

"Mind if we ask you a few questions?"

Pavel stared back at them without making a sound. His first impression when seeing the pair walk up was that they would try to play good cop/bad cop on him. It was now apparent they were eschewing the bad-cop portion and going straight for the kindness approach. Offering condolences up front, not dragging him into an interrogation room, asking if they could talk to him, as if he had a choice in the matter.

Their manner was clear enough. It was their motive he wasn't so certain about.

"FBI?" Pavel said, his voice thick and gruff from a day of going unused. He was more surprised than he let himself show, not expecting a federal presence over a simple break-in.

Cofey glanced over at the sheriff and said, "Because Yellowstone Park is federal land, the FBI keeps a special agent on hand for all investigations within its boundaries. I understand you have a connection to one such investigation."

Pavel furled his brow tight and said, "A connection? You mean my sister?"

Cofey opened the folder in his hand and extracted a single glossy photo from it, holding it up to the bars. "You mean this woman? A—" he paused a moment, consulting the file "—Lita Haney?"

For the first time, Pavel stood, pushing himself up from the cot with great effort. He slowly put one foot at a time out in front of him, measuring his steps, keeping his gaze on the image. How he handled the next few minutes would determine the outcome of his plan, dictate if his ruse had any chance of succeeding.

He walked to the bars and wrapped his massive hands around them, staring at the photo. He did his best to wear a morose look before glancing back to Cofey and nodding. "Yes. That is Lita. Was Lita."

Cofey stared at Pavel a moment before lowering the photo and putting it back in the folder.

Where he stood was close enough Pavel could have reached out and grabbed him by the shirt, jerking his body forward into the bars, dropping him unconscious to the floor. For just a moment he entertained the idea, thinking of the sickening crack his skull would make, of the sight of his blood on the concrete floor, but he quickly let the notion go. The sheriff was beyond reach, and despite any obvious physical advantages Pavel had on him, the bars separating them and the gun on the man's hip more than compensated for them.

"I'm sorry for your loss," Cofey said, backing up a few inches and clasping his hands in front of him, the folder cradled in his right palm.

Pavel noticed that they hadn't asked any follow-up about his being related to Lita, meaning they had already run his license against hers and found the identities solid.

"How did she die?" he asked, sure to keep his voice low.

Cofey shook his head and said, "I'm sorry, but right now that is an ongoing investigation. I really can't share any details."

Pavel nodded and lowered his gaze to the floor. "I understand. When can I take her home?"

Again Cofey shook his head. "Same answer, I'm afraid. We'll take good care of her until the investigation is over, and then see to it she is returned for a proper funeral."

"Thank you."

"Can you tell me what she was doing up here?" Cofey asked, shifting gears.

"I don't know a lot," Pavel said, head still aimed at the floor. "My mother called and said she had come up to bring home our friend Matthew. He worked for us in the family business, running the finances."

Cofey went back into the file and produced a second photo. "Is this your friend Matthew?"

Pavel raised his gaze and stared at the image of Mateo Perez a moment before nodding his head. His reason for being in Montana was now confirmed. "Matthew was an excellent accountant, but he was troubled. Sometimes he would take off by himself, and my sister would have to go find him, bring him home."

Cofey put the photo back and again glanced at the sheriff. "So this wasn't the first time?"

"No," Pavel said. "But this was the first time we'd lost contact with her, too. After a day or two, we started to worry. After a week, my mother asked me to come check on her."

"I see," Cofey said, stepping back once more and nodding. "And that's how you came to be breaking into the Hawk's Eye Tours office this morning when Sheriff Latham's deputies found you?"

Pavel had to force the corners of his mouth not to curl up into a smile. It was such a basic interrogation technique, such rudimentary questioning by someone who clearly had no idea who stood before him, or of the things he'd been through.

"I'm sorry," he said, his voice a whisper. "I didn't take anything, and I will pay to replace the window. It's just, when I got there and saw the sign that it was closed for the winter . . ."

"What made you go there to begin with?" Cofey asked.

The question stuck in the back of Pavel's mind. It was an odd thing to ask, something that should have been self-explanatory to them.

"She told us the last time we spoke that was who she had hired as a guide."

Cofey and the sheriff both traded another look before Cofey drew his mouth into a line and nodded. "Thank you, Mr. Haney. I hope you don't mind, but we'll need to keep you here another day or two on the breaking-and-entering charge, at least until we get this investigation wrapped up."

Pavel knew the American justice system well enough to know that was not at all how things were usually handled. If they planned to keep him, he was entitled to a lawyer, some more formal explanation of his charges than an off-handed comment about breaking and entering.

Whatever reason they had for keeping him meant they wanted him close, and they wanted him talking. Starting the process formally eliminated both of those things.

"Have a good evening," Cofey said, motioning Sheriff Latham toward the door. Together they shuffled away, shoes dragging against concrete, until they were just a few feet from the door before Cofey turned, raising a finger at Pavel.

"Oh, one last thing. Your sister wasn't by chance missing a hand, was she?"

Pavel stared back at Cofey a long moment, his face neutral, before twisting it up into a look of surprise. "No, both there the last time I saw her. Why?"

Cofey nodded without responding and turned toward the door, disappearing through it, the sheriff right behind him. Pavel stared after them a long moment before returning to the cot and taking a seat.

The question had been meant to try and get under his skin, to pry free some bit of information that he had yet to give them. In truth, it had told him everything he needed to know.

The guide was still alive, and he was on the hunt.

Chapter Fifteen

The living room of Hutch's place was outfitted much the same as the kitchen and study. Dark wood lined the floors and walls, the furniture bathed in deep hues of cranberry and brown. A comically large flat screen television filled one entire wall while framed paintings of landscapes covered the others.

The spoils of a bloated government salary.

The oversized leather sofa seemed to swallow me whole as I leaned back into it, the plush cushioned seats enveloping my body. I fought the sensation for a moment, trying to keep myself perched on the edge, before letting go and falling back into the sofa. A puff of air rose up around me as I did, hissing into my ears, as the chair molded itself to my contours.

I propped my elbow on the arm of the sofa, using it to hold my cell phone in place against my head. Kaylan had called five hours earlier while we were in the bowels of the DEA. She'd left a message stating it was important I call her back, but she hadn't mentioned what had happened or why it was so dire we speak.

She was about the only person in all of Montana I had even the slightest bit of loyalty to, and her calling proved she was okay. I wasn't particularly in the mood for talking on the phone, but if she claimed it was urgent, I did at least owe her the courtesy of believing it.

Without ringing once, an automated voice told me to enjoy the music as a bad rendition of "Over The Rainbow" played. Bypassing the usual ukulele and bongos for a jazz piano and flute, it sounded like something from a hotel lounge show, bringing a wince to my face and causing me to hold the phone an inch away from my head.

Not until I heard Kaylan's voice come on the line did I press it back to my ear.

"Hawk! Where the hell have you been?" Kaylan snapped, not bothering with a greeting of any kind.

"Well, hello to you, too," I said, a tiny bit of sarcasm present, just enough to let her know I didn't appreciate the tone, but I wasn't too upset about it.

"Sorry," she said, backing off an inch or two. "It's just, I called you like six times this morning, every one of them went straight to voice mail. I started to get worried."

My body grew a touch rigid as she explained. There were times when I'd been out of contact in the park for days at a time and she hadn't blinked an eye. For her to be so worried about a few hours' absence meant something had her spooked.

"What happened?" I asked.

"The shop was broken into this morning." Kaylan shoved the words out in a quick string, bunched so tight it sounded like one unending sound.

My heart rate ticked up a single beat as I processed the information, blowing a long breath out through my nose. "How bad?"

"Not bad at all," Kaylan said. "The guy broke the rear window and climbed in, setting off the motion sensors. Patrol was right down the street and showed up within five minutes. From what I can tell he didn't get anything."

"Local guy?" I asked, rubbing my brow. It wasn't the first time a business in town had been vandalized, usually by some kids out after a football game, looking to blow off some steam.

"Not at all," Kaylan said. "I haven't seen him, but Latham said the guy's a giant, looks like one of the villains from an old Superman movie. Claims he's that girl's brother, just here trying to find her. They're holding him at the department now."

The information fed itself into the tangle already bouncing around in my mind, trying to find a niche where it made sense. The likelihood of this random Lita showing up, asking me to take her to Mateo, whom she killed, and then my office being broken into a week later by a man claiming to be related to her was just too much to write off as coincidence.

It had to all fit together, I just had no idea how.

"Damn," I muttered, my voice low.

"I know," Kaylan said, empathy in her tone. "Sheriff Latham said he tried to call you, but when he couldn't get through he contacted me."

"Yeah," I said, nodding, barely hearing what she was saying, my thoughts far away.

"I went over and did a quick walk-through with Deputy Ferry just to assess the damages, but I haven't been back since. Felt kind of spooky in there, even with him by my side."

I blinked twice, forcing myself back into the present, and shook my head hard to clear it. "Yeah, no, that makes sense. If you could, call Henry down the road and ask him to fix the window. Pay him whatever it takes, just put it on the company account."

"All right," Kaylan whispered. "You okay, Hawk?"

"I am," I said, nodding at the painting of a purple sunset over the desert on the wall opposite me.

I hadn't told Kaylan where I was going when I left. Hadn't told her when I'd be back, either. The truth was I didn't know the entire answer to those questions, and I damned sure didn't want to put her in danger by someone thinking she did.

"Thanks for calling," I said, a note of finality in my voice. "I'll be in touch."

I cut off the call and sat alone in the living room a moment, a fist raised to my mouth. I stared at the painting until my eyes glossed over, my vision going blurry as I tried to force everything together.

Try as I might, I couldn't. There was just too much I didn't yet know.

"Everything all right?" Hutch asked, snapping me awake. He strode in stocking feet across the hardwood floor, a tumbler in each hand, and extended one to me.

I accepted the drink with a nod, touching the rim of it to his with a clink. "Shop got broken into," I said, lifting the glass to my lips. Out of reflex my body bristled as a few drops entered my throat, a conditioned response to years of being forced to share the alcohol Hutch enjoyed for himself, a cross between horse piss and rubbing alcohol.

To my surprise the amber-colored liquid slid down easily, leaving a sweet taste behind, as if laced with honey.

"Damn, that's excellent," I said.

"Ha!" Hutch spat, coughing out the laugh. "Johnnie Walker Blue. The good stuff."

"I'll say," I agreed, taking one more sip before sliding it onto the table beside me. "Apparently my shop was broken into this morning by a mammoth claiming to be Lita's brother."

"Aw, hell. What'd he take?"

"Nothing, as far as we can tell."

Hutch swigged down more of the whisky and smacked his lips, a sour expression on his face that I knew wasn't derived from his drink. "That can't just be a coincidence."

"Not at all," I agreed. "We get a hit back on her prints yet?"

"Not yet," Hutch said, shaking his head. "She wasn't in our system, so we had to expand the search. Apparently the NSA has been less than cooperative thus far in granting us access."

"Dicks," I muttered, pondering the situation. "Kaylan said they're holding him now. Any chance they can keep him until we get an ID back on her?"

Hutch stared off a moment, rolling around the idea. "Depending on how long it takes. They can't hold him indefinitely on what sounds like a simple B&E, especially if he didn't take anything. That takes it clear down to criminal trespass, a misdemeanor."

"Right," I said, nodding in agreement. I pondered everything in silence a moment before beginning to think out loud. "At the moment there are two bodies in the morgue at Yellowstone jail. One I knew from a lifetime before, the other had made a point of bringing me in to go find him and letting me see him die."

"To make a point? Or did she think she was doing you a favor?" Hutch asked.

The question set me back a moment; I hadn't thought of that possibility yet. "But a favor how? I didn't, don't, know the woman. And why would they go to that length to do it anyway? I've been out of the game for five years now."

"Amongst Injuns, a tribe's greatness is figured on how mighty its enemies be."

I nodded at the movie line, agreeing with the sentiment, even if I was still unsure how I fit in. I chewed on it another moment before letting it go and reaching for my drink.

"All right," I said, pushing the words out with a lengthy sigh, "what do we do now?"

Hutch twirled the glass in his hand a moment, its contents spinning around. He kept his focus aimed at it a long moment and said, "The way I see it, we've got two things going simultaneously. We've got this break-in up north and that whole mess."

"And we've got whatever's happening in the south that sent Mateo on the run to begin with," I finished.

"So," Hutch said, finally taking his gaze from his drink and looking up at me. "I go one way, you go the other?"

Chapter Sixteen

The eleven-hour time difference meant that it was ten a.m. in Russia as Viktor Blok shut the door to his office and stepped inside. He had started checking his watch incessantly two hours before, careful not to get too caught up in the evening's revelry to miss his appointment.

It was a standing call every Thursday night, first thing Friday morning back in Russia. A weekly check-in to let Sergey know how things were going, get an update on information that needed to be passed down.

Viktor shrugged off his purple velvet smoking jacket and let it drop to the floor behind him, leaving it where it lay as he walked through the room and took up a post behind his desk. He drew in a deep breath and pulled the phone receiver from its cradle, dropping it atop his table. The dial tone buzzed out from the speakers, filling the room.

The exercise had started three years before, when Viktor had been appointed to look over the North American operation. At the time he had been a twenty-nine-year-old kid, not yet quite ready for the post, and he knew it. His uncle had gone out on a limb for him in securing the position, a fact every person in the organization was aware of. The calls had served as a way for the old man to stay connected, to exert control, and to calm the other partners' nervousness about the plan to expand.

Now, three years later, the calls seemed more like blind oppression, paying taxes to a king an ocean away.

Pushing an angry breath out through his nose, Viktor pressed a single button and the line began to ring. It chirped a full dozen times in his ear before it was picked up, knowing better than to disconnect before it was answered.

"You're late," the voice said, a scratchy tone that was the end result of decades of cigars and vodka.

Viktor slid back the cuff on his black silk shirt and checked his Patek Philippe watch, the illuminated face on it stating it was exactly eleven o'clock.

"My watch must be a minute or two behind. My apologies."

A derisive sniff rolled out over the line. "Yeah, I'm sure that's it."

Viktor rolled his eyes, picturing the fat little man with his beady eyes and sun-spotted head, and bit back a retort.

He'd made that mistake before. No need to relive it.

"Where are we with things?" Sergey asked, moving straight to business, as he always did.

Viktor lowered himself into his padded leather desk chair and rested his elbows on the arms of it, his fingers steepled in front of him. "Things are progressing well. The takeover is near complete now, with only one last distributor still displaying any reluctance at all."

"Which one?" Sergey snapped, ignoring the first part of the assessment.

"La Jolla, on the north side of San Diego."

"That going to be a problem?"

"Not at all," Viktor said, shaking his head. "It's a wealthy community, the kind that thinks they can control things with a little bit of cash. Nothing we haven't seen many times over, here and back home."

Again a nasty chortle rolled out over the line, drawing another eye roll from Viktor. For the first two years the operation had felt like a partnership, a joint venture between two generations of Bloks, the older handing things down to the next.

In just the last twelve months that impression had begun to evaporate as Sergey took an increased interest in the business. It started with him sending Pavel stateside to look over Viktor's shoulder, had continued with random phone calls at odd hours, an increased demand for access to the financials.

"When are you thinking this will be under control?" Sergey asked.

Viktor tapped the pads of his fingers together in front of him and said, "I sent up a small scouting party yesterday. They were going to dig around, determine how much it would take to make the problem go away quietly, how many men it would take to make it an example."

"I don't need to remind you that right now we would prefer the quiet option," Sergey said, his voice taking on a stern tone.

"I'm aware," Viktor said, moving his focus toward the ceiling, keeping his gaze aimed at the stucco surface above him. "How long before we'll be ready to start importing our own product?"

"Just waiting on you," Sergey replied, no small amount of condescension in his voice.

Viktor gritted his teeth and pushed a long breath out between them, animosity rising within him. "One week. Two at most."

There was more he wanted to add, about the rumors of delays in production that were drifting across the Pacific, about the dissatisfaction with the organization, the mentioning of decreased sales. Still, he kept his tongue, careful not to draw any unnecessary heat. If things were wrapped up in a week and the shipments began arriving as planned, his upward mobility would be impossible to track.

He would be hailed as a wunderkind, the new blood that revived a dying system.

He only had to bide his time.

"Good," Sergey said. "Is there anything else?"

Viktor glared at the phone a moment before shaking his head in disgust. The old man knew full well what was going on with Mateo Perez. He had insisted on using Lita, was no doubt being fed updates from Pavel. He was simply testing Viktor, wanting to see how much he would disclose, how honest he would be.

Across from him the door to his office opened, one half of the sliding doors parting, moving silently on its rollers. A gap no more than a foot wide appeared and a long leg slid through, followed by the lithe figure of a young girl, a satin black shift clinging to her.

She pushed the door shut behind her the moment her body passed through it, walking one hip at a time into the room.

"There has still been no word from Lita," Viktor said, fighting to keep his voice neutral, to not let the old man hear his distaste. His gaze danced over the girl as she stood there, her long hair hanging down in dark waves, her nipples erect beneath the light material.

"And?" Sergey demanded.

"I sent Pavel up yesterday to deal with it. I have not yet heard from him, but—"

"Pavel will take care of it."

The intent of the statement was clear, but Viktor let it slide, his mind preoccupied with the girl across from him. He watched as she pressed the back of her thighs into the armchair across from him and slid her body onto it, her skin standing in stark contrast against the dark material.

"You are right, Uncle," Viktor said. "Pavel is a good man. I can trust him."

If not for the preoccupation in front of him, the words would have tasted putrid on his tongue. He shook his head even as he said them, angry at what his position had been reduced to.

"Yes, he is," Sergey said. "And you can."

A moment of silence passed, Viktor staring at his prize, knowing she was just moments away.

"Is that it?" Sergey asked a second time.

"Yes, that is it," Viktor said, leaning forward in the chair, smiling at the girl, a ravenous glint in his eye.

"Same time next week, then," Sergey said. "And try not to be late."

The call cut away to a dial tone as Viktor pressed his palms into the desk and rose to a standing position. He placed the phone back in its cradle, already forgetting the pointed barb his uncle threw at him to close the conversation, and peered down at the girl.

"Now who, might I ask, are you?"

Chapter Seventeen

Hutch got me on an Air Force flight out of Andrews at five o'clock in the morning, the last man on a bird packed tight with Navy grunts headed to San Diego. Most of them looked like they hadn't been finished at Annapolis more than a day or two; their faces were still unlined, their hair still buzzed ridiculously short.

My title for making it onto the plane, and for the duration of my investigation, was as an official consultant to the DEA. I was given a badge identical to the one I'd carried five years before and told to wear a tie, shuffled right back into the rank and file like I had never left.

The only two differences were that I wasn't being paid and I got to keep my hair. The first one I agreed to without a fight, the second one Hutch did the same.

Neither of us had the time or inclination to sweat the small stuff.

Given the three-hour time difference between the coasts, I landed in San Diego at eight a.m., six hours after takeoff. A sedan was waiting for me when I arrived, a perk of having one of the ranking officials in the administration calling in favors. A brand-new agent was waiting for me when I stepped off the plane, his black suit and sunglasses making him obvious amidst a sea of sailors in uniform.

A formal introduction and an exchange of handshakes was the sum total of our interaction as we piled into the generic black car and drove away, each of us lost in our thoughts. Me, still trying to piece together everything that was happening, determine my next move. Him, no doubt pissed about pulling the grunt duty of having to go and pick me up.

With traffic, it took us a little over an hour to make the trip across the desert. The morning sun burned away the overnight dew and promised to bring another warm day with it, regardless of what the calendar said. In silence, we pulled up in front of the DEA Southwest headquarters and I climbed out, waving thanks to a car already pulling away from the curb.

Bag in hand, I took a quick look at the place. The image was exactly as I remembered it from five years before, down to the size and shape of the bushes lining the front.

Government spending at its finest.

A pretty young SoCal blonde smiled at me as I entered, giving me a quick up-and-down as she did so. I couldn't help but notice the smile didn't make it all the way to her eyes; apparently my shaggy hair and airplane rumpled clothes didn't meet her approval.

"Good morning, how may I help you?"

"Yeah, my name is Jeremiah Tate. I'm here to see Mia Diaz," I said, glancing past her to the corridor extending out through the middle of the building. Despite the hour, many of the offices stood dark, the home bases for agents out working in the field. A small handful of staff could be seen passing between the others, most staring down at papers while they walked, the mood somber.

From where I stood, I could not hear a single voice.

"One moment, please," she said, lifting a phone from the desk and bringing it to her ear. She struck a sequence of keys and whispered into the receiver before nodding and returning it to its cradle.

"She'll be out in just one second," the girl said, the smile a little wider.

Keeping my bag in hand, I took a step back and waited. In most government buildings, a second meant I could be waiting upward of a half hour. From what little I knew about Mia Diaz, it was more likely to be a nanosecond.

She didn't disappoint.

My gaze had not yet done a complete lap of the foyer before the determined click of heels against a tile floor echoed down the hall. I turned to face a tall, striking woman marching toward me in a gray pant suit with a blue V-neck T-shirt under it, her hair pulled back behind her. As she walked forward, she stuck a hand out toward me and said, "Hawk."

"Diaz," I replied, returning the shake.

"Please, right this way."

She turned on a heel and led me back in the direction she'd come, a few faces appearing in doorways as we marched onward. I set my attention forward and ignored the stares as we went, careful not to let on that I even sensed their presence.

I wanted to believe there was no reason for anybody to be curious about my arrival, though I could imagine any number of stories had floated through the halls since my departure.

Diaz led me to a door standing open and slid to the side of it, motioning me onward. I passed through with a nod of thanks and waited as she shut the door behind us, then circled around me to her desk.

The last time I was in the office, it was occupied by Hutch, not long before our final meeting in the trailer a few miles east of where we now stood. The same blond wooden desk faced the room, dividing it in half, with the same dented metal shelves lining the wall above it. A steel filing cabinet stood in the corner, every item in the place replete with a metallic serial number sticker on it. The only things that had changed in the entire room were the knickknacks strewn about and the condition of the desk.

Hutch was a notorious slob, letting papers pile up for months. Diaz didn't have a stray item anywhere.

"Please, have a seat," she said, unbuttoning her jacket and dropping down into her chair.

I lowered my bag to the floor and did the same, settling into a plastic chair that was too narrow, pinching my hips and ribs. "Thank you for seeing me on such short notice."

"Not at all," she said, shaking her head. "As I'm sure you noticed on the way in, there's been quite a bit of speculation about you around here for a long time. Seeing you walk through that door is like viewing Bigfoot in the wild."

I smirked at the analogy, my head rocking back a few inches. "So you're telling me most people here didn't believe I existed?"

"Quite the contrary," Diaz said. "I think most people were fearful that you really did, that it was all true."

I nodded once in understanding. That explanation made a lot more sense.

"I apologize if Hutch strong-armed you into bringing me on," I said. "I recognize this is your house now. I'm not here to get in your way, just maybe poke around at some things I'm sure you don't have the staff or time for."

Diaz pursed her lips in front of her and tilted her head to the side, considering the statement. "We're overworked and undermanned, the standard government protocol, I won't deny you that. Depending on what you've got, though, I might be inclined to jump in with you."

My eyes narrowed a bit as I glanced over at her, the situation beginning to make sense. I had anticipated being met with open hostility, bringing with me a potential hornet's nest that could consume an outpost of this size. To avoid all that, Hutch had simply not told her why I was en route.

Whether that was a gift or a death sentence, I was about to find out.

"So he didn't tell you?"

"Just that it was very big, and that I would definitely be interested," she said, lifting her palms toward the ceiling before dropping them just as fast.

My shoulders raised in a quick shrug and I said, "It's big, all right, but whether you find it interesting or end up wishing we'd never met remains to be seen."

Any sense of levity receded from Diaz's features as she stared back at me. She raised her right hand and curled her fingers back toward herself, motioning for me to continue.

I had already given her fair warning, so I dove right in. I told her about Lita, about Mateo Perez, about a man currently in lockup in West Yellowstone and Hutch on his way to see him now. I told her everything, encapsulating the entire story in under three minutes, hitting every high point without going into excessive detail.

When I was done I fell silent, watching her digest the information, her face retreating into a stony mask. I waited a full two minutes for her to say anything, glancing up every so often as she set her gaze on the door behind me and put together everything I'd just said in her head.

When she finally spoke, her words surprised me. She didn't lash out and demand answers. She didn't challenge me on any points. She didn't even ask me any immediate follow-up questions.

Instead she said, "Mateo Perez voluntarily walked out of witness protection two weeks ago. It was against our strong advice, but he did so anyway."

"Any idea why?" I asked.

"Some guesses, nothing concrete."

I nodded. "Any reason to believe his location had been compromised?"

"He seemed to think so."

I arched an eyebrow at her, awaiting an explanation, but she waved a hand at me, letting me know we would get to it later. I could venture a pretty substantial hypothesis as to what she was thinking and why she refused to say it out loud, nodding my understanding.

"What kind of parameters did Hutch give you for my being here?"

"None," Diaz said, shaking her head. "He said your official position was as a consultant. I could give you as much assistance as I wanted, but I wasn't to obstruct you in any way."

"Something tells me he didn't put it quite so eloquently."

"'Either help him or stay the hell out of his way,'" Diaz replied, making air quotes with her fingers as she did so.

"Nice."

"He also made some quote about hunting griz, but I didn't quite catch that one," she added with a shrug.

The corner of my mouth tracked up, though the smile didn't make it all the way across. "Movie quote. Long story."

"Ah," Diaz said, nodding. "That makes two you'll have to tell me, then."

The corner retreated back down into place as I stared at her, knowing what she was alluding to. It was a story I replayed in my mind every night, but not one I was especially fond of retelling.

Had not done so once in five years, in fact.

"Oh, yeah?"

"Those are my terms," Diaz said. "Truth is I don't appreciate having the brass call in and dictate down to me, but in this case I could use the outside eyes. And the fact that I won't have to babysit you, even if you are a few years out of the game, helps a lot."

I nodded, rolling the proposal around in my head. Given the situation, my showing up at a moment's notice, asking to parachute in with something that could be paradigm changing for the entire region, it was more than fair.

I knew for a fact Hutch wouldn't have responded so well had the same thing been imposed on us. Damned sure knew I wouldn't have, either.

"Done," I said, nodding. "Not right now, but before it's over."

Diaz nodded in agreement, folding her hands together atop her stomach. "Okay then, where to start?"

"Hutch is in Yellowstone working on Lita and her mystery brother, so that leaves us with Mateo. I assume you're still keeping tabs on the Juarezes?"

Chapter Eighteen

A hulking guard in a tan shirt and brown slacks led Carlos Juarez down a narrow corridor, his every breath sounding labored as he pushed it out through his nose. The equipment strapped to his belt jangled with each step he took, a cacophony that reminded Carlos exactly where he was, where he never wanted to be again.

The walk ended abruptly at the end of the hallway with a single inward-swinging door, the top half of it made from glass crisscrossed with chicken wire. On the opposite side of it Carlos could see a room split in two equal parts with a clear floor-to-ceiling Plexiglas divider between them. On one side sat two women, each perched on a stool several feet apart. They both held phones to their ears and peered across at young men in gray canvas pants and matching short-sleeved button-downs.

"Go on in," the guard said, each word jumbled together, a complete lack of enunciation. "Take the far left stool. He'll be out in a minute."

Carlos nodded, grabbed the door handle, and slid into the room. A negative energy seemed to hit him as he stepped inside, a combination of fear and nervousness, the smell of body odor and sweat in the air. Neither of the women glanced his way as he walked past, toning down his usual swaggering gait and averting his gaze from the two inmates sitting on the other side of the divider. He settled himself down onto a squat round stool with a cushioned top, his knees folded up toward his stomach, and waited.

Two minutes after he took his seat, the door in the far back corner of the room opened and his cousin shuffled through. There were no cuffs or chains on his wrists or ankles, but his posture seemed to indicate he was used to wearing them; everything was bunched up tight, not moving more than a few inches.

Carlos stood as his cousin made his way to the corner, extending a fist to the plastic and pressing his knuckles against it. A faint smile crossed his cousin's face as he extended his own hand, reaching out slowly, as if he were afraid the imaginary cuffs would restrain him, and returned the gesture.

Manuel Juarez was older than Carlos by three years in real-world terms, though he had always carried himself in a way that made him seem much older. His time inside had done nothing but exacerbate the chasm between them; his movements were slower, his mannerisms more reserved.

As the two settled onto their respective stools and took up the phone receivers on the wall beside them, Carlos couldn't help but feel he was staring at a man twenty years his senior. Lines now encased his cousin's mouth and eyes. Gray hairs permeated his hair and goatee. A sense of weariness hung around him like a cloud.

"Good to see you, Manny," Carlos said, forcing a smile.

"Yeah, you too," Manny replied, nodding. He didn't bother to return the smile, letting Carlos see the worry on his face. "You know you shouldn't be here, Cuz. It isn't safe."

"It isn't safe anywhere right now," Carlos said, the smile retreating from his features. He pressed the receiver as tightly as he could to his mouth and whispered, "They found Mateo."

Manny pulled the phone away from his face and dropped it on the counter in front of him. He looked away to the side and ran a hand across his forehead, his mouth turned down in a frown.

After a long moment he picked the phone up and stared back at Carlos. "When?"

"The package arrived two days ago. Doing the math, I'm guessing a week, week and a half."

"Shit," Manny whispered, extending the word out several times its usual length. "Did he go up north, like he said he would?"

Carlos glanced back over his shoulder. The two women on his side of the room were both engrossed in their conversations, each one staring straight ahead. The elderly woman seemed to have tears in her eyes while the younger one looked to be just seconds from exploding.

Behind him was a sheet of one-way glass extended across most of the room, a cadre of guards on the other side watching his every move.

"I don't know," Carlos said, shaking his head. "I assume so. It was what we'd always agreed."

Manny nodded, glancing up past Carlos toward the glass behind him. "Yeah."

Carlos rose an inch off the stool and adjusted himself, lowering back down on to it. He leaned his upper body in another few inches and said, "What do you want me to do?"

A long moment of silence passed as Manny stared at the glass, shaking his head.

"Cuz?" Carlos asked, his voice low, probing.

Still, Manny stayed locked in his thoughts, no response.

"Cuz!" Carlos spat in an urgent whisper, drawing a quick look from the elderly women to his right.

The word seemed to snap Manny awake, causing him to blink several times, shifting his gaze back to Carlos. "Worst thing we ever did was enter that partnership."

"I know," Carlos whispered, bobbing his head, "but we didn't have a choice. You know that."

"Didn't we?" Manny said, the right side of his face twisted up in disbelief. "What if we hadn't? Everybody would be alive? I'd still be in here?"

Carlos leaned back a moment and ran his free palm down the length of his thigh. More than once he had considered the same question, often coming to the same conclusion as Manny. He himself might also be in jail if they hadn't gone through with it, but given the losses they'd taken in the time since, it might have been worth it.

Still, he couldn't express any of that. He couldn't lay any extra grief onto his cousin, couldn't make it worse than what it was clear he was already feeling.

So instead, he ignored it.

"What do you want me to do?" Carlos asked, pausing between every word, weighing each one carefully.

"Have you talked to the feds?"

"Last night," Carlos said. "Told them what had happened and that I needed to see you, fast."

"What did they seem to think?"

Carlos blew a quick breath out through his nose, loud enough for his cousin to hear and infer what he was trying to say. "Nothing. And I don't mean nothing of substance, I mean nothing at all."

A scowl grew across Manny's face as he shook his head. "Assholes."

Carlos nodded in agreement. "I got the impression they wanted to check out my story before they committed to doing anything."

"Yeah," Manny said, sarcasm laced through his tone, "and in the meantime . . ."

"My ass ends up dead," Carlos said. "Yeah, I know."

Manny fixed a gaze on him and said, "Mateo would never give you up. You know that."

"I do, but it doesn't matter now," Carlos said. "The package was sent. There's a trail out there. I can't go back to Texas, and I already told Diaz that."

"How'd she take it?"

Another head shake from Carlos. "Nothing."

Manny ran the back of his index finger under his nose, swiping at an itch, and sniffed deeply. "Give her a day or two. She's just checking facts. Of everybody over there, the chica's the only one with balls."

A smirk slid out of Carlos, rocking his body backward an inch. "Yeah, she's all right. Takes this shit seriously, makes it fun to mess with her."

"Yeah," Manny agreed, trying to force a bit of mirth onto his face. "What about the other? Any sign?"

"Nothing yet," Carlos said.

Manny's eyes narrowed as he again shifted his attention past Carlos, thinking. "I wouldn't be surprised if he surfaces soon. He won't stay away for long."

"Agreed," Carlos said. "He's in way too deep to let go now."

"Right," Manny said, nodding. "And what about the other guy? The one Mateo went up to find?"

Carlos twisted his head from side to side, his lips pursed. "Nothing out of him, either."

"You think they found him with Mateo?"

"I don't know," Carlos admitted, having considered the same thing on the trip in the day before. It wouldn't surprise him if it had happened; the entire thing had been nothing more than a sliver of hope Mateo had clung to long after he had any reason to.

A long shot, at best.

"Where do you think I should go?" Carlos asked, leaving those and many other thoughts unspoken. As much as he wanted to share them with his cousin, he just couldn't bring himself to, not in this situation, not knowing where they were both headed off to soon.

Manny sat silent for a long moment. He laid the phone down again and wrung his hands in front of him, visibly weighing the options while Carlos kept the phone pressed to his face and waited.

Once his internal debate was finished he picked up the receiver and said, "Stay the course. See how fast they found Mateo on his own? At least this way you've got someone watching your back."

"No matter how incompetent," Carlos muttered, rolling his eyes.

"No matter how incompetent," Manny agreed. "All right, Cuz, keep me posted."

"Will do," Carlos said, sensing that the conversation was over. They both knew that every word was being listened to, neither one wanting to say anything beyond the bare necessities needed.

He stood, extending his fist back to the plastic divide, returning the phone to its cradle on the wall. Across from him, Manny did the same, the cousins locking eyes for a moment, both of them solemn, and nodding.

They walked toward their respective doors, neither one looking back. Carlos could see the elderly woman and her young counterpart both still locked in conversation in his periphery as he went. He didn't once glance at them or at the mirrored glass on his opposite side.

The tension of the room seemed to fade away as he crossed out into the hallway, the door swinging shut behind him. The sounds of the women's voices, the feeling of desperation, the stench in the air, all drained away as he stood there, taking in what stood across from him.

He'd expected to find the same guard as before, waiting with a hand on his hip, the buttons of his uniform screaming for mercy beneath his bulbous frame. Instead he got Special Agent Diaz, her arms crossed over her chest, frowning at him.

Beside her stood a man Carlos hadn't seen in five years. He was a little older, his hair shaggier, but he was unmistakable, standing there in a rumpled suit.

Carlos's jaw dropped a half inch as he looked at the man, realizing Mateo had been right.

"Carlos Juarez," Diaz said, interrupting his thought. "We need to talk."

Chapter Nineteen

Hutch swirled the dregs of his latte in the bottom of a tall paper cup that had the gaudy mascot for a drive-up stand named Mountain Moose Coffee emblazoned on the side. After twelve hours in transit that had included two car rides and two flight connections, he'd choked down the coffee, though the only redeeming qualities he could find in it were the cheap cost and the bubbly twenty-something who served it to him.

Dark circles bordered his eyes, the telltale end product of an extremely long day. One of the upsides to taking the position in D.C. was he no longer had to travel the globe at a moment's notice. Even though he now rarely had to so much as leave the country, that didn't make it any more enjoyable.

Besides, he could be to almost any major European city on a direct flight faster than he could make his way to West Yellowstone, Montana.

Less than a day before, he had been sitting in his living room with Hawk, swirling a perfectly aged Johnnie Walker Blue in a crystal tumbler. Now he was standing outside an interrogation room in West Yellowstone drinking a cup of Mountain Moose piss from biodegradable paper.

Sometimes life was a bitch.

Hutch waited in a small darkened room deep in the bowels of the Sheriff's Department, staring through a window of one-way glass. On the other side was a room void of life, a single metal table with folding chairs on either side in the center of it. Two elongated fluorescent bulbs were stretched out parallel above it, casting a harsh glow over everything.

The door on the right side was pushed open after a moment, its hinges whining in protest. A giant of a man walked through first, his hands cuffed in front of him, dark hair shrouding most of his head and face. Behind him was FBI Special Agent Andrew Cofey, his tie loosened at the neck, a file in his hand.

Hutch tried swirling the coffee one more time before giving up on it and dropping it into the trash. As it landed in the can, the door beside it opened and Sheriff Latham stepped in, just missing the residual splash from the last bit of the latte.

"You were right," Hutch said, arching an eyebrow. "He is a big son of a bitch."

"Told you," the sheriff replied, folding his arms across his chest and turning to stare through the glass. "Reminds me of that one old boy from the Superman movies."

Hutch let out a small smirk, taking in the man as he sat in his chair, staring right at the glass. His gaze was so intense Hutch couldn't help but feel he was looking right at them, even though he knew the man could see nothing but his own reflection.

"Non, I think they called him," Hutch said, nodding. "The one that couldn't talk."

"Yup," Latham agreed. "This one here can talk, he just isn't saying anything."

Hutch shoved his hands into the pockets of his slacks, the sleeves of his sport coat bunching up by his wrist. It had been determined that Cofey would take a first run at the man, and if he got nowhere he would hand it over to Hutch to try.

After that, if they couldn't get anything to shake loose, they would have no choice but to cut him loose or charge him. If they charged him, he would be appointed a lawyer, and the odds of them getting anything of use went down tremendously.

This was their shot.

Inside the room, Cofey slid into his chair across from the prisoner, the back of his head facing the mirror. Despite Cofey appearing to be in his mid to late thirties, Hutch could already see a baseball-sized spot beginning to appear near the crown of his head, most of it covered by an elaborate swoop-and-swirl combing pattern. Once upon a time Hutch would have tried the same approach, but he had long since let such efforts fall by the wayside, accepting his age and his bachelor status with grace.

Some day Cofey would get there too. It would just take a while longer yet.

"All right," Cofey said, spreading the contents of his file out in an orderly line in front of him, "I'm going to start at the beginning here, just to get everything down for the record. That okay by you?"

The man across from him looked back as if he were bored and shrugged, offering no audible response.

"Okay," Cofey said, "could you please state your name for the record?"

The captive pushed out a long breath to show his disdain for the entire affair before stating, "Pavel Haney. Mora, New Mexico."

"Mhmm," Cofey said, jotting down a note. "And what do you do down there, Mr. Haney?"

"I work for my family's farming business," Pavel replied. "We grow chilies, ship them all over the world."

Another notation from Cofey. "I see. So what brought you up to West Yellowstone now? During a time I'm guessing you should be harvesting your crop?"

Pavel glanced up at the ceiling a moment, a move that Hutch noted could have meant he was frustrated, or trying to access the cover story he'd been trained to know.

"My sister, Lita, came up here a week ago to find our friend Matthew. He works for us and said he needed to get away. She came to try and bring him home. When we lost touch with her, I was sent to make sure everything was OK."

"Matthew. Right," Cofey said, finishing marking down the words and looking up at Pavel. "And did Matthew have a last name?"

Confusion passed over Pavel's face a moment as he gave a shake of his head. "I've never thought about that. We always just considered him family, but I don't think he was actually a Haney."

Hutch couldn't see Cofey's face from where he stood, but he could tell by his body language that he was growing antsy in his seat.

"Nice recovery," Hutch said, shaking his head at the exchange of obviously phony information going on in front of them.

"Complete bullshit is what it is," Latham said, running a hand back over his head, frustration growing on his face.

Hutch nodded in agreement and watched a moment longer before patting the sheriff on the arm. He said, "I've seen enough of this. I'm going in."

"Good luck," Latham said to his back, as Hutch stepped out into the hallway and knocked on the solid wooden door leading into the interrogation room. He remained outside a long moment before Cofey emerged, the exchange something they had discussed before the interview began.

They would do the swap without ever being in the room together, trying to throw Pavel off, not letting him get his bearings before switching the direction of things.

"Thanks for cutting me off early," Cofey said. "Much longer and I was going to start getting really pissed in there."

"I could tell," Hutch said, nodding. "Your shoulders were twitching like you wanted to fly across the table and club him to death with the butt of your gun."

"Damn," Cofey said, retreating two steps and opening the door into the observation room, "I didn't think I was being that obvious. Have to work on that."

He disappeared without another word. Hutch waited a few seconds to let him get situated before stepping inside.

The room was much colder than the rest of the building, the solid concrete enclosure putting a chill in the air. The smell of citrus disinfectant tickled his nose as he walked in, his gaze aimed at Pavel, his hands still shoved down deep into his pockets.

Across from him Pavel glanced up as he entered and looked back down at the table, his attention shifting up a moment later and remaining there. He tracked Hutch as he walked over and took a seat, shuffling the items strewn across the table back into the folder and dropping it to the floor beside him.

"Good afternoon," Hutch said, dropping his hands onto the table before him and lacing his fingers. "Tell me, red or green?"

Pavel stared back at him a long moment, a blank expression on his face. The wheels in his mind seemed to be visibly turning as he sat in silence, trying to piece together what was being asked of him. "Red?"

"Ah," Hutch said, nodding. "Good answer. I'm a hot man myself. Something in the range of an NM 6-4? You?"

The heavy brow of Pavel furled as he looked at Hutch, mistrust on his face. "Yes, that is a good one. I agree."

A smile curled up the corners of Hutch's mouth as he leaned back a few inches and said, "My name is Don Hutchinson, United States Drug Enforcement Administration."

The corners of Pavel's eyes twitched as he looked back at him. "DEA?"

Hutch had used the full title to gauge Pavel's familiarity with the organization. The fact he knew the acronym in under a second said he was familiar with their work and what they did.

"That's right," Hutch said. "Tell me, Pavel, does the name Mateo Perez mean anything to you?"

Cold Fire

The folds of skin around Pavel's eyes relaxed a fraction as he stared back at Hutch. His features flattened out, his face taking on a look that bordered on serene. "No."

"No? Nothing?" Hutch pressed.

"I live in New Mexico," Pavel said. "I've known a lot of Mateos, a lot of Perezes, but the name Mateo Perez doesn't come to mind."

"Okay," Hutch said, nodding. "How about Manuel Juarez?"

The serene look receded even further, taking on a pose that appeared almost catatonic. His eyes glazed over as he stared at a point just above Hutch's left shoulder, focusing on nothing. "Never."

"Carlos Juarez?"

"Not that I recall."

Hutch stared back at him a long moment. He looked right into Pavel's eyes, searching for any flash of recognition, any form of outward sign, but there was nothing.

"Okay," Hutch said, slapping his palms together and standing. He left Pavel sitting at the table without another word, striding from the room and shutting the door softly behind him. He stepped out into the hallway and leaned against the wall, his hands back in his pockets, and waited for Cofey and Latham to appear.

It took them less than ten seconds to emerge from the viewing area, both men almost tripping on one another trying to get out into the hall, expectant looks on their faces.

"That's it? You're done?" Cofey asked.

"No point in going further," Hutch said, his voice deadpan, almost resigned. "He's already told us everything he's going to."

"He's already told us . . ." Cofey began, letting the comment drift off. "So far he hasn't told us shit!"

"Exactly," Hutch said, nodding in agreement. "Everything he's given us so far came from things he didn't say. Now that those are exhausted, we're done here."

Both Cofey and Latham stared at him with jaws agape, glancing at each other before looking his way, their faces almost pleading for him to explain.

"First thing," Hutch said, "is he basically told me his entire back-story is bullshit. Anybody who's ever even driven through New Mexico knows red or green is the universal question for how you like your sauce, from red or green chilies. Can't even order without it coming up.

"When I asked him that, he looked at me like I was crazy. If some-one claiming to be a chili farmer doesn't know that, then his whole damn story is bullshit, no point pushing it any further."

Cofey and Latham both stared at him, their expressions unchanged, waiting for him to continue.

"Second, the moment I started asking names, his gaze shifted away from my eyes and his face went blank. *Too* blank. He knew exactly what I was talking about, he just couldn't look me in the eye and mak-ing a convincing case that he didn't."

With that, Hutch pushed his backside against the wall and drew himself up to full height. He nodded at the two of them and said, "Thanks for your help, gentlemen."

Turning on his heel, he kept his hands in his pockets and walked down the hall toward the front of the building, his mind already for-mulating his next move, cringing at the new journey that lay ahead.

"Hey, where the hell are you going?" Cofey called behind him, his voice echoing through the narrow corridor.

"California," Hutch whispered without looking back, pushing through the door at the end of the hall and stepping out into the cold Montana air.

Chapter Twenty

Carlos stretched out across the backseat of the Crown Vic, his legs spread wide, one foot tucked beneath the driver and passenger seats. He raised his arms and spread them wide along the bench extended from one side to another, his reflection staring back at him in the rearview mirror.

He seemed to be enjoying himself as we drove out of San Diego, the uneven skyline of San Diego receding from view, the city growing smaller behind us with each passing second. Vents blew cold air up at us from the front dash as we went, chilling the inside of the car.

The look on his face when he walked out of the visiting room was priceless. We had caught him completely unawares, shock and confusion jockeying for the primary position on his features.

Diaz was early, but she was expected. He knew it wouldn't be long after his chat with Manny before she showed up, poking around, wanting to know what was going on. That was part of the reason he'd asked to see her in the first place, knowing she would follow up on whatever was going on.

I was the part that had thrown him off. He must have figured Mateo going to Yellowstone had to do with me, but my arrival, unexpected and unexplained, caught him by surprise. In less than thirty seconds we could almost see the various thoughts running through his mind, from thinking maybe Mateo was nearby, to my showing up had to mean he didn't make it.

To his credit he rallied fast, the initial shock rolling off him by the time we got to the parking lot. Within three minutes he made the journey from unaware and cooperative back to his usual cocksure self, complete with faux bravado.

Diaz had tried to warn me beforehand how much it could grate on the nerves, but a quarter hour into the drive I was already starting to see how much of an understatement that had been.

"Sure was sweet of you guys to drive all the way to San Diego to pick me up," Carlos said, his head bobbing a bit as he talked, staring out the window. "Just felt like getting out for a drive, I take it?"

Beside me Diaz glared at him in the rearview mirror, her frown deep set, but she said nothing.

"I mean, if you needed me to stop by the office for a chat, I would have," Carlos added. "But this is much better. Now we get to spend some quality time together, get to know each other, then have our little discussion. I like it."

Once more Diaz cast her gaze at him through the mirror, but remained silent. That was the arrangement we had worked out on our way in, figuring out how to best approach Carlos.

In the preceding months, Diaz had been forced to work with Carlos a great deal, however tenuous such a relationship might have been. Over that time they'd gotten used to each other, figuring out what buttons to push, how to try to get under the other's skin.

I was a complete wild card, though. Carlos didn't know me from Adam, didn't know how long or short my leash might be, didn't know how I reacted when provoked.

There would be no good cop in our temporary partnership we decided, something more along the lines of bad cop/scary cop, with me playing the latter. It was a role I hadn't taken on in quite some time, but something I figured I shouldn't have much trouble slipping right back into.

"Just three friends, some old, some new—"

"Shut up," I said from the front seat, making my voice sound as bored as possible. "You talk too damn much."

"Shut up?" Carlos repeated, his voice incredulous. I didn't bother looking back at him, but I was sure he was checking Diaz through the rearview mirror. "And I talk too damn much? Isn't that the reason you came and got me? So you could take me back, put me in that big room, make me spill my guts?"

I rolled my head along the back of the seat to Diaz and said, "You were right. He isn't very damn bright."

"Not very—" Carlos began to protest again, his voice rising in protest.

"Shut up!" I snapped once more, cutting him off. "This *is* the talk, you dumbass. So shut the hell up for five seconds so we can get this over with."

Behind me I could sense movement, the natural reaction of any person who felt they were being attacked. I could imagine him pulling his hands in from either side and folding them across his torso, drawing his legs up tight. It was the body's instinctive reflex, to make a small target of oneself, give an enemy as little surface area as possible.

"Man, I don't know who the hell you think you are," he started again, strain in his tone. He was a man that was used to having control, being able to use his quips and braggadocio to steer a conversation. Already he was on his heels, hopefully more focused on winning the situation than the words coming out of his mouth.

"You know who I am," I said, keeping my gaze aimed out the front window. Beside me, Diaz remained quiet, her hands locked at ten and two, attention on the road ahead. "You knew it the second you stepped out of that room. It took you a moment to place me, but you knew."

On the way in we'd discussed how to handle it. We knew he would probably recognize me, and that my presence would catch him off guard.

The question we faced was in trying to play ignorant and work around that, or smack him in the face with it and hope it opened something up.

Subtle was never my style, and Diaz seemed to operate much the same way, so we opted to go right at him and see where it went.

If nothing came of it, it wasn't like we couldn't find him again.

"I, uh," Carlos managed in the backseat, the cockiness gone from his tone.

"Shut up," I said again. "Don't even try lying to us—we both saw it."

I paused a long moment, waiting to see if he would try a response, some blatant falsehood to attempt and reestablish the upper hand. To his credit, he remained silent.

"That's what I thought," I said, nodding, letting him see me smirk. "So tell me, Carlos, why the hell did you guys send Mateo, your third in line, to find me?"

The world outside transitioned from urban to open desert in a matter of minutes, city streets and mini malls giving way to sunbaked stretches of earth punctuated only by the occasional tufts of sage grass. A stiff wind blew in from the ocean, whipping sand along the ground, stirring what little foliage dotted the landscape.

"Our third in line?" Carlos asked. "Man, I don't know what the hell you're talking about."

"Oh, Jesus," I groaned, again shifting my head over to look at Diaz. "He's really going to make us do this, isn't he?"

"Apparently," she said, her voice resigned, raising her eyebrows and shaking her head. "I think I'd be a little bit more enthused to help if it was my ass on the line, but that's just me."

"Me too," I said, looking away, staring out at the side window.

It was a pretty thin tactic, an obvious bit of bait to make him snap at, but given the situation we didn't see where he had many options. He had brought himself in, because he knew he was in trouble. Diaz had humored him the first night, because she needed to know what had him spooked, but it was now time to take back the upper hand.

If we were going to figure out what had Mateo on the run, what made Carlos jumpy, we needed to be in control.

From the backseat, we could hear clapping. Slow, mocking slaps of Carlos smacking the palms of his hands together. "Oh, wow," he said. "I mean, really, bravo. Quite the performance you two just put on there.

"So let me get this straight. You guys mention Mateo, say I should be worried, then I suddenly start spilling my guts? That how this works?"

In one abrupt movement I spun around in my seat, rising up so my knees were in the well of it, my torso pressed against the seat back. I gripped the headrest with both hands and snarled down at Carlos. His entire body recoiled into the space behind Diaz as I spoke.

"No you little shit, this is how it works. You're supposed to tell us everything because we're protecting your ass right now. You're supposed to tell us everything or you can go out on your own like Mateo. You're supposed to tell us everything or you can end up exactly the way he did."

I left the last part vague, wanting, needing him to at least reach for that little morsel. Beneath me I felt the car slow, just as we had planned, nothing but a lonely, desolate strip of highway visible in either direction.

Fear flashed behind Carlos's eyes as he looked back at me. "What happened to Mateo?"

I met his gaze a long moment before letting a snort curl my head toward the ceiling. "The last time I saw him, a nine-millimeter parabellum shell had taken the entire back half of his skull off."

His eyes and mouth formed into three perfect circles as he stared back. "You do him?"

"No," I said, shaking my head. "Believe me, if I do any of you guys, it won't be that easy."

I was careful to use the present tense, wanting him to pick up the insinuation. If he recognized me, then he knew who I was, knew my story.

"Then who did?" he asked, uncertain if he believed me or not.

"*That's* what you should be worried about right now," I said. "Now get the hell out."

Opposite me Diaz unlocked the doors, the clicking sound of the locks releasing ringing out around us.

"Wait, what?" Carlos asked, pushing himself down lower in his seat. "You guys can't do that. Where the hell are we right now?"

"Doesn't matter," I said, still glaring at him. "I told you, this was the talk. Since you're not saying anything, this is where you get out."

Carlos looked at me like I was crazy, like there was a third arm growing from my forehead. Any hope he had of trying to control the situation was long past, fear splayed across his features as he looked up at me.

"Hey man, you crazy," he muttered. "Diaz, this guy is crazy."

"You had your chance," she responded, her voice void of emotion.

"You guys are agents—you can't do this!" he protested, looking from me to the back of Diaz's head.

"No, I *was* an agent," I said, leaning forward a few inches over the headrest. "But you and your boys put an end to that, didn't you?"

His eyes grew a touch larger as he looked up at me. I could tell he knew exactly what I was referring to, his mouth opening and closing a half dozen times, no sounds coming out.

"Get the hell out," I said, motioning with my head toward the door. He stared back at me, unmoving, for a long second, until I drew the Glock Diaz had loaned me from my hip holster and aimed it at him.

There wasn't a single bullet in the entire weapon, but he didn't know that. All he saw was the polished steel tip of a gun aimed at his head.

Moving slowly, he reached out with his left hand and popped the door open. He stepped outside one foot at a time and shut it behind him. Diaz sped away the instant he was gone.

Chapter Twenty-One

The scent of pine wafted up out of the fireplace, perfuming the entire office as Sergey Blok sat in his armchair before it, staring at the flames. Most years the Russian winter could be relied on to show up by late November, the bitter kickoff to a season that would last at least six months, bringing with it blowing snows and Arctic chills. This year it was a full three weeks early in arriving, pulling down icy temperatures from the north, sending homeowners scrambling for firewood and boiling-water-based heaters.

Being on the upper end of the social spectrum, Sergey was fortunate. He had two warehouses sitting full of firewood, product culled from the great forests on the western plains. One was exclusively for the use of his home and businesses, a cheap source of warmth that would keep his empire running through the long winter months. The other he would let sit until February, waiting until the wood had become a precious commodity, and the price had skyrocketed, before selling to the locals.

The mere thought brought a smile to his face as he extended his feet out over the edge of his ottoman and felt the warmth of the flames licking at his toes. He kept his digits close to the fire until he could stand it no more before pulling them back and pressing them into the velvet footstool, trapping the heat there.

Sergey rubbed his palms over the arms and thighs of his velour sweat suit, stirring warmth in his extremities, before taking up the phone on the stand beside him. He called up the number he was seeking with a single button, the smile fleeing his face as he pressed the device to his ear and waited.

The phone rang seven times before going to voice mail.

Sergey killed the call and looked down at the display on the phone. The digital readout informed him it was just shy of eleven o'clock in the evening.

"It's noon there, dammit," he muttered, pressing the same button to call again. "Where is he?"

This time the phone rang six times, just short of again going to voice mail, when the voice of his nephew came on the line.

"Hullo?" Viktor mumbled.

"Viktor!" Sergey snapped. "Where the hell are you?"

There was a momentary pause, the sound of feet shuffling barely audible over the line.

"I'm at home, working," Viktor replied. "Why? Where should I be?"

Sergey again could hear his nephew moving about, the din of a door opening finding his ear. "Why the hell didn't you answer the first time I called?"

"I was taking a piss," Viktor said. "I don't carry my phone at all times."

The backs of Sergey's teeth ground together as he stared into the fire. He pressed his lips into a tight line and blew an angry sigh out through his nostrils, squeezing the phone in his hand.

For the first few years, the decision to appoint Viktor as the head of his operations in North America had proven a shrewd one. The young man was eager to prove himself, hungry and driven. He had worked long hours and brokered solid relations, taking over for the existing regime there with surprising deftness.

In the time since, though, his grasp on reality had begun to waiver. He had started to enjoy his newly acquired lifestyle a little too much, believing in the legend he was trying to build around himself.

To combat it, Sergey had tried to reassert himself. Weekly phone calls. Sending Pavel to act as a go-between. Sending Lita to Yellowstone. Slowing the arrival of the first shipment to make sure Viktor was up to the task.

So far the combined outcome of his efforts had only served to prove that Viktor was far from capable of handling such an enormous responsibility.

"From now on you do," Sergey said, steel in his voice. "This is too important to mess up because I can't reach you."

"Yes, Uncle," Viktor replied, boredom, disdain, hanging from the words. "So, to what do I owe the pleasure of a midday surprise?"

Sergey pulled the phone back and stared at it, his face twisted into a scowl. He snarled at it a moment, fighting back the urge to reach through the line and grab his nephew by the throat.

"I'm calling to see what happened in La Jolla."

Another moment passed, the sound of Viktor blowing out a long sigh filling his ear. "The plan to do things quietly didn't work. They wouldn't deal with us. Said they didn't trust the new model."

As angry as Sergey wanted to be at the news, he couldn't say he was surprised. It was the answer he was expecting to hear, the same thing he would have said if he was in La Jolla's position.

"So what are you going to do?" Sergey asked, trying to keep his voice level. He didn't want Viktor to hear judgment in his words, to have any reason to believe he was being second-guessed on it.

"I am sending a team tomorrow," Viktor said. "I am instructing them to be as delicate as possible but to be thorough, no matter what it takes."

Sergey shook his head in silence. It was exactly the answer he had figured he would hear.

"Yes, I think that sounds perfect," Sergey said, rolling his eyes as the words crossed his lips.

"Thank you, Uncle."

A moment of silence fell as Sergey turned his gaze back to the fire, watching the orange flames curl around the charred bark of the logs, flickering upward in a serpentine pattern.

"Okay, that is all," Sergey said. "I was just calling to make sure everything was under control. Thank you for taking care of it."

"Of course, Uncle," Viktor replied. "Feel free to call any time. I'll be sure to have my phone on me from now on."

"*Noka*," Sergey said, his face contorted in anger. He signed off without waiting for Viktor's farewell, not wanting to hear one more lie, one more word dripping with condescension from his nephew.

Sergey waited for the display on his phone to clear before pressing a second button, the line connecting. This one went straight to voice mail without ringing; the recipient was most likely out of cell phone range, or was keeping it off to maintain his privacy for the time being.

Once the digitized voice informed him the caller was unavailable and asked him to leave a message, Sergey leaned forward in his chair, the warmth of the fire hitting his cheeks.

"Pavel, this is Sergey. Call me when you get this. I need you in California, as soon as possible. We have to teach somebody a lesson."

Chapter Twenty-Two

A peculiar smell wafted out of Diaz's office as we approached. It smelled a bit like incense, with a hint of something herbal mixed in. The moment it flitted past my nostrils I knew what it was, and my mind pulled back to a time many years before. If not for the tiny pulse of mirth I felt at experiencing the scent again, my stomach would have flipped in complete revulsion.

Beside me I could see Diaz was having that very reaction. The aroma had twisted her face into a knot, incomprehension on her face.

"What the hell is that smell?" she asked as we drew closer.

"You'll see," I said, shaking my head. "Good luck ever getting it out of your office again, too."

Diaz made a deep-throated, guttural sound that resembled a gag as we rounded the corner into her office, the light inside already on. Standing behind the desk was Hutch, studying her bookshelves, the source of the odor sitting on the desk beside him.

Put simply, the man looked like holy hell. Dark crescents underlined his eyes and covered most of his cheekbones. His thin hair was matted flat to his skull, and every article of clothing he wore looked like it had been wadded into a ball and stomped on a few times.

"Hutch, how the hell do you drink that stuff?" I asked, stopping just inside the door, trying in vain to put as much distance between me and the steaming cup as possible.

"You kidding me?" he asked without looking over. "I've been looking forward to this since I heard we might be swinging through town. Can't get the real deal like it on the East Coast."

Diaz made a face, leaning forward a few inches toward the cup and sniffing before recoiling. "You mean you actually put that shit in your body?"

Hutch pulled his gaze away from the shelf and glanced over at Diaz, his expression stony. "I'll have you know I never felt better in my life than when I was drinking three cups a day."

Both sides of Diaz's nostrils pushed up in a sneer as she peered down at the cup of greenish liquid. "What the hell is it?"

"You don't want to know," I injected. "It's basically a witch's brew of Native American and Southwest ingredients. Some kind of man-making concoction."

"He may be a Christian and talk white; but he's still an Indian and his rules is his rules."

I could see the confusion on Diaz's face as she looked a question my way, tilting her head to the side.

"Same movie," I explained.

"Right," she said, raising her head in a nod that relayed she didn't quite understand.

"So what did you find in West Yellowstone?" I asked, steering the conversation back to the task at hand. I could judge by his appearance he must have traveled straight through to get here, meaning whatever he uncovered was important.

"He's connected," Hutch said, shifting to face both of us, his customary position with toes pointed out and hands shoved deep in his pockets. For a moment it was like déjà vu, standing in that office, looking at him there, that awful stench in the air.

"How much or to whom, I don't know," Hutch added, raising his eyebrows in resignation. "He's got airtight papers and a backstory to fit them, but it was complete bullshit. Guy couldn't answer the most basic of questions about his supposed livelihood."

"So what makes you think he's connected?" Diaz asked, leaning against the wall and crossing her arms in front of her.

"Because the moment I started asking him about Mateo Perez, the Juarezes, whoever, he shut down. Almost catatonic. No looks of confusion, no searching his memory, nothing."

"Subtle," I said.

"More than you can imagine," Hutch said, glancing at me through heavily lidded eyes.

"So what's that mean?" Diaz asked. "We've got somebody out looking to pick off the Juarezes?"

"Apparently. Maybe," Hutch said. "Hell, I don't know."

I leaned forward and rested my palms across the top of the chair in front of me. I ran the various players through my mind, the different affiliations they had.

"All right," I said, thinking out loud. "We've got the Juarezes, with Mateo Perez. Two weeks ago he goes off the reservation and shows up in West Yellowstone, being tracked by someone with a forged background who isn't in our system.

"A week after that, someone claiming the same fake story shows up looking for her."

"I don't know that he was looking for her," Hutch said. "My guess is he was a cleanup guy. He was there to check on Mateo."

"Maybe you, too," Diaz added, jutting her chin toward me.

I nodded, having already considered that angle as well. I wasn't sure how or why I had been lumped in with Mateo, especially after five years away. In that time I had had no contact with any of my former cases, had barely spoken to the people I worked with.

I wanted, needed, a clean break from it all. I had made promises, to my wife, myself, every single deity I had called on that night, that I would walk away and never return if given the chance. Until two weeks ago, when a woman I had never met showed up and put a bullet into my chest, I had kept those promises.

The question though was why? Why had it happened? Why had they sought me out?

"I'm guessing the guy up there wasn't in the system, either?" I asked.

"Nothing," Hutch said. "The park has an FBI agent on-site for investigations. He put him through their system and came back empty. Whoever these people are, they're ghosts."

I considered the statement, thinking back to my time on the FAST team. In our experience, nobody was ever a ghost, not entirely. They might be beyond our sightline, but people like this were never completely invisible.

"Maybe just here," I said, putting the idea out to let the group chew on it. "Lita claimed to be from New Mexico, but I swear her accent was Eastern Bloc, maybe even Russian."

"Same with the other guy, Pavel," Hutch said.

"And those names," Diaz added, "Lita and Pavel? Not exactly Jim and Jane."

"So maybe they just aren't in our system," I said. "Do we know anybody at Langley? Somebody that might have lines back to the old KGB files or something?"

A long, weary sigh slid out of Hutch. He raised a hand to his chin and rubbed it over his two-day whiskers, shaking his head. "Not really, at least none come to mind. Tensions between the different agencies have reached an all-time high under this new administration, with them squeezing on the funding like they have. Nobody works together anymore—we all see each other as competition."

"Christ," Diaz muttered, shaking her head.

I bobbed my head in agreement with her, but didn't vocalize it. Hutch had heard my gripes with bureaucratic machinations a thousand times before. Once more wasn't going to add anything new to the narrative.

"What about Pally?" I asked. "Can he get around a few firewalls? Maybe take a look?"

"I'll give it a try," Hutch said. "I need to circle back with him and see if he's found anything on the money trail anyway."

"Okay," I said, my mind racing, trying to fit the pieces together. "What else does that leave us with?"

A twist of a smile curled up on Diaz's face. She glanced over at me, my mind picking up on her insinuation within a moment. The same look stretched across my features as I stared back, neither of us saying anything.

"What?" Hutch asked, glancing from one to the other.

"Carlos," Diaz said, her gaze locked on me, her body twisting toward Hutch. "I'm guessing he should be good and ready to talk here soon."

I coughed out a laugh as Hutch looked from one of us to the other.

"Oh yeah? Why's that?"

"Because the last time we saw him, he was walking alone on a dusty stretch of California highway," I said.

"Looking like he might piss his pants after Hawk pointed a gun at his head," Diaz said, suppressing laughter.

"Aw, hell," Hutch said, letting out a small groan, raising both his hands up to rub them over his face.

"Don't worry," I said, "there wasn't a round in the gun, and a second team came by ten minutes after us to grab him. We just needed to soften him up a little."

"You've dealt with Carlos before," Diaz said. "You know how he can be."

A look somewhere between exhausted and exasperated stretched across Hutch's face. He looked at each of us in turn before shrugging and saying, "Yeah."

"So there it is," I said, pushing myself back up away from the chair. "Let's get Pally on the phone and see what he's got, then go pay Carlos a visit."

"Okay," Hutch said, "but not right now. I need to sleep at least four or five hours or I'm not going to be worth a damn."

I nodded, considering the proposal. I hadn't slept much in the last few days either; my system was spurring itself along on pure adrenaline and the promise of finally giving myself a bit of closure that I'd been denied for so long.

"That's not a bad idea," I said, nodding. "I might rack out, too. We'll give Carlos a little time to settle down, get past being angry, then go pay him a visit. He has to know a lot more right now than he's letting on."

"I'd love to know what he and Manny were talking about in that visiting room this morning," Diaz said, her eyes glazing as she stared down at the desk.

The three of us stood in silence for a long moment. We had a random amalgam of information and evidence, none of it seeming to fit together worth a damn. There were competing interests, unknown cohorts, and the dredging of matters that we'd long ago stowed away.

It had to all be connected, but we just didn't have the faintest idea how yet.

Diaz was the first to break the silence, motioning with the top of her head toward the door. "Cots are still in the back. You know where to find them."

PART III

Chapter Twenty-Three

Icy crystals whipped up off the concrete lot, spraying across the face of Sergey Blok as he stepped out of the rear seat of his restored 1938 Buick Town Car. Oversized and boxy, it wasn't the most beautiful automobile on the road, but it was far and away unique, which was exactly the impression he was hoping to imprint. There would be little doubt from anybody that saw the car who was seated in the backseat, a gesture of power and prestige without the flashy arrogance his nephew now seemed to favor.

"Leave the car running, the heater on," Sergey said to the driver as he passed, receiving a nod of understanding before the window between them was rolled back up. This stop would take no more than five minutes, a surprise drop-in to make sure everything was still on schedule.

A second gust of wind pulled at the lapels of Sergey's overcoat as he walked across the open asphalt parking lot toward the front entrance. Once a large manufacturing hub for automobile tires, the warehouse before him stretched out nearly as wide as a city block, a square gray structure that rose a uniform three stories in height. Underfoot, the parking lot was marked off to accommodate several hundred cars at a time, though today, as it usually was, there were no more than a dozen present.

While having more staff on hand might expedite the operation, it would also involve bringing in a lot more people. Those people tended to have eyes and mouths, both things that Sergey frowned upon. On sight he could name the owner of every auto in the lot, each of them having a minimum of five years of dealing with the Blok family.

None of them needed to be reminded what would happen if they breathed a word of what went on inside to anybody. They had all seen it play out in front of them before.

Sergey pushed through the front door and unbuttoned his coat in quick order, stripping away the heavy wool garment. Compared with the velour track suits he favored wearing every day, the article was heavy and bulky, cumbersome to a fault.

Using both hands, Sergey smoothed out the rumpled front of his bright orange ensemble for the day and stepped through a second set of double doors into the main hold of the warehouse. Stretched before him was an enormous open space, the entire place one continuous room.

The right half of the building was filled with wooden crates piled high, arranged in tidy rows. A pair of forklifts zipped between them, their engines whining with acceleration, packages fitted onto their metal tongs being delivered. A series of black skid marks smudged the concrete beneath them, but otherwise not a single thing was out of place.

On the opposite end of the room were stacks of white plastic reservoirs, each one standing five feet in height and measuring more than two feet in diameter. The raw materials needed to produce the products were now stacked on the far end, arranged in perfect queues, and there was enough on hand to keep the place busy for the foreseeable future.

Among them moved a single clamp truck, identical to the forklifts on the other end save the oversized vertical tongs on the front acting in place of the metal forks. Sergey watched as its driver squeezed tightly on a barrel and lifted it from a stack before pivoting and lowering it to just a few inches above the ground. With a jerk of a few levers, he set off at a speedy clip, disappearing behind the far side of the makeshift structure that filled the remaining interior of the warehouse.

A series of metal tracks had been installed after the purchase of the building, and they hung down fifteen feet from the ceiling. Shaped into an elongated oval, the tracks were designed to cover an area thirty feet across on the short end and over three times that on the long end. Heavy plastic sheeting hung down from the track, enclosing the entire area, and a flurry of activity was visible inside.

Almost a dozen men in total could be seen, all of them dressed in white from head to foot save the yellow-and-blue breathing apparatuses covering the lower halves of their faces and the heavy goggles protecting their eyes. Arranged throughout the space, they went about a bevy of tasks ranging from testing product composition to wrapping and loading the end result into crates.

Every last one moved with brutal efficiency as Sergey stood and watched, nobody pausing to talk, not a single one slowing their pace of work.

Sergey nodded in approval at what he saw and walked forward toward the enclosure. Despite the matching uniforms of everyone present, he picked out the man he was looking for on sight—the man's diminutive stature was easily discernible—and slapped at the heavy plastic.

The sound reverberated through the building, audible even over the whine of forklifts, drawing the stares of everybody inside. Just as fast all but one of the men returned to their work, the intended target dropping the pipette he was holding and walking in exaggerated strides toward the overlap that served as a door into the facility.

Sergey took his time walking to the far corner, allowing the man to remove his hood and goggles before sliding his breather down around his neck. He reached as if to shake Sergey's hand as he approached, pulling back as he realized his body was still encased in white plastic.

"Mr. Blok, what a pleasant surprise," the man said, offering a cracked-tooth smile that stretched across much of his face. His voice was a bit higher than expected, his chin and nose both pointed.

More than once Sergey had thought that if not for his undersized ears and thick fuzz of hair atop his head, he would have all the trappings of an elf.

"Anatoly," Sergey said, leaning forward an inch or two at the waist in lieu of a handshake, "how are you, my friend?"

A hint of red appeared on Anatoly's cheeks as he matched the pose and said, "I am well, Mr. Blok. Very, very well."

"Good," Sergey said, casting a glance around the room. "Things here also appear to be going very well."

The words came out like a statement, but both men recognized that it was a question. Sergey's management style was one predicated on delegation. Only if those selected seemed to be failing in their duties, as with his nephew, did he feel the need to insert himself.

In the seven years that Sergey and Dr. Anatoly Bishkin had been working together, there had been no such incident, no reason for a loss of trust. It was a fact acknowledged, but never spoken, by both sides.

If Sergey was stopping by, it was because he wanted a status report, not that he was snooping on his employee.

"It is," Anatoly said, dipping his head for emphasis. "If you look over there—" he extended a stubby arm out toward the wooden crates on the far side of the room "—you can see a section cordoned off with red tape."

Sergey took two small steps to move his body perpendicular to the enclosure beside him and peered down the bridge of his nose, loose skin collecting in a heap by his temples. "Yes?"

"That is the requested product for the first shipment."

A long, soft whistle pushed itself out between Sergey's lips. An optimistic expectation upon arrival was that the first shipment would be ready within a week, two at the most.

"And the rest of it there?" Sergey asked.

"That's most of the second shipment," Anatoly replied. "As you know, it can be stored for years if necessary."

Sergey nodded, his smooth head rocking several inches forward and back. The gesture was in agreement with what Anatoly said and in recognition of the fine work being done.

"Very good, Doctor. Very, very good."

"Thank you, sir," Anatoly said, the red deepening across his cheeks.

Sergey shifted back toward the enclosure and gave it a once-over, running his gaze from the tracks hanging above to the plastic scraping against the floor just a few feet away. "Is there anything you need here? Anything we are running short on at the moment?"

Anatoly took in a deep breath, a bit of apprehension flooding from his features, the realization that the tough part was behind them. "No, sir. We're doing well here, and have plenty of materials to keep going."

"Good," Sergey said. "This is good news, seeing you so far ahead of schedule. We've got one last hiccup that's being worked out as we speak, and then we'll be ready to start getting some of this out of your way."

The oversized smile returned to Anatoly's face. "You keep taking it away, we'll keep making more, sir."

A hint of a smile crept across Sergey's features as well. His previous statement was meant as a bit of a curious challenge, wondering if Anatoly would inquire to the holdup he mentioned across the ocean. There was no doubt he had heard the statement, but the fact that he knew better than to ask spoke volumes of the man and their relationship.

"Well then," Sergey said, "don't let me keep you. Just stopped by to see how things were coming."

"Thank you, sir. Anytime, sir," Anatoly said, dipping his upper body into two quick bows, already backing away to return inside the plastic.

Sergey watched him go for just a moment before turning and heading toward the door. His coat was a misshapen black blob visible beyond the glass.

Chapter Twenty-Four

The oversized face of Mike Palinsky filled the back wall of the conference room, the section from his chest to the top of his head stretched almost five feet in height. It was difficult to tell if the ghostly pallor that seemed to encase his features was a result of the flat screen television he was on washing him out, or if he had just failed to see sunlight since leaving the unit a few years before.

Given his predilection to stay squirrelled away in the office when he worked here with us, I was prone to assume the latter.

The previous five years had lent themselves to a bit of aging, though nothing as pronounced as Hutch. Given that he was just a handful of years older than me it was to be expected; the major changes for both of us were still a little ways ahead on the horizon.

Like me, his hair was longer, but his was pulled back into a ponytail that ended at an unknown length somewhere behind him. He had lost at least a dozen pounds since I'd last seen him. His cheeks were hollowed out, which accentuated the pockmarks dotting them.

The little I could see of the room behind him appeared to be a home lab of some sort. Computer monitors took up almost the entire backdrop of the space, and the bit of desk that was visible was covered by an array of electronic wizardry.

I had been the one to initiate the call, choosing to go in a few minutes early to get the perfunctory small talk out of the way before the others arrived. It wasn't that I had any problem with Pally—of all the guys on the team, he was one I liked the most—it was that each passing moment seemed to pull me back further into my old self.

When the incident with Lita first took place, it was a surprise to me, a jolt to the system that I survived through muscle memory and blind luck. Spending those days on the rock shelf with Mateo, finding her body on the way out, they had served to awaken something inside me that I had buried deep within, had even tricked myself into believing was dormant.

Seeing Hutch had only made it worse. Being back in California, knowing what lay just up the road, seeing so many familiar names, it was all tugging me straight back into a life I no longer wanted any part of.

Pally was just another part of that. Seeing him up on the screen, despite the obvious physical changes, was like staring into a vision of 2010 all over again.

It was a vision I wasn't sure I wanted to see, friend or not.

"So Hutch tells me you got yourself deep into something again," Pally said, leaning back in his chair and lacing his fingers behind his head. The sleeves of his baggy green sweater fell down around his forearms as he did so, a quartet of brightly colored rubber bands around his wrist.

"More like I was pulled in," I replied, pushing a chair to the side and hopping up onto the table in the vacated space. I ran a hand back through my still-damp hair and wiped it against the leg of my slacks, and a thin, dark water line appeared as I did.

"Mhmm," Pally snorted, his entire body rocking backward, "sure ya did. Just like ya weren't the one always charging headfirst into every situation we ever encountered?"

The left side of my mouth curled up into a smile, knowing full well he was right. Still, that was a different time; I was a different person. If there was any way I could go back and change all that I would, no questions asked.

"Maybe then," I conceded, "but not this time."

"He's telling the truth," Hutch said from behind me, the corrosive scent of his miracle concoction arriving just a moment after his voice. "This one went all the way to Montana to drag his ass out of retirement."

He appeared on the opposite side of the table from me, mug in one hand, the other shoved into the pocket of dress pants. Like me he had showered after waking, opting to stay with the same rumpled togs he'd been wearing instead of putting on something new.

Knowing Hutch, there was an equal chance he had forgotten to bring along anything else, or had and just chosen not to unpack it.

"And hello to you, our fearless leader," Pally said, raising a hand to his brow and lowering it in an overdone salute. "A pleasure, as always."

"Yeah, yeah," Hutch said, offering the tiniest bit of a return salute.

"You wouldn't be saying that if you could smell that shit in his cup right now," I offered, drawing a knowing grin from Pally.

"Yeah, yeah," Hutch repeated, taking another drink from the vile concoction.

"No, he's right," Diaz said, her voice all business, pulling all three of our gazes toward her. "It smells like ass in here."

In the hours since our last meeting, she had shed the jacket, now sporting just her slacks and a T-shirt. Her hair was piled high in a messy bun, her face wearing a *don't mess with me* veneer.

Whatever new information she had wasn't good.

Sensing the about-face from our host, Hutch shifted his attention back toward the screen. "All right, Pally, hit us with it."

On-screen, Pally remained in the same position: reclined in his computer chair, his hands atop the crown of his head. He shook his head, his entire upper body twisting. "Not a lot to tell. The account was set up in Haney's name, which we all know to be fake. It was set up as a subsidiary of the family business, which—"

"Also fake," Hutch inserted. He remained standing to my right, his arm bent at a ninety-degree angle, his drink in front of him. On my left, Diaz rested a hand on the top of the closest chair, crossing her right leg over her left, the toe of her shoe pointed into the floor.

"Meaning?" I asked.

"Well," Pally said, raising his eyebrows a fraction of an inch, "even if the names and addresses are fake, the money has to come from somewhere. And believe me, that *somewhere* is where things get interesting."

Diaz and I exchanged a glance as Hutch took another pull on his drink, his slurp audible throughout the room.

"We're listening," I said.

Without turning around or consulting anything, Pally lowered a hand and held it in front of him, his thumb and forefinger pressed together. "The money was wired into New Mexican National Bank from an account in West Cayman."

"So it's a dead end?" Diaz asked.

"Ha!" Pally spat, his head rocking back a few inches. "The Caymans aren't nearly as untouchable as they want people to believe. Most of that mythos comes from corporate stooges and bad television."

I had heard the same rant on multiple occasions over the years. The vitriol was a little dialed down from times past, but the general message was still the same.

"So how did it get to Cayman?" I asked.

At that, Pally shifted his thumb from his index finger to his middle finger. "Prior to landing in the Caribbean, these fortunate funds spent some time in the Swiss Alps. Surfing and skiing, not a bad way to live."

"Right up until it decided to become a chili farmer in New Mexico," Hutch deadpanned, drawing a smirk from Pally.

"Right you are, boss," Pally said. "Sort of." He ticked his finger from his middle to his ring finger and said, "But you guys haven't heard the

Dustin Stevens

kicker yet. Before Switzerland, that money originated in none other than Mother Russia herself."

"*Russia?*" I asked, my face twisted up in confusion. I turned to face Diaz, who had a similar look on her face, and asked, "You guys working anything in Russia right now?"

"Nothing," Diaz said, shaking her head. "You guys do much there when you were around?"

"Almost nothing," I said. "Stopped through one time when we suspected an outfit from Hungary was hiding there. Nothing local."

"There's not much on the national scene involving the Ruskies, either," Hutch said, finishing his beverage and sliding it onto the table. Without the mug, he shoved both hands into his trousers, remaining in place, staring back at Pally.

If he seemed at all surprised by the revelation, he didn't show it.

"All right, Pally," I said, "I'll be the first to bite. Where did it come from in Russia?"

Pally replaced the hand back atop his head and said, "Don't know. Not yet anyway."

"You don't know?" Diaz said, her eyes widening a bit.

"Well, I can tell you the shell corporation it is said to have originated with," Pally said, motioning over a shoulder to the monitor on his right. "But if you want actual usable intel, it's going to take me a day or two yet. The Russians are a bit more lax on their SEC filing requirements than we are."

Despite the weight of the moment, I allowed a single snicker to roll out. Pally never missed an opportunity to take a jab at the country that held his ancestors in persecution for so long, no matter how veiled or innocuous it might sound.

Besides, the fact that he had traced the funds that far meant it was only a matter of time before he found out who was behind them. If he could crack both the Cayman and Swiss banks, figuring out a false business front in Moscow would be no problem.

"Russia would definitely fit the names of Pavel and Lita," I said, glancing over to Hutch. He nodded in agreement, his face bunched tight, deep in thought.

"You had any luck on that front yet?" I asked, turning back to Pally.

"Actually, I farmed it out," Pally said, raising his hands from his head and holding them out wide before dropping them back into place. "I know somebody at the NSA that owes me a favor. Seemed easier to let her do the digging from the inside than to tiptoe around them the entire time."

" 'Her'?" I asked, arching an eyebrow.

"Stop it," Pally said, rocking forward to sit erect, his face much closer to the camera. "I get anything on either front, you'll be the first to know."

"Thanks, man," I said. "Good seeing you again."

"You too, Hawk," Pally said. Once more he raised two fingers to his brow and said, "Hutch, Diaz."

They both murmured a farewell as the feed in front of us cut out and the screen changed to bright blue. It cast a harsh pallor over all three of us as we sat in silence, each chewing on the new information.

"All right," I said after a moment, "the money originated from somewhere in Russia. Not exactly what we were looking for, but at least we now have a heading."

"Not a lot of activity coming out of there," Hutch said, his gaze aimed at the wall, just beneath the television beaming blue onto us. "Shouldn't be too hard to narrow the field quickly if we have to."

"True," I conceded, bobbing my head in agreement. I paused a moment to add that to the tangle of information nestling itself into my brain and turned to Diaz. "So what happened while we were asleep?"

The question seemed to jolt her out of her own thoughts, her head snapping upward to face us. "Huh?"

"Something happened since the last time we talked. It was obvious when you walked in. Pertinent to us, or something else we don't need to know about?"

I had no illusions that she didn't still have an entire branch to run, with cases stretched across the gamut of subject areas that the DEA dealt with on a daily basis. I appreciated how helpful she'd been and how much autonomy she was granting us, both facts I wanted to impress upon her. In return, I understood that she had things on her plate separate from us, and I respected that.

Still, if whatever had happened was relevant, I'd prefer to know sooner rather than later.

She glanced at each of us in turn and said, "Carlos Juarez is gone."

My eyes bulged as I stared at her, my heart rate picking up a tick. "You mean after we . . . ?"

I left the question open-ended, the destination clear.

"No," she said, shaking her head. "Our guys picked him up right behind us, brought him here. A little later they tried to take him back to his safe house in Texas, but he refused and I guess things got ugly.

"As of this afternoon, he's in the wind."

Chapter Twenty-Five

Hutch decided to remain behind at headquarters. Being a ranking bureaucratic official in one of the larger agencies under government control meant he had responsibilities beyond the case at hand, no matter how hard any of us tried to ignore it. Diaz offered him her office to work out of, giving him free reign over his old digs with the lone exception that no herbal teas were to cross her threshold.

The comment was meant to be a joke, something to lighten the mood a tiny bit, though it barely drew more than a half-hearted chuckle from Hutch. He hadn't said anything to us directly, but we could both tell there was a bit of disapproval about the way we'd handled Carlos earlier.

We all knew the incident hadn't led directly to his leaving, but it damned sure hadn't helped the situation, either.

"What in the world could have Carlos spooked enough to never return to Texas, but secure enough that he would leave protective custody, even after what happened to Mateo?" I asked, staring out the side window as we rolled into the Metropolitan Correctional Center on the outskirts of San Diego.

Diaz remained silent for a moment as we pulled up alongside the front gate and a reed-thin guard in a light brown uniform stepped out to meet us. She flashed her badge at him as he bent at the waist and peered in at us, the same man who had been on seven hours before.

"You guys back again?" he asked with a smile. "Just can't get enough of this place?"

"Something like that," Diaz said, forcing a smile to her face, despite her voice relaying it was not the time to be messing with her. "Can you call ahead and ask to have Manuel Juarez made available for questioning, please?"

The smile faded around the edges as the guard stood to full height and stepped back from the car. "Yes, ma'am, will do. You know the way, right?"

"Sure do, thanks," Diaz said, buzzing the window up and depressing the accelerator at the same time. Once the car was sealed tight and we were on our way, she pushed out a quick sigh, blowing a stray strand of hair off her forehead.

"I honestly have no idea," Diaz said. "As you saw today, it's sometimes hard to get a full read on Carlos because he's always playing that rebel-without-a-cause character of his."

"More like without-a-clue."

"That too," Diaz agreed. "But this time seemed different. I heard the tape from when the package arrived. You saw him today when we forced him out of the car. That boy was spooked. Bad."

She maneuvered the car back to the same building, situated in the far back corner of the lot. Beside us, prisoners were out for their late afternoon yard time, hundreds of men dressed in gray, no more than a handful even glancing our way. Despite the cool weather, many had stripped off their shirts and were playing basketball or pumping iron, sweat glistening on their skin.

Diaz jammed the gear shift into "Park" and killed the engine, the same disgruntled look that had been on her features all afternoon still in place. Without the sound of the air-conditioning or the road beneath us, the outside world could be heard plainly: the sounds of inmates in the yard filtering in, their voices full of bass, floating on the breeze.

"Think there's any chance Manny tells us why? Or who?" I asked.

"Depends," Diaz said, tightening the side of her face, considering the question. "If he and Carlos set this up this morning, he'll fold his arms and give us some tough-guy bullshit runaround."

"But if Carlos is really acting alone here, he's going to be just as worried as we are right now," I finished.

"Different reasons, obviously, but same final product," Diaz said.

Together we climbed out of the car, our respective dress shoes sounding against the concrete sidewalk. As we walked, Diaz shrugged her suit coat back on, buttoning it as we approached the front door and entered.

Stale, frigid air greeted us as we stepped inside, the door swinging shut behind us with a wheeze. The same guard that had been on before lunch nodded us through without checking badges, barely looking up from his copy of *Field & Stream* magazine as he waved us on by.

A few weeks ago, I would have stopped to see which issue he was reading, maybe even asked him what his sport of choice was. Now, the only thing that even registered with me was the antler spread on the moose splayed across the front cover, an image processed and dismissed in less than a second.

The change was not a welcome one.

I fell back a half step and allowed Diaz to take the lead, moving quickly through the front hallway and turning us toward the interrogation chambers. A pair of oversized guards on their way out for the day stopped and turned sideways to let us squeeze by, keeping their backs pressed against the walls, their uniforms aching for relief from the strain. Otherwise, nobody so much as glanced our way as we cut a direct path through the facility.

Given the deference of the guards around us, and the clench of Diaz's jaw, I got the distinct impression that she was no stranger to the place. Once upon a time I would have been stopped by a handful of prodding guards wanting to know who I was with and what I was doing. Not once had I ever been allowed to wander unescorted through the halls. The fact that we were doing so now meant either procedure was becoming more lax or Diaz was known as a woman not to be trifled with throughout the building.

My money was on the latter.

"We good?" Diaz asked as we stepped past a trio of doors, simple gray metal affairs with chicken wire across the plate glass windows covering the top half of them. Each one had a basic plastic placard on it announcing interrogation rooms with numbers counting backward from 4.

"Yeah," I responded, knowing she was asking if I was ready with what we had discussed on the drive in. We pulled up to a stop outside the door marked Interrogation Room #1. I was careful to stay back on the opposite side of the hall, out of direct sight line of the window.

As it stood, Manny didn't know I was there. Carlos hadn't seen me until after meeting with him, and a simple call had confirmed that he had not contacted his cousin to relay that information.

The plan, as it were, was pretty simple. Diaz would go in first and try to determine where Carlos would have gone. She would be tough but firm, letting him know how dire this was and how this was the direct result of Carlos being a bit of a loose cannon, not some perceived slight by the DEA.

If he insisted on giving her a hard time, or being in any way uncooperative, she would give me the signal. Neither one of us was exactly sure what the punch line would be once I entered, but we both had a feeling it would be effective.

Standing in the hall outside the interrogation room, most of me wanted him to play ball, to tell her what she needed in a timely manner so we could find Carlos and get moving.

Some small part of me though, a tiny, undefined space deep within, hoped he would press her, that he would try to mess with her just enough to get me called into the room.

"Okay," Diaz said, standing alongside the glass and peering inside. "They're bringing him in now."

"How's he look?" I asked.

She paused a moment. "He's a little more worn down than the last time I saw him, has a scowl in place that would make Ice Cube proud, but otherwise he seems okay."

I fought down the urge to step forward and peer in, both for fear it might derail our plan and that it might send that tiny spark deep inside into a full-on blaze. Despite whatever scar tissue the previous five years might have melded over the old wounds, it never actually sealed them completely.

My only worry was what might happen once they ripped open again, allowing all the hate and rage bottled within to spill out.

If the Juarezes were smart, they would worry about that, too.

One more nod of the head and Diaz stepped through, her hands empty, her customary deep-set frown in place. From where I stood I could see the back of her head for three steps before she disappeared from view, leaving me alone in the hallway.

With my back pressed against the cool concrete block behind me, I tried to fit everything I knew into some form of pattern. Discovering that the funds originated in Russia had been a bombshell, a shot in the dark that none of us could have seen coming. Were they what had Carlos so worried? And how did he now think he could avoid them?

I stood in place, my gaze aimed at the tile floor, my mind racing, when a flash of color jerked my attention upward. Standing in full view of the window was Diaz. She wasn't looking at me, keeping her attention on what I assumed was Manny, but as she talked I could see her raise her head up and down, an almost imperceptible nod meant for me. Tapping into just a bit of the animosity lurking within, I bolted across the hallway and jerked the door open, letting it slam back against the wall with a clatter.

Diaz didn't so much as turn her head as I entered, her focus fixed on Manny. For his part he jerked his gaze up at me, surprise at the sudden entrance soon replaced by a mixture of realization and shock. He extended one hand up toward me, his jaw dropping open, a sound resembling a pained moan sliding out.

The sight of him made my every nerve tingle as I stomped across the room at him. With my left hand I shoved the table aside, the legs of it squeaking as it slid across the polished floor. Open and exposed, Manny sat and looked at me, his eyes growing wide.

Again he attempted to say something, but never got the chance.

My fist connected with his cheek with a deafening smack of skin-on-skin contact. I aimed it high enough to avoid snapping his jawbone, but low enough so it would rattle a few teeth.

The blow had the intended effect, sending him toppling over from the chair, depositing him in a heap on the floor. A trail of bloody spittle extended out away from him a full three feet in length, dotting the light tile floor.

Without waiting for him to recover I flipped him onto his back with the heel of my foot and bent low over him, grabbing a handful of rough canvas shirt and lifting him toward me. I made sure to get a little skin and flesh as I hefted over half of his body up into the air, bringing him to a stop just inches from my face.

"Where the hell is Carlos, Manny?"

Chapter Twenty-Six

The ground crunched beneath Carlos Juarez's feet as he exited the rented Jeep and stood staring at the structure. A plume of dust and debris hung in the air around him, raised by his tires as he traveled over the long-abandoned road, thrown upward no matter how slowly he traveled. It tickled his nose as he stood and surveyed his surroundings, tasted grit as it settled on his lips.

Carlos ran the back of his hand across his mouth, adding even more dust. Thin and chalky, it caked on his tongue, causing him to spit repeatedly at the ground. Little wet specks appeared by his feet.

"Home again, home again," Carlos said, a sour expression crossing his face. For several long moments he stared warily at the silent structure, waiting as the cloud of dust settled behind him.

Once it did, he could see out through the California desert for miles in every direction.

Situated atop a bluff in the Sonoran Desert, the place was fifty miles from the closest metropolis of any size. On especially clear nights the lights of San Diego were just visible in the distance, a tiny cluster glittering on the horizon, seventy miles to the southwest.

The sky was not yet dark enough for such viewing, the sun still a few inches above the horizon behind Carlos. Long shafts of sunlight bathed everything in a late-day glow, reflecting off the Jeep beside him, their intensity barely contained by the thick coat of dust covering it.

The choice in arrival time was deliberate, making sure to show up before his headlights could be seen cutting a solitary path through the night.

After leaving Manny that morning, Carlos had every intention of doing as he'd been told, staying with the plan they had laid out years ago. He would remain under protective custody, raise all kinds of hell to make sure they did their job, and he would stay alive. As tempting as the thought of finally being out from beneath their watchful eye was, the recent travails of Mateo served as a cautionary tale to keep him from doing anything rash.

That had been five hours ago, though. Before Diaz and that bastard from another time dropped him alongside the highway, noon sun beating down on him, not a soul around. Before the second car, manned by a pair of condescending pricks with shaved heads and terrible facial hair pulled up and demanded he get in, making borderline-racist comments the entire way back.

Long before they tried to force him to return to the house he'd been staying in for months, the same one Mateo had sent the package to, its location had no doubt been spilled to whoever found him.

Despite whatever he had promised his cousin, there was no way he could return there. Going back would all but confirm his death, be walking right into a trap that was lying in wait at that very moment, a team of men in place, waiting to spring for him.

Instead, he'd gone off the grid. Gotten himself to town, rented a Jeep, and made a line for a house that only one other person in the world knew of, and he damned sure wouldn't tell anybody about it.

The building was made entirely from concrete block, stretching forty feet in length and twenty feet in width. The back half of it was buried within the sand dune it was perched atop, a practical design meant to serve as a natural coolant and to aid in reducing visibility. A single wooden door stood in the middle of the front, a pair of matching windows on either side. Every surface, the glass included, was painted sandy brown.

If somebody didn't know exactly where it was, there was no way they would ever find it on their own.

The place had been constructed as a bomb shelter sometime in the fifties, the kind of place Army officials could hide in and watch remote detonations through binoculars. Rumor was there were dozens just like it scattered through the Sonoran Desert, all from a time when Cold War fears were a part of daily life.

It was the only one Carlos had ever seen. Manny had acquired it ten years before as a private safe house exclusively for the family. Not even Mateo knew about the location, something the two cousins had discussed at length before deciding to keep it strictly between them.

The fact that Mateo might still be breathing had that conversation gone a bit differently was something Carlos had actively avoided since receiving the package a day before.

"Well, here we are," Carlos muttered, reaching across the front seat of the Jeep and extracting a pair of plastic grocery sacks from the passenger seat. Each one contained bottles of water and Gatorade, stacks of canned and dried goods in the back. Stored inside the house were pallets of MREs—meal ready to eat—picked up at a military surplus store years before, but the idea of actually eating any of those had been bad enough to force Carlos to risk the extra time needed to stop for some real food on his way out of San Diego.

More than once he had thought of getting word to Manny about his plan, but in the end decided against it. He was going against the script now and he knew it. Better to lie low a few days and figure things out, hope the DEA got their heads about them, and resurface. After that he would stop by the prison and explain what had happened, why he did what he felt he had to.

Manny would understand, he always did.

And even if he didn't, it was easier to apologize than ask permission.

A thin top layer of sand whipped across the ground as Carlos walked to the front door, the sound of it smacking against the Jeep, the front windows of the building, ringing in his ears. Underfoot the ground was compact, the soil hard packed and sunbaked, a heavy dose of sand lying atop it, pushed back and forth by the unending desert winds.

Switching both sacks into his left hand, Carlos rotated a clump of keys in his right, shifting them until the single brass implement he was looking for came into view. Using his thumb and forefinger he separated it out from the others and slid it into the lock. The mechanism turned smoothly, releasing with a click.

The wind had driven a heap of sand beneath the doorway, clumping it on the ground and offering resistance as Carlos pressed his shoulder into the door and shoved. It pushed back against him a moment before giving way, swinging out into a darkened space. The only light spilled in through the doorway. His elongated silhouette stretched across the floor as the musty scent of stale air and dust met his nostrils.

Carlos stood in the doorway a long moment, allowing his eyes to adjust to the darkness. He twisted the sacks a bit in his hand, the plastic echoing out, the sound breaking up the eerie silence of the building.

"OK," Carlos said, nodding, before taking a step forward, his foot touching solid concrete for the first time since leaving the grocery store.

His second step never made it.

There was no chance for Carlos to defend himself, not even the opportunity for him to scream out. Instead there was just a single flash of light, a glint of sunshine flashing against polished steel, before everything receded to darkness.

Chapter Twenty-Seven

"How's the hand?" Diaz asked, glancing over from the road to my right fist, lightly balled atop my thigh. I glanced down at it without looking over at her, flexing my fingers into a tight bunch before spreading them wide, leaving the hand flat.

"It's fine," I replied, looking out the front windshield. "I'm not made of glass."

Until she asked, I hadn't once thought about my hand. The combination of avoiding his jawbone and the concentrated adrenaline coursing through me had kept there from being even a slight hint of soreness. My skin, leathered from five years of exposure to the elements, had held firm as well.

It was the first punch I'd thrown in a very long time, though my body didn't seem to realize it.

"I could say the same for Manny Juarez," Diaz said. "Hard as you hit him, I thought he'd be unconscious for hours."

An inch up or down, inch and a half to the left, and he would have been. I don't say that to be boastful, but as a statement of fact. Most people have never thrown a meaningful punch in their lives. They curl their thumbs beneath their overlying fingers, angle their hand away from their forearm, don't know how to balance their weight.

On the second day of DEA training, they began teaching us hand-to-hand combat. Not how to box, not some twisted version of the hottest MMA style, but how to fight. Even a few years out of practice, those skills never leave a man.

If I'd wanted him unconscious, he would have been. Simple fact was, he was of absolutely no use to us lying on the floor, unable to open his eyes. So I did what I had to to make my point, to get his attention.

Two minutes later he told us exactly what we wanted to know.

"Tell me," I asked, switching the topic of conversation, making no attempt to be covert about it. "How did you guys close the net on him anyway?"

A long moment passed as Diaz pushed the speedometer above seventy. The setting sun shone in our faces. I reached out and flipped the visor down in front of me as the front dash piped chilled air into my face.

"You never heard?" she asked, the top half of her face covered in plastic black sunglasses. Their mirrored lenses reflected both the sun and the road ahead.

"No," I said, shaking my head less than an inch to either side. "Once I was out, I was out."

"Damn," Diaz muttered, just audible above the air-conditioning fan in front of us.

She left the comment open-ended, pausing for a moment, allowing me to fill in the blanks if I wanted to. There was plenty I could have inserted for her, ranging from the need to get as far away from the desert as I could, to the knowing if I was around it even a little bit there was no way I would be able to control the torrent of emotion within me.

My actions a half hour before, the first of what I feared would be many, had already displayed a tiny bit of that, even after five years to suppress it.

"First of all," Diaz said, reaching up and adjusting the sunglasses on her face, the reflection bouncing in equal measure, "it was you guys that did it, not us."

Unable to stop it, my jaw dropped open a half-inch, my head twisting to the side. "Say what?"

Diaz nodded, rocking her body forward an inch or two with it. "Maybe a year after you left. Took almost another year before Manny entered prison and all the details were ironed out, but, yeah. It was the last thing Hutch did before heading back to Washington."

I stared at her a long moment before turning back to face forward, running a hand over my face. For three solid days now I had been interacting with my old boss, but not once had he shared that bit of information with me. Why? Was he trying to protect some old wounds he thought I still carried?

"Son of a . . ." I muttered, letting my voice trail away.

"Yep," Diaz agreed, nodding once more.

Silence fell between us, my mind racing to determine what to make of this newest piece of information. My breathing grew louder as I sat and stewed on it, forcing air in and out through my nose, my eyebrows knitting together as I stared ahead.

Sensing where my mind was, feeling the anger start to roll off me, Diaz pushed ahead. "The plea bargain was to cover Carlos and Mateo as well. I got the impression from reading the case file after the fact that Mateo was more of a throw-in than a demand, a pity toss by our side based on the volume of information he gave up."

This time I was more prepared for any surprises. I kept my mouth closed, not letting the wonder of this statement show.

In all my time with the DEA, I had been a full-time field agent. Never was I inside the boardroom for final negotiations with anybody that we brought in, but not once could I remember our side throwing in extra concessions just for the sake of it.

"All three protected under one plea deal? What the hell did he give up?"

A smirk pushed Diaz's head back as she glanced over my direction. "Who *didn't* he give up? In total over a dozen distributors, stretched up the coast from here all the way to Fresno."

"Fresno?" I asked, letting shock show in my voice. "Damn, when I was running them they were making their way into Bakersfield. That's over a hundred miles of expansion in just a couple years."

"Yeah," Diaz said, nodding in agreement, "and my hunch is if we hadn't gotten to them they'd have been all the way to the Bay Area within the decade."

An elongated whistle slid out between my lips, my head leaning back to sit on the headrest behind me. All told, that represented a stretch almost five hundred miles long, encompassing no less than five major cities, including LA, Oakland, and San Francisco. There were no doubt other competing interests in each of those areas, but just the fact that they were there spoke volumes of the scale they had become capable of operating on.

"So you pinched Manny? And he rolled to protect his higher-ups?"

Diaz lifted the sunglasses from her face onto her forehead and pulled her cell phone from the middle console between us. She checked the automated directions onscreen against the mile marker outside before dropping the phone and her glasses back into place.

"Two more miles," she said, both hands returning to the wheel. "I don't know all the details, even now. Large chunks of the terms have been redacted, written off under the old company maxim—"

"—'above your pay grade,'" I finished for her, having heard the words a hundred times before, each just as bitter as the previous.

"All I know for sure is Manny went in for fifteen, probably be out in less than half that. Carlos and Mateo were both put into protective custody, I assume in case any of the distributors they ratted out decide to go after them, and given the caveat that they provide any assistance we ask for with dealers along the coast."

She slowed the car to less than half our previous speed as a green mile-marker sign came closer along the right shoulder. We both leaned toward the window as it crept by, eyes aimed on the ground, looking for anything that might be construed as an in-road.

Seventy yards after the sign we found it, a matching pair of indents in the shallow desert sand giving the place away. Without flipping on the blinker Diaz hooked a right, the car bouncing up and down, tires spinning, before settling into the grooves and rolling forward.

I waited until the car evened out before returning my thoughts to the conversation. So much of what she was telling me wasn't making sense. Priority one was to find Carlos, but getting him, Manny, and Hutch all together in the same room wasn't far behind.

Whatever had happened with the Juarez cartel three years before was a mess I had to get cleared up if I was to have any chance at deciphering why they were now under attack. There were dozens of questions still left unanswered, but I decided to let them go for the time being.

Beside me, Diaz removed the sunglasses and tossed them atop the dash. She pulled her chin back into her neck, folds of skin gathering there, the frown back in place on her features.

We rode in silence for a full five minutes, traversing the three miles from the roadway, just as Manny told us it would be. The entire way we both leaned forward in our seats, straining to see the faintest hint of a path through the sand. The sedan whined in protest as it pushed along. Outside I could hear the sound of sand crunching beneath our tires, mixed with gravel and soil beaten down hard over the years.

"You think he's here?" I asked, watching as a dune rose out of the desert ahead of us, seeming to swallow up the path we were on. The front side appeared to be a solid surface, though it was hard to decipher anything out of the wall of light brown.

"I don't know," Diaz said, keeping her head locked in place. "I don't see anybody, though, not even a car outside."

I nodded in agreement, the same thought spurring my question in the first place. "And he damned sure didn't hike in here from anywhere."

There was no response from Diaz as she slid the car to a stop twenty feet away from the front door, the brakes again offering a tiny moan of protest. She killed the engine and left the keys in the ignition, both of us sitting in silence, sweeping our gazes over the grounds.

A small part of me almost told her to stay put, that I would be right back, but I refrained. The move was not one of misogyny, but rather the feeling that anything we found here couldn't be good. No point in subjecting us both to it.

Instead I waited though, allowing her the lead, sitting in silence until she unlatched her door before climbing out on the opposite side.

The structure seemed pretty simple, exactly as Manny had described it. A square concrete crash pad, partially covered by sand, painted to match. There was no foliage of any kind to be seen, the only path in being the one we were now parked on. Not a single thing seemed to be out of place until I took a deep breath, catching just the slightest hint of a smell on the breeze.

"Oh, shit," I muttered.

Diaz snapped into a crouch on the other side of the sedan, her right hand cocked by her hip, poised to grab her weapon. "What?"

"Draw," I said, my voice low, reaching into the small of my back and extracting the Glock. I gripped it in my right hand, my left wrapped around the base for support, bending at the knees to match Diaz's pose. One foot at a time I advanced on the front door, pressing my back against the concrete alongside it, waiting as Diaz got into position opposite me.

What? she mouthed again, her voice inaudible.

I raised both sides of my nose at her in an even snarl and replied, "Smell that?"

I paused as she drew in a deep lungful of air, her chest rising as it filled her body. Just as fast she shoved it out through her mouth, a look of revulsion on her face. "Blood."

The scent had caught me twenty feet away, a practiced response from my time in Yellowstone. There, fresh kill often meant predators in the area. Being able to recognize it at a moment's notice was a necessary life skill.

I rotated out away from the door and positioned myself in front of it, my legs square. Then I pointed down at my right leg, motioned at the door, and gestured for Diaz to go inside right after. One at a time she raised each foot from the sand and prepared to move, nodding in agreement as she shifted her focus on the wooden structure before us.

Unwrapping my left hand from the gun, I lowered my hands to either side and drew in a quick breath. I allowed the moment of seeing Manny Juarez to enter my mind, of seeing his face for the first time in years to play across my senses, before snapping forward and driving my heel through the door just inches from the handle.

The aged wood exploded backward on contact, disintegrating into a flurry of dust and shards. They still hung thick in the air as Diaz darted through, gun extended in front of her, moving fast. Her lower body was visible in the dim glow as I raised my weapon and joined her, swinging in the opposite direction.

The open doorway was the only source of light in the place, but it was more than enough to illuminate everything there was to see. We each did a lap in our respective directions, meeting on the opposite side, directly across from the door, before holstering our weapons and walking side by side into the center of the room.

"Oh, shit," I said again.

Chapter Twenty-Eight

The tip of the Pidka cigarette glowed brightly in the darkness, filling Victor Blok's lungs with acrid, bitter smoke. He held it there a long moment, savoring the taste, letting it burn, before shoving it out. The sea breeze caught the smoke and pulled it away from his face in a sideways mist.

The cigarettes in America were too pure for his taste; the tobacco was thinned out, watered down by additives. Making things worse, nearly every brand on the market had taken to jamming a filter on the end of it, removing all flavor, stripping the smoke of any inherent bite.

Pidka cigarettes were the only thing Viktor ever missed from the Motherland. Everything else he could get at a moment's notice, even good vodka, except for real smokes. Eight months earlier he had had a shipment brought in, one hundred cartons, to be used only in extreme situations.

Tonight seemed like one such circumstance.

Standing on the edge of his dock, Viktor watched as a small team, five men all dressed in black, loaded supplies into a boat. A high-end trawler painted glossy silver, the vessel would carry the men up the coast into La Jolla. Once in place offshore, four of the men would enter the water and go ashore, taking with them the supplies that were currently being loaded. The fifth would stay with the boat, pushing it north along the coast, and return in exactly an hour to retrieve them.

The plan had been hashed and rehashed no less than ten times in the preceding hours. Viktor could sense from the last phone call with his uncle that the old man was growing antsy, threatening to exert his presence once again. For the time being, Viktor had Pavel out of his hair, hopefully still somewhere in the mountains, digging around for the remains of Lita.

It was a very narrow window Viktor had, getting the operation completed before either Sergey or Pavel became aware of his actions. Once they did they would try to insert themselves, either eschewing his plan entirely or at the very least insisting on their involvement.

If Viktor was ever going to break free from the tether his uncle insisted on keeping him tied to, this was where it had to begin. His operation, with his people, going off without a hitch. A simple in-and-out procedure that was effective and quiet, securing the last holdout in the network, allowing new distribution to begin.

Taking one last drag on the cigarette, Viktor cast it into the ocean, watching the small white speck being swallowed beneath the dark waters. He blew the smoke from his lungs and stepped up alongside the ramp leading onto the boat. The evening breeze pushed his hair atop his head and tugged at the collar of his silk shirt.

"This is the last of it," Anton Chekov, the leader of the expedition, said, peeling himself off from the procession of men loading up the ramp for a final time. He stood several inches shorter than Viktor but was considerably thicker, his upper body cut from corded steel. He wore his dark hair shorn close to the scalp, and his face was free of any stubble.

Behind him the other three continued on their way, the first carrying an automatic weapon in each hand, their barrels pointed at the sky, their butts resting in the crooks of his arms. The other two marched on either end of an elongated box, wooden, white in color.

None of the three looked at Viktor or Anton as they went, moving in silence with complete precision.

Through the front window of the boat's cabin Viktor could see the fifth man, an affable young guy named Ivan with blond hair and ruddy cheeks. He was dressed in white linen pants and an Aloha shirt, just another rich playboy taking his boat up and down the coast for a late-night joyride.

"Good," Viktor said, nodding, fighting the urge to pull out another Pidka and light it. "Has he checked on the conditions yet?"

"Twice now," Anton said, offering a grim nod. "Everything is clear from here to Oregon. Should be no problem getting in and out this evening."

"Good," Viktor repeated. Both men had been over the plan so many times there was nothing more to say. They each knew how important the run was, to their position in Mexico and to the operation as a whole.

"I'll be available by phone the entire time if anything should happen," Viktor said, extending a hand toward Anton.

A thin crack of a smile broke across Anton's face as he returned the shake, squeezing hard for a moment before releasing it. "Nothing's going to happen, sir. We'll call and let you know when it's done."

Viktor attempted to force a matching smile onto his features, though the best he could manage was a lopsided grimace. He nodded and slapped Anton on the shoulder, watching as he turned and bounded across the gangplank before lifting it from the edge of the boat and shoving it onto the dock.

The water around the boat began to churn as the engine picked up steam, Viktor remaining in place as it started to ease away. The turbo-stroke diesel puttered in a steady cadence as the vessel moved forward, leaving a wide wake behind it.

Viktor stood with his hands in his pockets, the scent of diesel smoke and saltwater in his nostrils, and watched until it was nothing more than a cluster of lights moving through the darkness. With it went his plans for the next decade, the first step in breaking free from the family, establishing his own empire on a new continent.

The thought of it brought a smile to his face, a genuine response that stretched across his features as he climbed the steps away from the water's edge, his shoes shuffling against wood. Deep within his right pocket he could feel his phone begin to vibrate against the palm of his hand, and his smile dropped away in an instant.

"Already?" he muttered. "Jesus, they just left."

Shaking his head, he pulled the phone out and held it at arm's length, his gaze settling on the name displayed before him. As if Pavlovian, his heartbeat began to thunder in his chest, sweat dampening his armpits. For the first time, he became aware of the taste of smoke and salt in his mouth, his tongue fighting to conjure any bit of saliva within him.

After the fourth buzz, he accepted the call and pressed it to his ear. "Hello, Uncle."

"Where the hell were you this time?" Sergey barked, annoyance and anger in his voice.

The same pair of emotions welled within Viktor as he finished ascending the stairs and stopped on the top landing. He rested his rear against the railing encasing it, the ocean breeze hitting him full in the back.

"And why does it sound like you're in a wind tunnel?"

Viktor held the phone away from him for a moment and muttered a string of expletives, each with more hostility than the one before. When he could think of no more he brought the device back to his face, his features contorted in anger.

"I'm down by the dock," Viktor said. "I was here to send off a team headed north to La Jolla, going to take care of that last little problem we discussed."

Five minutes before, he'd hoped to be completed with the task before mentioning it to his uncle. Now, he just hoped his decisive action would be enough to curry a bit of favor with the old man.

"You did what?" Sergey asked, his tone pointed, low.

For a moment Viktor felt a bit of panic within him before pushing it aside. "There was a problem, I fixed it," he said, shoving more bravado into his voice than he actually felt. "That is why you sent me here, isn't it?"

He could feel the challenge in his tone, knew that he was walking on very thin ice. Still, if this was to be his moment to break free, to put some distance between himself and things back home, this was where it had to begin.

A long moment of silence passed, followed by the exaggerated inhalation of air. When his uncle spoke his voice was flinty, honed to a razor's edge.

"No, you arrogant little prick," Sergey spat. "You're there because my brother is dead and my son is in jail. If there was anybody else in this family to send, *anybody*, they would be there instead of you.

"As it is, I'm still considering taking the whole damn thing away from you and giving it to Pavel."

A surge of rage roiled within Viktor, his hand squeezing so tight it threatened to shatter the phone in his hand. Scads of retorts sprang to mind, ranging in ferocity from telling his uncle off to threatening to come back to Russia and finish him himself.

"Pavel isn't family."

"But at least I can trust him!" Sergey shouted back, his voice cracking with each word.

Viktor clenched his left hand into a ball and held it by his temple, squeezing it so tight it trembled beside his head. He kept his eyes and mouth both screwed shut for several moments, pressed together so hard little white lights began to dance before his eyes, before releasing the tension in his body. Vitriol still pulsed through him as he took two deep breaths and asked, "Why are you calling me? To tell me I'm out?"

On the other end he could hear Sergey panting, fighting to get himself under control. He waited as his uncle coughed and spat out a wad of phlegm, the sound repulsive over the line.

"No, that's not why I'm calling you," Sergey muttered. He sounded weak and tired, much older than the man that had been screaming just a moment before. "I was calling to tell you La Jolla has been taken care of."

Viktor's eyes spread wide for a moment before sliding shut. Tonight was supposed to have been his chance to step away from the bonds that were growing tighter by the day. Instead, his place at the bottom of the pecking order had been sealed, done by actions thousands of miles away, completely unbeknownst to him.

"And when you say . . ."

"I mean it's been taken care of," Sergey repeated. "The message has been delivered. La Jolla is now on board with our plans."

Viktor ran a hand back through his hair, shaking his head, trying to comprehend what this meant for his operation. "Does that mean shipments are ready to begin?"

"We'll discuss the shipments another time. Right now, just get on the phone and call your crew back home. The last thing we need is another embarrassment."

Chapter Twenty-Nine

The plastic wrapper on the outside of the Gatorade bottle crinkled in my hand, the sound serving to mask a bit of the noise going on inside the bomb shelter beside me. After hours of being left on its side, the liquid inside was rather warm. Even the condensation on the bottle had long since evaporated, just a few smudges of clumped sand the only reminders that it was ever there.

"Where did you get that?" Diaz asked, stepping up alongside me and leaning against the trunk of our sedan. She wrapped the front of her suit coat over her torso and folded her arms across it. The autumn breeze blew cool across us.

"Courtesy of one Carlos Juarez," I said, lifting the bottle toward the sky in a faux salute before taking another drink. "Want some? Fruit punch was never my favorite anyway."

Diaz stared at me a long moment, a fleeting bit of shock, almost revulsion on her face, before raising a corner of her mouth in a smirk. She reached out and took the bottle, upending the bottom of it, downing a couple of inches of the beverage.

"You know, technically this was part of the crime scene," she said, handing it back to me.

I accepted the bottle and took another pull, not bothering to wipe the lip of it. "That's not a crime scene in there. That's a massacre. A brutal ending that even a smartass like Carlos didn't deserve."

Diaz nodded in silent agreement beside me, both of us envisioning what we had found just an hour before.

The building was entirely void of life when we entered. It was obvious the moment we stepped across the threshold, though we both did our due diligence and cleared the premises before focusing on the macabre centerpiece the scene had to offer.

Lying chest down in the center of the floor was Carlos, his arms and legs extended out from his body like a twisted starfish. Two plastic sacks with bottled water and Gatorade lay beside his left foot, a couple of strays having rolled across the dusty floor toward the wall.

We knew it to be Carlos from his skin tone and the clothes he was wearing, the same khakis and open button-down he'd had on this morning. A certain ID wouldn't be possible until DNA results came back though, given that his head had been cleaved away from his body, removed with a single slice.

Most of his blood had spurted from his exposed carotid, striping the dust-covered floor in angry sprays of crimson. The speckled rooster tails covered a wide half arc over the ground, tracking the descent of his body, his heartbeat continuing even after the removal of his head.

Once the body had come to a stop, most of his blood had pooled out onto the concrete around him, moving in an uneven circle across the sandy floor. By the time we arrived it was already dark and sticky, the first flies just beginning to buzz around it.

After a moment, Diaz had stepped outside and called it in, leaving me behind to glean away what I could without disturbing anything.

With the exception of a few uneven footprints, large with heavy treads, there was nothing of use in the place. Crime Scene was now inside combing through things, but something told me they weren't going to find anything, either. Even if they did, odds were it would come back to another ghost originating somewhere in Russia, completely beyond the scope of any major American agency.

The desert sun was now below the horizon, nothing more than a faint speck of orange glow along the western skyline. Behind us the techs had set up a mobile field unit, bright fluorescent light filling the inside of the building and spilling out into the night. It splayed across the ground in long orbs, passing just a few feet away from us and extending far ahead over the ground.

"Thoughts?" Diaz asked, holding her hand out for the Gatorade.

I passed it across without glancing her way, my gaze aimed out at the darkening sky. It had been years since I'd seen a desert evening, though the image seemed to carry a certain familiarity with it that was both comforting and startling.

"Two big ones," I said, my eyes narrowed. "First, how the hell did they know about this place? Manny swore, *swore*, that he and Carlos were the only ones with access up here."

"Yeah," Diaz agreed, nodding her head. She took another swig from the bottle, tilting the bottom of it toward the sky, giving the distinct impression she would rather be drinking something a little stronger than Gatorade.

"And second," I continued, "how the hell did they get here? Judging by the positioning of the body in there, whoever did this was lying in wait, caught Carlos the minute he stepped inside."

"Agreed," Diaz said. "No way was this a classic double cross."

"Nor was it a body dump," I said. "You see the spray pattern in there? This was done here."

"And no bindings of any kind, grocery sacks in hand," Diaz added. "He thought he was alone. There's enough MREs in there to last a couple weeks. He was coming to hide for a while, nothing more."

"So again," I said, "how the hell did whoever did this get here? You saw the lay of the land. There's one road, completely wide open. If a car was parked here, Carlos would have seen it. If they'd parked on the high-way and hiked in, he would have seen it."

"And to even do that would have meant miles across open desert in the afternoon sun," Diaz added.

"While knowing exactly where they were going," I said. "It's not like a person would just set off on foot out here and hope to find this place. Hell, we had directions and barely made it."

A long silhouette appeared in the stripe of light protruding from the structure. It started as a black blob, the head and shoulders visible, swaying a few inches from side to side. After a moment, a pair of long, dark legs extended out from the bottom, the angle of the person chang-ing as they walked toward us.

The sound of footsteps became audible behind us, though neither of us turned around. We both knew who was approaching, the smell of his herbal concoction preceding him by at least thirty feet.

"Preliminary findings by the ME say death was by decapitation, a single slice made by a sharp metal object," Hutch said, coming to a stop beside us, paper cup in hand, a white plastic lid atop it.

"No shit," Diaz muttered beside me, voice so low it just barely caught my ear.

"Anything else?" I asked.

"Like I said," Hutch said, "single slice. Had to have been somebody very strong, familiar with working a blade."

"What about angle?" I asked.

"Too early to tell," Hutch said. "And given the place is a mess, we may never know. He could have been bent over as he entered, could have been searching for the light switch on the wall, anything. Too many variables."

"What are you thinking?" Diaz asked, sensing my question was for a reason.

"Single swipe, with a blade?" I replied. "Somebody powerful, used to working with primitive weapons. If we could determine it was at a downward angle, get an idea on how large this guy might have been . . ."

I let my voice trail off, shifting my attention over to Hutch. He took a long sip on his tea, pondering in silence, before his head started to work itself up and down in a small bob. "You think maybe Pavel Haney? Or whatever the hell his name really is?"

"It's possible," I said. "Didn't you say he was cut free last night?"

Again Hutch nodded, his face compressed in a bitter stare. "Had to. There was nothing to charge him with beyond a misdemeanor B&E. Can't hold a man forever on that."

"They impounded his car while he was inside, though, didn't they?" I asked.

Hutch shifted his gaze over to me and nodded, realization settling over his features. "I'll get on the horn and put out a BOLO for him."

At that he turned on his heel and walked away, cutting a straight path toward his own sedan, parked on the outside of a small clump of Crime Scene vehicles arranged haphazardly around the building, sand beginning to pile up alongside their tires.

"Man, that stuff smells like shit." Diaz finished off the Gatorade and swiped the back of her hand across her lips. "How did you put up with it for five years?"

I turned and looked at her, pointing along the bony ridge of my nose with a single finger. "Broke my nose second year on the job, lost over half my sense of smell."

"Lucky bastard," Diaz said, pushing herself up from the trunk of the car and turning to face me. "You ready?"

I nodded in silence, sliding past her to take my seat. Even without asking I knew where we were going: off to pull on the only thread we still had available to us until Hutch's BOLO turned something up.

It was time to pay Manny Juarez another visit.

Chapter Thirty

The task itself was easy. Sergey had fed him the exact location where Carlos would be, giving him more than enough time to get into position. He had even arranged for a weapon and a ride out into the desert for Pavel, dropping him off at the edge of the road, giving him water to cover the three-mile hike back along the sandy, windswept path to the safe house.

Only two real concerns had presented themselves along the way, both disappearing with relative ease. The first was the fear that his footprints would be visible leading back to the structure, a clear line in the sand that alerted Carlos he was there. For a time Pavel had considered dragging a broom, or even a blanket, behind him to blot them out. In the end, the combined effect of the hard-packed ground just beneath the surface and the persistent wind pushing in from the west swept his steps away no more than minutes after he passed.

The second worry was of actually getting inside the structure. He had been warned that the terrain was flat and void of places to hide, the ideal location for a house of its purpose. If he couldn't make it across the threshold before Carlos arrived, the odds of him remaining unseen went down tremendously.

For a time the thought of burying himself in the ground and waiting had seemed like it might be the most plausible option, but in the end a bit of luck saved him from spending two hours in a cocoon of superheated sand.

The front door was locked, as he expected it to be. The building was made of concrete and the frame and door from thick oak, all three making any kind of forced entry too difficult to manage without being obvious. The only other routes into the building were a pair of cracked windows, their glass painted over.

After the experience in Montana, Pavel was less than enthused by the options.

To his great surprise, one of them was left unlocked.

The squeeze was tight for his oversized body. He positioned his head and left shoulder through, pushing himself forward, then twisting his right shoulder in behind it. His body spun around so it was facing out the same direction as the house. An inch at a time he shoved his body backward until his feet touched the sandy floor beneath him. Then he reached back outside and took up the gift his driver had bestowed upon him.

After that it was just a matter of sitting in the darkness, taking occasional slugs of water, and waiting. He put his back against the cool concrete of the back wall, which was insulated from the sun by the sand outside, and reduced his body to autopilot. His eyes lowered themselves into slits, his aching joints took in the solace of rest, and he prepared himself for what the night held in store.

Two hours after assuming his position, the rumbling of an engine churning over the sand crept into his ears. His eyes opened wide, and his heart rate elevated back to its normal level as he rose from the floor and took a place behind the door.

Gripped in his right hand was an authentic Russian shashka, its curved blade almost two feet in length, the outer edge honed razor sharp. It balanced itself perfectly in his grip, the contoured lines of the oversized handle fitting his massive hand, the blade catching errant bits of light, flashing in the darkness.

The entire encounter, from the time Carlos pulled to a stop outside to the moment Pavel saddled up in his Jeep and drove away, took less than five minutes. The moment his victim appeared in the doorway he did what was required of him, finishing the job in a single swipe, one massive cleave that removed the head clean from the shoulders. He waited a full minute for the blood to stop spurting across the floor before collecting the trophy, careful not to step in any of the fresh bodily fluids.

In a plastic sack much like the ones Carlos had in hand upon entering, Pavel carried the head away with him, taking the car keys on his way out, stopping to lock the door behind him.

Not once throughout did his heart rate spike, his breathing grow rapid, or a sweat even crease his brow. There was no way Carlos could have stopped him from doing what he came to do; the element of surprise and his physical prowess was just too much to be denied.

That same mirror-calm demeanor now encompassed his features as he approached the mansion overlooking the Pacific. He had swapped out Carlos's Jeep for his Avenger, the last stop he would have to make before returning it to the spot he found it. His ride back to Mexico was waiting for him at a private port.

The idling engine pushed him through a pair of oversized brick structures; the wrought iron gate that usually closed the driveway between them was standing open.

The owners were expecting him.

Without touching the accelerator, he allowed his car to follow the winding brick path to the base of an expansive home, which stood on an extended bluff with the ocean right underneath. The house's three wings spread out wide before him. The entire place was painted dull white in the Mediterranean style, and hundreds of windows faced out in all directions. Lights were burning brightly within each one, illuminating the home like a beacon.

Pavel could hear the sound of waves smashing into the rocks below as he stepped from the car, paused behind the open door, and surveyed his surroundings. From where he stood he could see a pair of guards on the front porch, both wearing light-colored suit coats over T-shirts, automatic weapons in hand. Above them two more were positioned behind windows, making sure they were seen, wearing the same ensemble.

No doubt there were at least that many scattered about the grounds, lurking just beyond his sight line.

For a moment his mind flitted back to the USP compact 9 mm in the middle console of the car, but just as fast he let it pass. The act would be seen as one of antagonism, something he could ill afford at the moment. The gift he was bringing along for them was gruesome enough; there was no need to exacerbate the situation.

With a curt nod to the guards, Pavel closed the car door and walked toward the front door, hands in plain sight. He kept the bag a few inches away from his side, the thin handles looped across his middle and index fingers, swinging free. One at a time he climbed the three steps onto the porch and stopped, raising his hands by his side, remaining motionless as one of the guards gave him a quick pat-down, careful to avoid the sack, while the other stood by with gun gripped in both hands.

Content that he was clean, the guards nodded to each other, and the one who had executed the search led Pavel inside. The other brought up the rear, keeping his weapon never more than a few feet from Pavel's back.

Throughout, Pavel kept his face neutral, his breathing even. He made no sudden movements, showed no signs of disdain. Instead he forced his features to be as serene as possible, allowing the guards to take the lead, granting them the illusion of being in control the entire time.

He was there to serve a purpose, not to win a test of manhood.

The house opened before him as he was led inside, the front door leading to an open foyer. A wraparound staircase extended up both sides of it, an enormous chandelier hanging from the ceiling. Everything was outfitted in white, the myriad of lights reflecting off each surface, the entire space seeming to glow. With the exception of the handful of armed guards watching his every movement, it seemed like a scene directly out of a movie.

The guards led him straight across the foyer and through a rear door. The back wall gave way to an outdoor patio that stretched most of the length of the home. Made to match the rest of the spread it was done entirely in white, extending out over twenty feet before changing to plush green turf. Less than a hundred feet away, the lawn ended abruptly on the edge of the bluff. The moon reflected off the ocean visible in the distance.

Two brass fire pits were situated on the patio, twenty feet apart, both filled with glass fire rocks with flames rising above them. Between them were two white outdoor sofas, separated by a glass table.

As Pavel made his way out, a man in blue linen pants and a striped Oxford shirt stood, an oversized smile on his face. His brown hair hung in two stiff arcs from a part that split his head down the middle, framing blue eyes. His expression revealed a gap between his two front teeth, his veneers flashing white against his bronze skin.

At first glance, Pavel sized him up as a beach bum turned entrepreneur, a child of fortune who had eschewed the family business for a chance to make fast money.

Exactly the kind of man he had encountered frequently, despised every time, since coming to North America.

"My friend, how nice of you to stop by," the man said, extending a hand to Pavel. Pavel accepted the shake, noting the weak grip, and tried not to crush the man's hand. "Wyeth Mender."

"Pavel Haney. Thank you for having me," Pavel said, his English as usual a bit stilted, but passable. He chose to stick with the alias name just in case; he wasn't sure how much these people knew. "You have a very nice home."

Mender released the grip and stepped back, holding his hands wide and motioning to the place. "This old place? Aw, it ain't much, but you've got to live somewhere, right?"

Images of the hovels Pavel had lived in growing up, with their lack of heat, running water, and beds, passed through his mind. Already he could feel his dislike for the man growing, held in check only by the half-dozen guards that now loped nearby, all within easy firing distance.

"That is very true," Pavel replied.

"Please," Mender said, extending a hand down toward the sofa opposite him, "have a seat."

Pavel nodded in appreciation and lowered himself down, the soft white padding cocooning around his legs and back, undoubtedly by design, meant to make movements difficult for him.

"Can I get you anything?" Mender asked, playing the perfect host. "Coffee? Water? Vodka?" He added a wink and a smile at the last one, pointing a finger in Pavel's direction.

"No, thank you," Pavel said, forcing his mouth to curl upward without showing any teeth.

After the previous few days he was not in the mood for pleasantries, even less so for blatantly false ones. Hoping to move things along, he swung the plastic sack up onto the glass table, letting the weight of it hit with an audible thud. Dried, congealing blood could be seen smeared along the inside of it, and a few tufts of short brown hair protruded from the top.

All mirth, and color, bled from Mender's face as he looked at the bag and up at Pavel again. He worked his mouth twice through an exaggerated motion in an attempt to conjure moisture, fear plain across his features.

"Just like that?" Mender asked.

Pavel nodded, keeping his face impassive, wanting to appear as unimposing as possible. "I am led to believe you are a very busy man, so I came here to talk business and to get out of your hair."

Again Mender looked from the bag to Pavel and back again. "OK?"

"My employer was told that you still have some trepidation about joining the network," Pavel said. The story was rehearsed, and he was quoting directly from what Sergey had told him hours before. "That there was still some concern about backlash from the Juarez cartel.

"We are here to show you there is nothing to fear from the Juarezes, nor will there be anything to fear from any competitor moving forward."

The words felt odd in his mouth, a type of syntax he never would have chosen for himself. Still, he rattled them off as practiced before reaching out and pulling back the sides of the sack. The thin material slid down without opposition, bunching up at the base of the table, its contents obvious to all.

Around them, the guards inched forward, weapons held at the ready. Each one seemed to glance at the object before looking to Mender, waiting for some sign of how to react.

A long moment passed as Mender stared down at the head of Carlos Juarez, his mouth curled down in an open frown, his face twisted away. He seemed to look at the grisly offering through only one eye, his head twisted to the side, his mind fighting for the proper response, his body wanting to flee.

"What . . . what the hell is that?" he muttered, his voice cracking, his face contorted.

"That," Pavel replied, "is Carlos Juarez. Mateo Perez has also been taken care of, though his body is not so easy to provide proof of."

"Mateo?" Mender mouthed, terror crossing over his features. "So, you mean he's also—"

"—dead, yes." Pavel felt the guards inch ever closer, but he forced himself to remain still. He knew before entering that this would be the most difficult part, the moment when they would either shoot him where he sat, or be so repulsed by what they saw, so fearful of what might happen to them, that they would allow him to leave and be under Blok's control forever.

"But I thought . . . witness protection?" Mender managed, prying his gaze from Carlos and looking up at Pavel.

"Mr. Mender," Pavel explained, speaking as if a teacher talking to a child, "we have known the location of both men since the day they entered witness protection, just as we know that Manny Juarez is inmate number 546708 at the Metropolitan Correctional Center not twenty miles from here."

"How . . ." Mender began, his thoughts apparent on his features, trying hard to catch up. Ten minutes before, he'd thought he had the upper hand, armed with his men and the home field advantage. With one simple move Pavel had turned the dynamic on him, letting it be known where the power in the meeting resided.

"The minute we took control," Pavel said, "we began keeping tabs on them. For a long time there was no need to act against them, so we let them live in peace. Recently, both men left the program, and you started to show reservations about our arrangement.

"Needless to say we couldn't have that, so steps were taken."

Pavel made sure his demeanor stayed neutral, his tone noncombative. His goal in the meeting was to issue a threat without appearing threatening, to make Mender believe this was done in the best interest of business, to put him at ease over any lingering uncertainties about the new arrangement.

In truth, it was a none-too-subtle kick in the ass for Mender to fall in line, and fast.

"And this arrangement," Mender asked, looking down into the face of Carlos Juarez, his eyes locked open wide, a thin tendril of blood snaking down from a nostril. "Mr. Blok is looking to get started on this right away?"

"Yes," Pavel said, offering a curt nod, making sure not to let the humor within him show through.

It wasn't the first time he had met with a Wyeth Mender. No less than half of the men they dealt with were just like him, just like Viktor

Blok, sons of privilege that insulated themselves with faux security but crumbled at the first sign of actual peril.

Even sitting on a sofa on Mender's patio, surrounded by a half-dozen men with weapons, Pavel knew he was not in danger.

The fear that his presence incited, the terror at what would happen if he didn't walk out of there in one piece, was too much for a man like Mender to fathom.

"Good," Mender said, nodding, again trying to work his mouth up and down. "I apologize that you had to come out here like this. Just can't be too careful with undertakings this big, you know?"

"I do," Pavel said, nodding, agreeing with the young man in an attempt to allow even the slightest shred of dignity to remain. "And that's why we're here. Anything else comes up, don't hesitate to let us know."

"I will do that," Mender said, snapping to his feet, the rubber soles of his white deck shoes slapping against the patio. He extended a hand and said, "Like you said, we're both busy men. I won't keep you any longer."

Pavel made a show of standing slowly. He accepted the handshake, squeezing a little tighter, allowing his host to feel the power within it. "Like I said, anything else comes up, don't hesitate to let us know."

At that he turned and walked back through the house, leaving the head of Carlos Juarez perched on the patio table in his wake.

Chapter Thirty-One

"Back to finish the job?" Manny Juarez asked, shuffling one foot at a time, neither ever leaving the floor. They scraped across the tile, the sound echoing through the small room.

Without the light of day pressing in through the closed blinds on the wall, the overhead bulbs seemed much brighter, harsher. They reflected over everything, casting an orangish tint on the room. The smell of cleaning solution was in the air, something citrus, most likely used to clean up the bloody spittle left behind after our last visit.

Diaz waited until Manny was seated in the same chair across from us before raising her chin toward the guard behind him, a wiry guy with blotchy tattoos on both forearms. "You can take the chains off him."

The guard stared at her a long moment before glancing over at me, a barely perceptible nod my only response. He gave each of us another look before shrugging his shoulders and extracting a key ring from his belt, starting at Manny's feet and moving up to his wrists. The chains jangled loudly as he unlatched them and pulled them free, looping them around his left hand as he exited the room.

"You guys have any problems, we'll be right outside."

"Thanks, but we'll be all right," Diaz said, settling into a chair.

"Yeah, we'll be all right," Manny said, glaring across at Diaz. His face was twisted up into a scowl, his breath coming in short bursts as he fumed. Once the door was closed and the guard gone, he shifted his gaze to me.

"That how this trip works? You guys come back, you the nice one, put him in the corner to threaten me?"

I met the stare, peering into his eyes, the same face I'd seen twenty, a hundred times a day while I was on the job. The rest of him might have aged, adding a few pounds, a couple of gray hairs, but those eyes were exactly as I remembered.

"Considering what you did to my family, what I would like to do to you, I'd say you got off easy," I said. "So quit your bitching."

At that Manny snapped up onto his feet, his hands clenched into fists in front of him. "Man, if you were going to get in here and start running your mouth, you shouldn't have let her take the chains off."

"It was his idea," Diaz said, rolling her eyes up toward Manny.

The words drew his attention back down at her, the scowl still in place. "Yeah? Why's that? So you two could attack me and it go down as a fair fight?"

For the first time since he'd entered, I pushed myself away from the wall. I made sure he watched as I walked into the corner of the room and pulled a plastic chair off the stack, sliding it across the floor and taking a seat beside Diaz.

"Sit down and shut up," I said, extending a hand across the table, motioning for him to take a seat.

Manny remained standing, peering down at us, and crossed his arms over his chest. "Man, why the hell should I?"

"Because Carlos is dead, you dumb son of a bitch," I spat, venom rising in my voice. "Sorry for your loss, asshole. Now sit down."

The scowl faded from Manny's face, his arms sliding down to hang by his sides. Again his hands curled into fists, veins filling with blood along the backs of them, running up his forearms.

"First you come in here and punch me, then you make up some shit about my cousin?" he managed, so much hatred in his tone he could barely speak. "I ought to—"

"What?" I yelled, snapping upward onto my feet, sending the chair skittering across the floor behind me. I dug my phone from my pocket and held it at arm's length in front of me. The images I'd taken just hours before were already pulled up for him to see. "What are you going to do, Manny, besides sit your ass down here, the safest place on earth for you right now?"

His jaw fell open as he looked from me to the phone, shock, horror, disbelief on his face. "That's not Carlos, that can't be. He was just here."

"Yeah, wearing those clothes, right?" I countered. "And you see that ring on his right hand? That's his too, isn't it? Recognize the building that's in? Any of it look familiar?"

As I spoke I scrolled through a series of photos, each one of them taken in anticipation of this very moment while Diaz called in for backup. Every shot was meant to rebut whatever objections Manny might have, to provide definitive proof that his cousin was gone.

One at a time he watched the images scroll by, his mouth working as if he might speak, but no sounds coming out. His body began to quiver as his eyes glassed over, his lips pressing tight together.

"That dumb bastard," he whispered. "I told him . . . I sat right in that room and I told him."

"And now you're going to tell us," I said, dropping the phone on the table, leaving the last picture up and visible. I walked back and grabbed my chair, pulling it forward, and took a seat beside Diaz, who was still staring at Manny.

It took him almost a full minute, but eventually he lowered himself back into his chair as well. When he did, he seemed different, his body slouched, his spirit broken. His face twitched as if he might break down at any moment, his lower lip quivering.

There was no joy for me in delivering the news to him that way. After what he'd done to my family I didn't give a shit about saving his feelings, but we just didn't have the time to waste on him stomping around about one little punch.

If the prick had any idea what I would have liked to do to him, one shot to the jaw would be the least of his concerns.

"Start at the beginning," Diaz said, reinserting herself into the conversation, taking the lead. Compared to me, her voice was soft, soothing, leading him right where we wanted him to go.

Manny kept his attention focused on the picture of Carlos a long moment, the shot taken from the doorway, the entirety of his headless body splayed out on the floor, nearly all of his blood spread on the concrete around him. When he finally began to speak his voice was distant, detached, void of emotion.

It was a feeling I knew all too well.

"Shit all started six years ago when you guys started coming around," Manny said. "Until that time things were good. I was the head man, Carlos my right hand, Mateo ran the books. We had a sweet spread, bringing the product up from the south of Mexico, running it across the border on boats. Once it was in San Diego, a network of local distributors shifted the stuff up and down the coast, LA and beyond."

This much I knew already. It was their entry into the LA market that first got our attention, brought our team onto the case. By the time I had bowed out they were in Bakersfield, and apparently by the time they were apprehended they were clear to Fresno.

Saying they had a sweet spread was an understatement. Still, I let him continue without interrupting.

"It wasn't the first time we'd had heat down on us," Manny said, shifting his gaze away from the picture, staring at the blank steel table in front of him. "Federales, Coast Guard, even the LAPD. Every time, we managed to grease a few palms, or change how we handled things for a while, the problem went away. Then, two things happened at the same time.

"A third party wanted to partner up, and your sorry ass started dogging us."

On the last part he flicked his gaze up to me, his eyes void of any life, nothing more than dark pools.

Ignoring the stare, I focused in on the front half of his statement, feeding it into the frenzy of information already swirling through my mind. For the first time a major piece seemed to fit into place, a dawning within me.

"The Russians," I muttered.

If Manny was surprised I knew, he didn't show it. He simply nodded and continued, "They came to us and said they were developing a new product. Claimed to have heard we were feeling the squeeze from you guys, said they'd help us lie low for a while, keep our goods moving.

"Once their stuff was ready to go, we could push it through the same network, everybody share a piece of the pie."

So many questions came to mind, I had to force myself to sit still and not jump ahead. Snippets of a former life started making their way to the surface, bits and pieces I had long ago buried. Faces, names, details from the case, all part of something I had sealed off long ago.

"So you made the deal?" Diaz asked.

"Hell yeah, we made the deal," Manny said, his voice rising just a bit. "Your boy here was close, and moving in fast. We knew we had to go underground for a while, clear our tail, but if we did, our distributors would find product from somewhere else.

"The Ruskies solved that for us. Within weeks they had boots on the ground, were pushing our stuff up the coast. It was beautiful. For a while."

"Then you got busted," Diaz said, prompting him forward, keeping the story on track. Seeing the picture of Carlos had set free an uninhibited Manny, information flowing from him.

Maybe he figured he no longer had to protect anybody. Maybe he no longer thought he had anything to lose. Whatever it was, we weren't about to derail it.

"Ha!" Manny intoned, his head rocking back in a smirk. "Busted my ass. After your bulldog here took his ball and went home, there wasn't anybody looking for us anymore. We could have gone back to doing things exactly the way we wanted.

"You guys weren't the problem."

Just like that, another chunk of information fell into place. At the same time, a massive piece of the dam holding my own emotion back split away, a roiling ball of vitriol threatening to spill out at any moment.

"The Russians started taking over," I muttered. "The DEA didn't catch you—you turned yourself in for protection."

Manny cast his gaze up at me a moment before leaning back in his chair. He looped an arm over the back of it and ran his opposite hand down the length of his face, his focus never far from the phone still sitting on the table.

"I agreed to do the time, give up a dozen of our major providers, even assist things moving forward, so long as you guys took care of Mateo and Carlos. So much for that shit."

I could feel Diaz's stare on me as she glanced my way, shaking her head. My own attention was aimed on the opposite wall, no longer looking at Manny, letting his words sink in.

"Why did Mateo come to Yellowstone?"

Manny shifted his eyes up to me, drawing my own gaze over to him. We sat in silence, each sizing the other up for a long moment, before he sighed.

"We knew you were on our ass. We also knew that you would never let it go, you were *always* going to be on our ass. Mateo always said if they somehow found him, he would go find you. Even if they got him in the end, he knew it would set you out after them."

It was exactly the answer I'd been expecting. It fit with everything else he was telling us, from the introduction of the Russians to the hostile takeover.

There was no way the Russians could just let Mateo and Carlos walk, not knowing everything they did. They would never stop looking for them, not until they were found and silenced.

My involvement, right from the start, was no coincidence. I had been placed intentionally on the sideline by warring factions, taken out of the game only to be pulled right back in when they needed me. I was simultaneously a thorn in their side and a saving grace, something they hated but needed.

There were still so many questions, so many holes that needed to be filled in, but there would be time for that later. There was something bigger at play here, some reason Mateo and Carlos had both been killed within a couple of weeks of each other.

"Who are the Russians?" I asked.

The eyebrows on Manny's face tracked up a fraction of an inch as he sat there, once again moving his gaze away from me, back to staring at nothing.

"Some cat named Blok. Viktor. A real pretty boy, second- or third-generation guy, born with a silver spoon and a lot of attitude. He runs things on this side of the ocean, a real asshole, nothing but a front for the real muscle back home."

"Where?" Diaz asked, her body rigid beside me.

Manny spread his hands wide and said, "Last I heard he had moved the operation down into Baja somewhere, but I've been here. I can't do your entire job for you."

Despite the barb, he wasn't entirely wrong. We had been operating with so much less than the whole story, a fault starting with Hutch and extending all the way to Carlos, that we had been doing little more than fumbling around in the dark. Now we had a clear heading, a way to put everything together, have it all make sense.

I leaned back in my chair and folded my arms across my chest, letting the new information meld with what I already knew. There had to be a reason Mateo came to find me when he did, a reason Lita showed up right after and tried to gun me down as well. It had to be more than just dredging up an old rivalry or trying to tie off a loose end.

That simple fact lodged itself in the front of my mind for a full moment, sitting there, marinating, before a single statement Manny had made a moment before fit into place.

"The product the Russians wanted to bring over, it's finally ready."

Sensing it was a statement more than a question, Manny looked up at me, his head rocking up and down in agreement. "Only thing I can figure. Some new stuff they call Krokodil."

Diaz snapped her attention over to me, alarm in her eyes. "You're shitting me."

"What?" I asked, making no attempt to mask my confusion.

"You've never heard of that stuff?" she asked. "The papers call it a zombie drug because it has hallucinogenic effects. Makes people do all kinds of crazy things like walk off bridges or try to eat human flesh."

I had vaguely heard of it when it first came onto the market, but never had I researched it too closely or taken a case involving it. When bath salts originally surfaced in America, I had heard that this was being developed as an even more potent version overseas.

"And Mateo knew all this, didn't he?" I asked. "He knew what they were making, what it was capable of. Knew they would be coming after you guys, wanting you taken out before they started moving it."

"So he went to find you," Manny finished.

So he came to find me. Somehow they too knew where I'd been, what I'd been doing all this time. They'd watched as I created a life for myself, left all this behind, only to pull me back in when the time came to do their dirty work.

Deep within me, another bit of my resolve broke away. No matter how angry I was, how much the craving for blood was growing within me, this was not my fight. I had made promises, walked away years ago, for a reason.

Mateo Perez showing up one day was not about to trump that.

My right hand slid out and pulled the phone back to me. I took the picture down off the front screen and put it in my pocket, rising to leave. This entire ordeal had awakened a darkness in me I had worked long and hard to tuck away. No matter how hard it would be, I was going home to bury it back where it belonged.

Nodding once at Diaz, I slid my chair toward the stack in the corner and walked to the door, making it almost there before Manny called out.

"Hey, Hawk," he said, his inflection even, void of any taunting or sneer. "The cat that did that to Carlos is a guy named Pavel, big son of a bitch that works for Blok."

I stopped by the door, processing the information. It was the same first name Hutch had given us after returning from Yellowstone, the man that had gone up in search of Lita. Like most everything else he had told us, the information fit.

The Bloks were cleaning house, getting ready to set their vicious new toy on the West Coast.

"You know how I know that?" Manny asked.

Something about the words he used, the way he asked the question, resonated deep inside me. I knew what he was trying to say, where he was going with it, even before he said it.

He stood, retreating toward the door and knocking on it. The sound of his knuckles connecting with hollow metal echoed through the room, a moment later answered by the same wiry guard.

"I can tell by the look on your face that you think you're out," he said, staring right at me. "But let me tell you why you're not. Let me tell you why Mateo was right, why you're not going to drive out of here and not come back, why you're going to go to Baja and get these moth-erfuckers, and then go to Russia afterward if you have to.

"You see what he did to my cousin there? That was what convinced us to partner with the Russians in the first place. Not only did they offer us a way to keep moving product once the DEA started sniffing around, they got you off our asses for good five years ago.

"They sent that sick son of a bitch out into the desert, and he did the same thing to your wife and daughter before he torched your house to the ground."

Chapter Thirty-Two

The voice on the other end of the line was worried, frightened even. The fear permeated every word it said, driving home the message that it carried.

Whatever Pavel had said to Wyeth Mender, it worked. The man was on board, come what may, forevermore.

Viktor Blok sat with his feet resting on the corner of his desk, his bare limbs crossed at the ankles. His right elbow was propped up on the arm of the chair, keeping the phone in his hand pressed against his ear.

His left hand was looped loosely around the rim of a crystal tumbler, the glass filled almost to the brim with Sibirskaya vodka. The remainder of the bottle sat nearby in a silver bucket filled with ice; only the top few inches of the label were visible from where he sat.

"Yes, glad to hear it," Viktor said, his tone distant and bored. He waited as the man again launched into another apology for causing any delay, another cased promise about it never happening again, and he lifted the glass and took a heavy swallow.

The icy cold liquid slid smoothly along his throat, no trace of the customary burn associated with the low-end forms most people in

North America drank. Clear as water, it went down easily, and Viktor paused only a moment before taking another slug.

"Yes, excellent, we'll be in touch soon," Viktor said once over half of the tumbler was drained, cutting the conversation short. There was obviously much more Mender wanted to add, effusive praise he wanted to heap on the operation, but Viktor wasn't in the mood for it.

Without waiting for a farewell, he dropped the phone back onto its cradle and took up his drink once more. He pulled it over onto his lap and held it between his hands, staring down at it, his mind racing.

Tonight was supposed to have been a crowning moment, the time when he called his uncle and declared everything was ready, the operation could begin. The act would remove any lingering distrust the old man had, allowing him to once again take charge in North America.

He, Viktor Blok, would control an empire running up the entire coast of California. Within months his new product would be in the hands of Hollywood stars and professional athletes, the entire country clamoring for Krokodil. Demand would explode, his network would spread. By the age of thirty-five, he would be a king.

Instead, his night had once again been thwarted by the meddling of his uncle and his goon. He had been pushed to the side, shown to be impotent to a major distributor, the last remaining holdout. At a time when he should be celebrating a grand triumph, he had instead been reduced to nothing more than a secretary, answering the phone and mumbling through the acceptance of more praise of the family name, a name he had done nothing to build.

In one movement he raised the glass to his mouth and tossed back the remainder of the vodka, swallowing it down without regard for cost or taste. The goal of the evening was not to celebrate. There would be no savoring of anything.

Dropping the glass back on his desk, Viktor lowered his feet to the floor and shifted his body toward the bucket, lifting the bottle from it. Frigid water and half-melted ice burned his fingertips as he lifted it out, pulling the top and filling the tumbler once again.

Halfway back into the bucket, a knock sounded at the door, three deep thuds followed by it opening wide, and a massive figure filled the frame.

Viktor stood with the bottle raised above the bucket, an eyebrow arched, and watched as Pavel stepped inside. The behemoth wore his customary dour expression, his face made even more harrowing by the dark circles underlining each of his eyes. He walked straight in and splashed himself down into the seat across from Viktor, not saying a word.

"Please, come in, take a seat," Viktor said, dropping the bottle back into place, letting the sarcasm drip from his words. "Get you a drink? I hear you've had a busy night."

Pavel stared across at him with the same emotionless eyes, pools that looked almost black, shrouded in mounds of dark hair. He sat in silence for a long moment, motionless.

"Well," Viktor said, raising the glass toward his unexpected guest, "I'm going to have one. Hope you don't mind. Here's to you!"

Once more he raised the glass to his lips, draining over half its contents. Already he could feel the high-grain liquor starting to work on his senses, dulling his vision around the edges, making his tongue feel heavy in his mouth. He swayed just a bit as he fell back into his seat, pausing to collect himself before propping his feet back up into place.

"So, to what do I owe the pleasure of your little visit?" Viktor asked. "Stop in to gloat about your newest accomplishment? To catch me up on what you have been doing without my knowledge?"

Still Pavel sat in silence, staring back at Viktor.

Viktor matched the gaze for a long moment, feeling the hatred he had for the man, for everything he stood for, rise within him. Looking across the desk he saw his uncle, he saw Anatoly, he saw cold winter mornings and firewood riots and endless bowls of borsch, all of the things he loathed about his former life and would never again return to.

"You know what I don't understand?" Viktor said, resting his elbows on the arms of the chair and pressing the pads of his fingertips together in front of his face. "You're not even family. Sure you're big and scary and take orders like a damn dog, but at the end of the day, you're nothing. You'll never be a Blok. You'll never be anything more than the son of a whore, some street urchin my uncle found all those years ago and felt sorry for."

Perhaps it was the alcohol allowing Viktor to finally say what he had always felt about Pavel. Maybe it was the realization that after tonight, the family would never allow him to ascend to the level he should. Most likely, it was a combination of the two, the sudden fear of losing a life he had become rather fond of playing no small part in it as well.

Viktor twisted his head to the side and glared across at Pavel. He waited, looking for any sign of rage, any display that his words had found their mark. As much as he should have been afraid, he found himself unable to muster any terror, no matter what the giant might be capable of.

Rather, he felt anger rise within him. A tiny bit that started deep in his stomach, further down even than the warmth of the vodka swimming through his system. It grew in size and animosity, rippling through him, pushing past the alcohol and forcing its way to the front of his mind.

What he said was true. *He* was a Blok. *He* was the handpicked successor to the family dynasty in America. This was his time, the long overdue coronation of his place in the pecking order.

This man was nothing, useful as a soldier but nothing more.

"Say something, dammit!"

In one sharp movement, Viktor snatched up the tumbler from the desk beside him and hurled it at the opposite wall. The delicate crystal shattered on contact, shards exploding in every direction, their pieces tinkling softly as they fell to the floor. A stream of vodka traced itself across the floor between Viktor and the wall, light shining off the misshapen pools.

An oversized amoeba of liquid showed itself on the wall, splattered out from the bits of shiny glass embedded in the woodwork.

Pavel turned his head and stared at the mess on the wall before shifting his focus back to Viktor. He pressed his thick hands down into his thighs and stood, letting a low groan escape through his nose as he reached full height and stood looking down at Viktor, contempt obvious on his features.

"They're coming."

Chapter Thirty-Three

Naval Base San Diego was the largest military installation on the entire western seaboard. Over twenty-six thousand people, more than three-quarters of them active-duty personnel, called the place home. In total it encompassed more than thirteen hundred acres, land and aquatic combined.

After leaving the Metropolitan Correction Center, we didn't bother returning to the desert. What we needed to do was apparent. Whoever had found Carlos within hours of him leaving clearly had a pulse on everything going on at DEA headquarters. If we were to have any hope of getting into Baja and finding the Russians that had taken over the Juarez cartel, a move was going to have to be made fast.

Waiting even a day at this point would give them too much lead time. They would be able to liquidate whatever they were doing and disappear into the Mexican countryside. If not with their entire stash of product, at the very least with every person who mattered.

Our only choice, a fact we both acknowledged without saying it out loud, was to go tonight. Whatever we might lose in planning would be more than accounted for by the element of surprise. With the backing of the United States Navy, we both felt reasonably secure in the chances of success moving forward.

The first call Diaz made while exiting the interrogation room was to the commanding officer at NBSD. More than once the base had provided open support for the DEA on stings up and down the coast. I could tell just from hearing one side of the conversation that there was surprise at the unusual proposition, even some trepidation about the truncated timetable it would be performed under, but no outright opposition.

This would be a good thing, for the country and for their respective careers, and they both knew it.

The second call was to her head analyst, a guy she referred to several times as Potts, someone I was certain I had never met before. I matched her step for step as we exited the building and climbed into the car, only half-listening as she relayed to him that she needed a location and she needed it fast. Between everything the Juarezes had handed over during the last few years and the new information we had, there should have been more than enough for them to find the new base of operations.

If this guy was anywhere near as good as Pally had once been, he'd have something for her by the time the first boat pushed offshore headed south.

While the flurry of activity of Diaz beside me slid in and out of my consciousness, my active thoughts focused on what Manny had said just a few minutes before. For five long years I had known that what happened to my family was a direct result of my work, but never once had I heard it stated that bluntly.

Born of equal parts denial and self-preservation, I pushed aside the notion that what I did for a living had ultimately taken my life away from me.

The sorrow of their passing was long since gone. There was not a single day that I didn't think of them or long for their company, but the sharp stabbing pain of a pickax to the stomach had subsided some time ago.

In its place was anger. Rage. Hatred. Full-scale hostility that roiled through my system, bubbling just beneath the surface. To stand ten feet away and look at me, I would have appeared perfectly calm, sitting in the front seat, staring at the city of San Diego as Diaz followed the signs toward the base.

To know me though, to look into my eyes, it was apparent that a tempest of adrenaline and acrimony was swirling beneath the surface.

For five long years I had bit back the bitterness, forced it to stay down to keep from consuming me from within. Now it had found me, slapped me in the face, and demanded to be dealt with.

Somehow, I had made it out of that room without sprinting across and smashing Manny Juarez into the wall. Something told me very few of the others involved would be so lucky.

Diaz finished her third call beside me and dropped the cell phone into the middle console. She gripped the wheel in both hands and extended her bottom lip out, exhaling a puff of air over her face, a strand of hair flying back off her forehead.

"Bet you didn't see this coming when you woke up this morning?" I muttered, my voice just audible over the sound of the engine whining.

"You make one hell of an entrance, I'll give you that," Diaz said. By the tone of her voice I couldn't tell if she was pissed I'd showed up and turned her world on its head, or just gearing up for what lay in store. I opted against responding, keeping my eyes narrowed as I stared out the window, as the city was just beginning to put itself to sleep for the night.

"What happened to your wife?"

The words surprised me, interrupting me midthought. My lips parted a half inch as I unconsciously turned toward her, silent.

Hands still in a death grip on the wheel, she glanced over at me, pausing a moment before moving her attention back to the road. "That was our agreement. Before this was over, you'd tell me what happened."

I kept my face aimed toward her, though my gaze slid back through the front windshield to the road ahead.

"That was our agreement," I echoed.

Five years had passed since that fateful night, though not once had I ever spoken of it. Not in its entirety, anyway. At moments I had alluded to it, maybe even acknowledged snippets of it, but never had I told the entire thing from start to finish. Not to Hutch after it happened, not to the appointed psychiatrists they made me talk to before accepting my resignation.

Even my subconscious, lurking just beneath the surface every night when I closed my eyes, couldn't bear the act of telling the entire story.

"I'd been away for six weeks," I said. "Myself and two guys from my squad, Diggs and Martin, both good guys, both out of the game now as well. We'd been tracking this known runner across most of Central America, starting in El Salvador, taking us through Honduras, Nicaragua, Costa Rica. Finally caught up with him in Panama."

I flicked my gaze over to her to make sure she was listening, her face intent on the road as she drove. Halfway through a turn her eyes met mine, urging me forward, before returning to the task at hand.

"Couldn't have asked for a better bust. Panama, as close to an ally as we have in the region, with their beautiful extradition laws. Eight hours after finding his ass holed up in a shack on the edge of a cocaine field, we had him and the entire operation under custody, and we were headed home.

"Up until that point, we'd had no idea how long the damn thing was going to take, so showing up back on American soil that night was a treat. We caught a one-way flight into NBSD, slapped each other on the back, and headed out."

I paused for just a moment, remembering the moment, the joy we had felt. In the parking lot we had toasted each other with a can of Natural Light, a more watered-down horse-piss beer having never existed. It was a big score for us, the kind of thing that would grant us a lot more agency leeway from then on.

"I don't know why, but I didn't call my wife. At the time I thought it would be nice to surprise her, but looking back . . ."

Again Diaz looked over, silently urging me to keep going. She avoided the freeway as she drove, sticking to city streets, pushing the straightaways as fast as she could, the engine revving and falling away each time.

"Anyway, that night I was feeling good. I was back in my truck, I was going to go home and see my wife, my daughter, eat real food, sleep in an actual bed. You've been on the job before—I don't have to explain it to you."

"Right," Diaz managed, her voice showing she was a bit surprised by being brought into the story.

"The first thing I remember was the smell. Even through my jacked-up, can-barely-notice-that-shit-Hutch-is-always-drinking nose, I picked up on the scent. Fire. Smoke. Charred wood. Roasted meat."

My voice cracked just a tiny bit on the last words, pure rage obstructing me from delivering them without alteration. I squeezed my left hand into a tight ball and held it above my thigh, keeping it there a long moment before dropping it back into place.

"Next was the sight of it. I hadn't seen it before because of the setting sun behind me, but once it blinked out beneath the horizon, I could see the orange glow to the south, undeniable against the darkening sky.

"Even though I spent a large amount of time on the road, I knew the area well enough to put it together in my mind. I don't know why, I had no reason to even think such a thing, but I just *knew*. I knew based on where the glow was coming from, I knew because of the feeling in my stomach, everything.

"I just knew."

Once more I pushed out a long breath. This part I had replayed in my mind hundreds, thousands of times before. It came to me every night, sprang into my thoughts at least once a day.

The easy part was over.

"I tried calling then, but it went straight to voice mail. Not even a single ringtone. It only confirmed my initial thought. My family was in trouble."

"So what did you do?" Diaz asked, a red light blazing in front of us, the car idling. I could feel her gaze turned to stare at me, though I couldn't bring myself to meet it.

"I prayed," I said, the words tasting sour on my tongue, an act that to this day I'm not terribly proud of. "God, Buddha, Allah, Odin, Pele, the Great Spirit . . . I hit them all. Made every promise I could think of, tried every bargain known to man. Begged them, please, somehow, not to let me be right.

"But I was."

My eyes slid closed as I remembered the details of that night. A tremor ran the length of my spine, goose bumps rising like chicken skin over my arms.

"The fire had been going a while by the time I got there. The second story had already collapsed, most of the first floor was gone. Everything was charred black, nothing more than cinders.

"I pulled up as close as I could, but had to stop a good fifty feet away. The heat was so sweltering it scorched the hair from my forearms, singed my eyebrows. Even in the late-evening sky I could see waves of it climbing high above, an invisible sheen rising into the night.

"We didn't live far from our neighbors, but somehow there was nobody on the scene. Someone must have had to have seen it burning bright, but not one single person called the fire department or the police."

"You're kidding me," Diaz whispered, her voice bearing the familiar lilt of sympathy, the same exact sound that I despised so much, that often served as the impetus for me avoiding the subject entirely.

"I was a DEA agent on the wrong side of the line in a border town," I replied. "It wasn't until that moment that I realized just how dangerous everything about my life really was."

I could see Diaz nodding, though she remained silent.

"By that point, it was obvious help wasn't coming. A hundred different thoughts ran through my head, but there was nothing I could do. Instead, I called Hutch and told him to send everybody, then I sat my ass on the ground, the heat-scorched grass brittle beneath me, and I cried until they arrived."

Just like that night I could feel hot tears threatening to streak down my face. I could sense my eyes growing glassy, the anger within me so strong that, even years later, it was fighting to release itself in any way possible.

"Two days later I tendered my resignation. At first Hutch didn't believe me, said it was just a reaction to what had happened. He put me on administrative leave for a few months to see if I would come around, but all that did was subsidize a very dark time I'd rather not get into."

Diaz hooked one final turn and pulled off the road and onto the shoulder. In front of us a blue and silver sign welcomed us to the UNITED STATES NAVAL BASE—SAN DIEGO, a row of spotlights gleaming off it, a cadre of flags hanging limply behind it. She shoved the gear shift into neutral and folded her hands in her lap, keeping her attention facing forward.

"How did you know your family . . . ?"

My eyes squeezed tight, the body's natural reaction to such a horrific trauma, even tucked away that long ago. It was the single part that I always tried to avoid, consciously or not, whenever the topic managed to surface in my thoughts.

"They staked them out, right in front of the house."

There was so much more I wanted to add. Details such as trying to rush forward and take them down, but the heat driving me back, blistering my forehead and cheeks. The way their bodies had burnt far beyond recognition, their arms and legs blackened away to nothing, just brittle sticks extended out in every direction. That by the time I got them to the crematorium there wasn't enough left to fill an entire urn, both bodies together.

But I didn't. I didn't tell her that, or the way I spent two full months staring at a loaded service piece, wondering what a 9 mm slug tasted like. I didn't mention that once they accepted my resignation and took back the gun, I got another one, with a large caliber, and stared at it for another four months.

I didn't mention the tattoo that now covered the entire left side of my chest in their memory, embedded in ink above my heart forever. I sure as hell didn't mention the fact that to this day every other relative I have blames me for what happened, has let it be known that my presence is not wanted or needed at home.

Even without all that, somehow, she seemed to understand. She waited a long moment to make sure my story was complete, that there was nothing left for me to add, before nodding. "After you left, it became something of a cautionary tale throughout the department. A warning to all incoming agents to minimize loved ones, to keep them far away at all times."

Never had I heard that, though it made sense. I doubt that I would have believed such a story if they'd told it to me when I signed up, being young and gung-ho, but I'd like to think it would have at least helped to hear it.

Diaz exhaled through her nose and turned to face forward, resting the back of her head against the seat behind her. "You know, when you hear a story so many times, it starts to take on a mystique. After a while, you come to believe there's no way it can be real, just the kind of thing old men romanticize while sitting around talking about the way things used to be."

I nodded. While not the most delicate response in the world, I couldn't say I faulted her. There was no way of knowing how contorted that story had gotten over the years, the purposes it had been used to serve.

"How far was what I told you from what you've heard before?" I asked, almost not wanting to know, fearing that I might have been martyred to serve the purposes of the agency.

"No difference at all," Diaz said, her voice barely a whisper. "Which is the most harrowing part. You hear something like that, you want to believe it to be bullshit, that there aren't people on this planet capable of doing such things."

My focus grew fuzzy as I stared at the sign welcoming us into the naval base. "Hopefully after tonight there'll be a few less of those people out there."

For a full moment neither of us said anything. Diaz reached up and dropped the gear shift back into "Drive," easing the car forward toward the guardhouse ahead. The brakes moaned slightly as she kept them depressed halfway down, the car moving just an inch at a time.

"Yeah," she agreed, pulling her head forward off the seat back. "We'll get the bastards."

"Not we," I said, watching the sign slide by beside us. "You."

The car came to an abrupt stop as she snapped her head over to look at me, her eyes wide. "What the hell do you mean 'not we'? Where are you going?"

With every bit of composure I could muster I turned to match her gaze, hoping she didn't see everything clashing together behind my eyes.

"I'm going to Russia."

Chapter Thirty-Four

Steam rose up from the plate of pirozhki situated in the middle of Sergey Blok's desk, little white threads streaming upward before dissipating into nothing. With it came the familiar scent of baked bread and melted butter, one that had filled the office no less than twice a week for thirty years.

The recipe was a hand-me-down from his mother-in-law, a gift that was presented more as a directive. It was the first dish his wife, Anya, had learned to make upon their marriage, a meal she had reconstituted with total faithfulness, with not even the slightest bit of experimentation, for decades.

Sergey had returned to his office from a trip down the hall to the restroom to find his lunch waiting for him, the meal and the dish it was served on both warm. He had no idea how or when Anya had managed to slip it by him, but he allowed the left corner of his mouth to curl up in a smile just the same.

Three bites into the meal his food-induced euphoria was shattered by his cell phone buzzing beside him, the growling visage of Pavel staring up from the screen. Sergey allowed it to ring a moment as he pulled the cloth napkin from his lap and wiped his face. He tossed it down atop the nearly untouched pirozhki and pushed it away, certain he would no longer be hungry once the call was finished.

Contact from Pavel had not been expected. Several hours before, he had given explicit instructions on how things were to unfold. The fact that his most trusted employee was now calling could only mean something had gone awry.

The twisted feeling he felt deep in his stomach wasn't because something had occurred, but that he had a good idea of what it was.

"Hello?" Sergey asked, trying to mask any animosity from his voice. There was a chance that the call was nothing more than courtesy, a perfunctory explanation of where things stood.

"Mr. Blok? Pavel," Pavel began, the same exact way he did every phone conversation they ever had. "We have a problem."

Sergey twisted his mouth up into a sneer and nodded his head, confirming what he had already suspected. "How bad is it?"

"Not Chernobyl, but bad enough," Pavel said, drawing another wince from his employer.

"I'm listening."

A long moment passed, the sound of an ocean breeze, the distant burst of a ship's horn sounding out. Sergey could sense Pavel pausing to find the right words, uncertain of how to approach it. Such a delay could only mean one thing, the same way it did every time Pavel acted unsure of anything.

"What the hell did that nephew of mine do now?" Sergey growled.

Never had Pavel directly stated there was a conflict, though it wasn't hard for Sergey to piece together. In the past twelve months he had sensed a growing impunity in Viktor, a self-righteousness based in his status as a Blok. His life on the upper echelon of a poverty-stricken country had embodied him with a rather full opinion of himself. Sergey more than once had gotten the impression that the young man thought he actually had something to do with the lofty status the family had attained.

On several occasions he had seen Viktor exert that sort of high-handed mentality on others, often those in his direct employ. There was little doubt he had done the same to Pavel in their time working together in Mexico, despite the fact that Pavel was a greater asset to the family than the young Blok would ever be.

Such tensions had made for an uneasy working environment. Viktor knew Pavel was a trusted ally of Sergey's and was careful never to openly speak ill of him, despite making no effort to hide his true feelings. Pavel respected Sergey and the Blok family too much to ever speak out of turn.

Still, there was little doubt that Viktor and Pavel both would eliminate the other without thinking twice if it came down to it.

"It's not what he did, it's what he won't do," Pavel said. "He is drunk, and he refuses to leave."

Sergey's eyes grew wide, revulsion on his face. His nostrils curled upward as he stared out the window in front of him, gaze hardened on the bare branches of a tree outside. "He *what*?"

"He's holed himself up in his office and says he isn't going anywhere."

"And you told him that agents are en route as we speak?" Sergey asked, his voice low and graveled, his free hand balled into a fist atop his desk.

"He said to let them come, we will fight," Pavel replied. His voice was even, neutral. It was not his first encounter with Viktor's antics; his response was to hand it over to Sergey and do as instructed.

Sergey dropped the phone onto the desk and looked away a moment, pushing an angry breath out through his nose. He passed a hand over his face and rested it along his jaw, five o'clock stubble already noticeable against his skin.

Viktor *would* think to do something like standing and fighting. In his head, he would have built it up to be a Hollywood blockbuster, with helicopters in the air and boats in the water. Spotlights would be showcasing him on the veranda, a gun in each hand, screaming as he took out a torrent of faceless intruders, all dressed in black, firing but hitting nothing.

The truth would be that he and everybody with him would either be shot or arrested. Anybody that so much as raised a weapon in opposition would be cut down. The others would be put in a holding chamber, every bit of knowledge they had extracted from them painfully and meticulously.

"The product is finally ready," Sergey said. He knew the line was safe, but his brevity lay in the fact that he trusted Pavel would pick up on the insinuation.

Everything they had worked to establish the previous years, from finding a suitable network to quietly taking it over, was done with the end goal of finding a distribution system for their own goods. A fiery showdown now with one of the preeminent drug-enforcement groups in the world would shatter that all in the course of an hour.

"So get him on the boat?" Pavel asked.

"Yes," Sergey said, fighting to keep his anger at Viktor's stupidity from exploding at Pavel. "By whatever means necessary. Get up the coast to Tijuana. I'll have plane tickets at the airport to get you both back here."

"Back there? To Russia?" Pavel asked.

"Yes," Sergey said. "I think it's time we all had a little get-together and got some things straightened out. Is that a problem?"

For the first time in ages, Sergey heard something in Pavel's voice that seemed to border on hope, happiness even. "Not at all, sir. Looking forward to it."

Sergey nodded, it being exactly the response he had expected.

"And the rest of the men?" Pavel asked.

"Continue on as planned," Sergey said. "We can't completely abandon things on the ground there, not with us being ready to go live so soon. Disappearing right now would set us back months, if not more."

He didn't bother to add that their meeting would not take more than a day or two. Both of them would be traveling back under the pretense of making final business preparations while only Pavel would be returning. Sergey had made the proper arrangements to allow him to take over the North American operations, finally ascending to the post he had earned a hundred times over.

His nephew, no matter how much Sergey would like to rid himself of the nuisance for good, would be stashed on a much smaller project, somewhere closer to home, where Sergey could keep a thumb on him at all times.

"Thank you, Mr. Blok," Pavel said. "We will see you soon."

Sergey signed off the call without responding, tossing his phone on the desk and shaking his head at the arrogant foolishness of his nephew. As he did so his gaze lingered on his lunch still sitting on the desk, nearly untouched, the scent permeating the air.

He had been wrong. There was absolutely no reason to let one of Anya's pirozhkis go to waste over a nephew throwing a temper tantrum. He pulled the plate back over and dropped his napkin into his lap, picking up right where he'd left off a few minutes before.

PART IV

Chapter Thirty-Five

I respected Diaz both as an agent and a person. She had gone out of her way for me when she didn't have to, long before it reached a point where her career was about to receive a serious bump for doing so. Because of that, I felt some responsibility to do the right thing by her, but that would have to come in time.

Right now, I was worried about the situation I had been pulled into, a situation that I was best equipped to handle by going off the grid for a while.

It had taken a few minutes of back-and-forth for me to persuade Diaz to leave me outside the gate. Her initial reaction was the expected shock, followed by disbelief that I would think of stepping away at such a moment. I didn't insult her intelligence by trying to pretend I was simply bowing out now that the end seemed so near, but rather told her there were things that I needed to handle on my own.

It wasn't the entire truth, not even close, but she seemed to grasp enough to agree, if begrudgingly.

As a young ensign sailor standing by the front gate gave me a curious stare, I left my weapon in the car, got out, and walked away. With me I took a single shoulder bag containing some necessary paperwork, my wallet, and a toothbrush. I left my overnight bag stowed away in the trunk, not wanting to take the time or hassle of dealing with it. Whatever else I might need, I would pick up along the way.

The single lane leading into the base was just over a mile long. Walking alone in the middle of the night, I was able to move easily along the edge of the road, free from worry about traffic whizzing by me. I made it out to the major thoroughfare feeding the base just after midnight and flagged a cab a few minutes later.

Twenty minutes after that, I was standing in the Alamo rental car line at San Diego International Airport. A quarter hour after that I was on the road north.

Doing the math in my head, I knew that no international flights would be leaving the West Coast for at least five hours. There was no way any of those departing from San Diego would be flying direct to Russia, so my best bet was to hit LA. The drive between them was right around two hours at that time of night, giving me more than enough time. After the nap earlier I was still pretty alert, and the trip ahead would give me ample time to sleep.

Besides, I had a phone call to make that I didn't want to risk anybody overhearing. A rental car made for the perfect place to allow that to happen.

I put the car on my Hawk's Eye Tours American Express, hoping that if anybody was trolling the system for my name it might slide past them. I had an idea how I would get out of the country undetected, but that wouldn't help me any on the rental.

Alamo hooked me up with a brand new Nissan Altima; its odometer registered less than thirty miles total. I racked the seat back as far as it would go and turned the temperature gauge all the way to cold, keeping the fan off as I eased onto the highway. Then I set the cruise control as I headed north.

One thirty in the morning in southern California meant it was four thirty on the East Coast. Most likely the target of my call was curled up fast asleep, as most of the world would be at such an hour. Despite that, I plugged in the number from memory and put my cell on speakerphone, then dropped it in my lap.

It was answered after the third ring, the voice sounding a bit tired, but not groggy.

"Mr. Tate, what can I do for you?" Pally asked.

No anger or frustration in his voice, which was a good start. "How do you know I need something done?"

"Does anybody ever call another person at two thirty in the morning unless they need something?"

My guess about Pally being on the East Coast was entirely based on Hutch's new location. The fact that he called it two thirty meant he was somewhere in the Mountain Time Zone, only an hour's difference from where I was. Odds were he lived nowhere near my home in Montana, but at some time I needed to make it a point to find out.

Now just wasn't that time.

"Actually, I need a couple of favors," I said, taking a breath and staring out over the steering wheel at the road ahead. The I-5 was a full five lanes wide around me; the Nissan sat comfortably in the middle, its speedometer locked at seventy-five miles an hour. A handful of long-haul truckers dotted the lanes around me, otherwise traffic was almost nonexistent.

"Aw, hell," Pally said, emitting a low groan. I hoped it was just him being his normal cantankerous self rather than the sound of a man crawling out of bed, but at the moment it didn't greatly matter either way. "Let's hear it."

"First things first," I said. "Can you run the logs on international flights leaving Baja tonight or first thing in the morning? Probably out of Tijuana International, but not necessarily. Might even be a private flight."

"Yeah, yeah," Pally said, the sound of bare feet sliding over hardwood floors audible in the background. "And who am I looking for?"

"Two men," I replied, remembering everything Manny had told us. "One of them is named Viktor Blok, both spelled with a *K*. The other is Pavel, last name may or may not be Haney. Could be traveling alone or together."

There was no reply for a long moment as Pally went to work. In my mind I could see the array of electronics I'd seen via video conference earlier, imagining his long hair askew, the sleeves of his oversized sweater shoved back as he worked. The din of a keyboard clattering drifted over the air to me, the only other sound the highway passing beneath my tires.

"All right," he said after two full minutes. Any trace of sleep was gone from his voice, it now taking on the familiar detached resonance he always seemed to assume when working a case. "I don't have either of those names, but I have a Vitaly Gusev and an Andrei Zhobrov leaving on the four a.m. flight to Hong Kong."

The names were undeniably Russian, certainly plausible aliases for two known associates of an international cartel to use for travel purposes. Still, assuming that was them would be a dangerous proposition. I knew that at least one target was based in Russia, but I needed them all there. If the other two snuck away by boat, or, even worse, traveled inland, it might be years before they surfaced again.

"Possible," I said, letting Pally hear my thoughts, "but not certain."

"Au contraire, my analog friend," Pally said, a scolding tone in his voice. "I didn't find them by searching manifests. As you know, that takes more than ninety seconds and an act of God to pull off."

There was a long pause, and I could tell Pally was putting me on. I motioned with my right hand in the darkness, a circular gesture meant to draw the data out of him, but he didn't bite. "Okay, Mike, how did you find them?"

"Thank you," he replied, letting me hear his satisfaction. "You remember those financials you had me run? I finally tracked it back to an account running out of Vladivostok."

"Port town," I muttered, having seen the name a time or two in my previous life.

"That's right," Pally said. "They ran back to a corporation known as Kolb Enterprises International, the very same company that just purchased said plane tickets."

I snorted and shook my head, half pissed at the simplicity of it. "Kolb, as in an anagram of 'Blok'?"

"This is Russia we're talking here. This thing was set up in the late sixties when the place was still reeling from the Cold War. Over there, sending an anonymous envelope of cash once a month grants you carte blanche to do whatever you want the rest of the time."

As much as I wanted to disagree with his assessment, I knew he was right. It was the way most of the countries of the world operated, even large chunks of our own if we really wanted to nitpick about it.

"And would you like to hear the best part?" Pally asked. "The owner is a woman named Anya Merinkova."

Folds of skin gathered around my eyes as I squinted, trying to place the name. I had heard a lot of Soviet names and accents in the last few weeks, though that one didn't seem to ring any bells. "And how is that the best part?"

"In 1965, Anya Merinkova married none other than Sergey Blok," Pally said, putting a triumphant flare on the end of the sentence, announcing his victory for all.

I pursed my lips together and released a low whistle, another enormous piece falling into place.

Lita *had* come to my office to tie up Mateo and me both. They were ready to start moving their product and were wiping away all loose ends before getting started.

"Damn, Pally, that's good work. Seriously, impressive."

"I know," he replied, not a trace of irony in his tone.

A hint of a smirk tugged at my face, pulling me back an inch. "Hong Kong, though? That doesn't make any sense."

"My guess would be it's not a final destination; it just happens to be the first flight out of that hellhole this morning. I could check everything moving out of Hong Kong later if you'd like, but let's be honest, they're going home."

"Right," I said, nodding in agreement.

Everything I had just learned jibed perfectly with what I'd been expecting. I knew that my going to Baja with Diaz would be a waste of time, because they weren't going to be there. They had been one step ahead of us the entire time, and tonight would be no different.

"All right, you mentioned a couple of favors?" Pally said, already sounding bored, ready for his next task or to be cut loose so he could, presumably, return to bed.

"Yeah," I said, shaking away my current train of thought and returning to the conversation. "Can you get me a plane ticket out of LA to Russia this morning?"

There was a long moment of silence, followed by the low hum of air being sucked in. "Hawk, what are you doing, buddy?"

For the first time since leaving the jail, I felt the anger rise to the surface. It was a reaction I could ill afford, needing to keep it buried just a little while longer.

"You know damn well what I'm doing," I said, just audible. "And I'm trusting you to keep that between us in the meantime."

"Of course," Pally replied. "Of course. It's just—"

"I know," I said, leaving it at that. There were hours of conversation we could both add on the topic, but knew better than to dredge up. Maybe once I tracked down an actual location for him, we could share a lot of the things that had been left unsaid over the years.

"All right," he said, the sound of tapping on keys able to be heard again, "looks like the best we can do is a direct to Moscow and then a hop over to Vladivostok."

"No," I replied, once more shaking my head. "Just get me into Moscow. I'll figure it out from there."

"Are you kidding me? Those two are more than five thousand miles apart."

I needed to make a stop in Moscow that I didn't want to mention to Pally. He had already done more than could be expected for me, more than enough to bring some heat on himself should things go sideways later on. The less he knew from this point forward the better.

"Yeah, that's fine," I replied. "And can you put it under my old alias? I'd rather keep my name off things for as long as possible."

"Your old alias?" Pally asked. "You mean the one from before?"

I glanced over at my shoulder bag stowed on the passenger seat. Deep inside it was a passport I had not used in five years, the last stamp in it placed there when I left Panama, the day my family was killed.

"It's still good for another six months," I replied.

Once more I could hear a heavy sigh, though to his credit he didn't fight me on it. "You got it, Hawk."

"Thanks," I whispered, loud enough for him to hear me, soft enough for him to know I meant it.

"You got it," he repeated. "Anything else?"

"Just one last thing," I said. "Did you know?"

I left the question as vague as possible, though I had a feeling he would know exactly what I was referring to. If he didn't, that answered my question just as effectively.

"Did I . . ." he began, his voice trailing away. Once more I could hear a heavy sigh, and when he spoke there was a strain that wasn't there before. "No, Hawk. To be honest, I still don't. I suspected, but I never knew."

For whatever reason, I believed him. I had no basis to, beyond the fact that he had no reason to help me as much as he just had. The next couple of days would tell me if he was being truthful, if my initial reaction was right.

If it wasn't, it wouldn't much matter anyway.

"Thanks, Pally," I said, ending the call.

I drove in silence a full ten minutes, an overhead sign, white letters on a green background, telling me I had eighty miles to go on toward LA. I used the time to process what I had just learned, using it to fill in ever more of the holes that existed. There were only a couple small gaps remaining, all of which would hopefully be answered in the coming days.

The second number I had to dig out of the shoulder bag, scribbled down on a scrap of paper buried deep in the bottom of it. The first time I'd heard Lita's accent I had hoped it wouldn't come to this, but had thought I should bring it just in case.

The line rang a dozen times before it was picked up. There was no answer, just total silence on the other end.

I counted to five in my head before saying, "Same place, same time," and hanging up.

Chapter Thirty-Six

Twelve and a half hours in the air plus an eleven-hour time difference put me on the ground in Moscow just shy of a day after leaving. Considering that Pally had been kind enough to arrange a first-class ticket for me, I spent almost the entirety of that time reclined flat on my back, eyes closed. The Lufthansa craft wasn't quite as spacious as some of the other planes I'd been on, the lie-flat seat pinching my shoulders a bit, but it was still far preferable to a half day crammed into coach.

The first nine hours of the trip were spent in complete darkness, a near comatose state as my body recovered from the last few days, prepared for what lay ahead. After that my mind raised itself into a state of consciousness enough to allow for activity, the same damn dream sifting in and waking me with a start.

The last couple of hours I sat with my gaze aimed out the window, trying to plan my next move, making sense of what I already knew.

Two weeks ago, a woman I had never met walked into my shop and spent an absurd amount of money to get me alone in the woods with her. She fed me a phony story to lead her to a man from my past, whom she executed, and she then tried to kill me. In the time since, more people had died, and the questions piled up thick and furious.

Sitting and trying to sort the information out in my head, I allowed myself a pass and tried not to focus on my own foolish actions throughout. Lita's willingness to pay such an absurd amount of money should have been my first tip-off, followed by her demeanor and a hundred things thereafter.

Five years ago I would have sniffed this thing out before it ever got off the ground. Now I was just lucky to still be breathing, hoping that the next few days would put things right for good.

The plane touched down at Sheremetyevo International Airport in Moscow, a harsh, stark structure that could have been located anywhere from Paris to New York City. Without the need to wait for luggage, I made a single stop to exchange two hundred dollars into rubles and stepped out to the curb to flag down a taxi.

The driver, an older man with tufts of graying hair and a handful of teeth in his entire head, made no attempt at small talk after learning I spoke only English, and he drove me the twenty minutes to the closest metro station, relieving me of a hundred rubles. From there I ducked underground and hopped a train toward downtown, moving slowly, acting as nonchalant as I could manage.

Inside me, two emotions fought for the upper hand, both threatening to explode out at any moment. The first was anxiety. The Bloks had known exactly what we were doing from the moment things got started. There was a better-than-not chance they knew I was on the ground, using an alias to book the ticket be damned. I had done my best at countersurveillance the entire time, using every reflective surface I could to monitor my tail, eyes darting back and forth, hidden behind my sunglasses, but I was far from infallible, especially in a city I didn't know well.

The other emotion was anger, a bear in hibernation within me, a cranky monster that was ready to finally explode forward and claim what it had been waiting so long for. Five long years I had managed to keep it dormant, removing all major stressors, cleansing my life of any remnants from the past. Everything that I had encountered in recent weeks, though, starting with being shot at and encompassing every site and person from my past, had brought it all rushing back, five years of residual animosity heaped in with it.

I chose a corner seat in the last car in the train and put my back to the wall, removed my sunglasses, and counted the minutes in my head. My posture slouched and I pretended to doze, all the while watching every face that entered and exited, filing away anything suspicious.

If somebody was tailing me and using a team approach, there would be no way for me to know it. Being stuck in the corner of an underground train would be the worst possible place in the world for me, at least for the next hour or so anyway, but there was nothing I could do about that.

Most of the crowd departed the train at Red Square, tourists and sightseers off for a morning of roaming the country's most famed attraction. I remained in place as a new wave of people entered, carbon copies of the people headed away from the Square, off to cross the next item from their to-do lists.

Two stops after the Square, I exited the train and surfaced three blocks west, taking my time, roaming in and out of a handful of different shops. I bought a glass bottle of what appeared to be tea in one, a candy bar and a newspaper in another. All three items were plastered in Russian writing, none of it decipherable to me, though that was hardly the point.

Six minutes before nine o'clock, local time, I appeared on the northwest corner of Red Square and walked along the outer edge of it. To my right was the sprawling expanse of the Kremlin outfitted in dark brick, a single spire of an oversized clock tower rising from the center. Scads of guards could be seen manning every gate, standing at attention, oblivious to the blustery winds already pushing across the Square.

Large handfuls of tourists were clumped up into herds around the outside of it, guides in garish outfits explaining the building and its architecture in a dozen different languages, pictures being taken by the hundreds.

In front of me rose Saint Basil's Cathedral, its multicolored domes twisting up toward the sky. The gray overcast of the early morning did nothing to diminish its magnificence as it sat like a dazzling beacon on the end of a sea of brick and concrete, beckoning people to it.

As inviting as the structure may have appeared, my destination lay much closer, sitting alone on a bench halfway between the two landmarks. Hunched over in a wool overcoat, collar flipped up to the ears, he tossed out small bits of bread crumbs as a flock of pigeons hopped around before him and snatched them up.

Six years had passed since I'd last seen Xavier Doss. Like with me, the first hints of middle age were starting to set in, though he could still pass for late twenties if need be. His cocoa-colored skin was free from lines save a few crow's feet around the eyes, and his dark hair was shorn close to his scalp.

I slid down onto the bench beside him without extending a hand in formal greeting; the gesture would have been far too obvious to anybody that might be watching. The bench seat felt cold beneath me as I settled onto it, watching the birds hop around in front of me.

"X."

"Hawk," he replied, flinging another clump of bread crumbs onto the ground. "Nice haircut."

A half smile tugged at my mouth as I kept my gaze aimed forward, watching throngs of tourists and government workers all scurry by, heavy coats and dark colors already starting to make their first appearances of the season. If I was staying longer than a day or two I would have to purchase something much the same, as my suit jacket was already proving inadequate to the brisk wind blowing over us.

"Thanks for meeting me," I said. "I didn't even know for sure if the line was still good."

"Just barely," X said simply. His voice was free of judgment or accusation, not even a hint of curiosity. I had asked for the meeting, and therefore whatever transpired therein was going to be on me.

Xavier and I had worked together briefly during our initial training at the agency. As former military personnel with fight training, I was winnowed toward being a field agent, bouncing around the globe, mixing things up on the ground. Coming from the Ivy League and three years spent on Wall Street, Xavier was made an analyst. He was inserted into the Moscow branch of an American brokerage house, used to monitor any suspicious financial dealings going on in Asia.

While his skill set might not have aligned exactly with my current mission, he was an ally, which was what I needed most at the moment. Even if he couldn't help me directly, I knew he wouldn't do anything to get me killed, either.

"You still involved?" I asked.

"Six more months," he said, twisting away a crust of bread and tossing it, three pigeons diving toward it at once.

I nodded. That would put him at almost ten years in, which was the standard career mark for most people abroad. After that they either circled back home for a nice cushy desk job or left the agency entirely, a sparkling letter of recommendation in their dossier.

"Congratulations. Moving home or moving on?"

"Home for now," X replied, his face aimed away from me, his gaze shifting every few seconds, no doubt scanning the crowd as much as I was. "Maybe on thereafter, haven't decided yet. Just need to get out of here."

"Too cold?" I asked.

"Too white," he corrected. "The snow, the people, all of it. Time to be closer to normality for a while."

The words weren't exactly what I wanted to hear, issued as a subtle hint for me not to do something that could potentially jeopardize his last bit of time in-country.

"Point taken," I said. "I guess I'll just jump right in—you can decide if there's any way to assist me or if we stand and walk in opposite directions, part as friends."

A small snort rolled out of X. "Just like that?"

"Just like that," I said. "Regardless of what happens in the next five minutes, I'll buy you dinner in Washington the next time I'm there."

A long moment of silence passed as he considered the proposal. He twisted the last bit of bread in two and tossed both pieces out, wiping his hands clean against each other.

"Start at the beginning," he said.

At this point I wasn't even sure where that was, so I started where I knew I could get the biggest punch. Hopefully it would be enough to draw him in.

"I found who killed my family."

He cocked an eyebrow in my direction for a split second before shifting back to watching the square. "I wasn't aware you were looking. Last I heard, you were off playing mountain man."

There was no way of telling if my plan had any effect on him at all, hardly the response I was hoping for.

"I wasn't. They found me."

"Aw, hell," he muttered beside me, a trace of a groan present in his voice.

Seizing on it as the opening I needed, I jumped ahead to the opposite end of the story, hoping the two would be enough to make him care about the middle. "What do you know about Krokodil?"

"Aw, hell," X repeated, shaking his head. He shoved his hands into the pockets of his jacket, a sour expression on his face. "The simplest way of putting it is the evil, ugly younger sibling of meth. Truly vile stuff, the kind of thing you wish could be un-invented."

My eyebrows rose a bit on my forehead. I had never encountered Krokodil, but I had seen enough encounters with meth in the States and abroad to know it was pretty abhorrent, the low-class form of crack. Saying this stuff was even worse took things to an entirely new level.

"Why? What have you got?" X pressed.

"The last case I was working was the Juarez cartel out of Mexico," I said. I left out the part about my leaving and why, all information he already knew.

He had sent flowers to the funeral. I don't remember much from that time, but I remember they were nice.

"Couple years back a crew out of Vladivostok, the Bloks, came in, said to be looking for a North American partner."

"And they took over the Juarez cartel, kept the distribution network for themselves," X finished.

"You know them?" I asked, focusing in on a young couple walking hand in hand across the concrete, both wearing knee-high black leather boots. I watched them a moment before moving on, shaking my head.

"Naw," X said, "Vlad is five-and-a-half thousand miles from here. This isn't like the States, where giant networks have fingers throughout the whole country. Here, everybody has their square they snatched up after the Cold War when things were going to shit. For the most part they keep to it, operating within their own territory."

"But I'm guessing by the way you put that together, if they have a chance to expand, they move in and take over," I added.

"Like parasites," X said. "They keep to themselves, but they're always on the watch for opportunities, always have their guard up on their own situation."

It made sense. Everything from looking to expand across the ocean to the way they'd muscled out the Juarezes tracked with what X was saying. Nothing about their actions was malicious or personal; that was just how business was done.

"How big you talking?" X asked.

I lifted my palms to the sky and let them fall back to my thighs, letting him know I wasn't exactly sure. Another gust of wind blew in from the west, raising goose pimples along my arms and sending a shiver down my spine.

"Enough to feed California," I said. "And all signs seem to indicate they're ready to move now."

"Aw, hell," he repeated once more, running a hand back over his head, his close-cropped hair sounding rough against his palm. "What's your next move?"

"Heading across right after this," I said.

I didn't bother to say that I would need some help. I didn't have to. The fact that I had called and asked for a meeting five thousand miles from my final destination should have made that obvious.

In my periphery, I could see X's head bob a few inches, a rapid-fire movement up and down. His lips pursed out as if tasting something bitter, his expression matching it.

"You know you're alone on this, right?" he asked. "If you find the mother lode, you call us and we'll send the cavalry, but until then we can't be involved. That's not how things work here."

I nodded in agreement. I had known that since getting on a plane the day before, since deciding to come to Russia a few hours before that. They had an international agency to run, one that was predicated on respecting the host countries we visited. If ex-agents began running rogue operations under the official banner, DEA access would be cut off completely, something that could ill afford to happen.

"That being said," he continued, "there is a bay of lockers on the second level of the rail station eighteen blocks from here. Automated pass keys. Little care package inside that might help you on your journey."

My first reaction was to smile, or to reach over and shake his hand, but I managed to keep both in check. I nudged my chin downward an inch in thanks, already mapping out the eighteen blocks from here to there in my head.

"Thank you," I said. "I appreciate it."

"I know," he replied. "But if you really want to thank me, be right. And remember this conversation when you confirm it."

Once more I nodded in affirmation, his point clear. This was the kind of thing that could submarine his career, or it could fast-track him out of the country. There was no way I would do the former, but if I could help bring about the latter I would.

"I'll see you soon," I said, rising from the bench and walking back the way I'd come, not once looking back as I went.

Chapter Thirty-Seven

As far as secret pass codes go, X's choice left a little something to be desired. While our history together wasn't terribly deep or nuanced, he could have managed something better than H-A-W-K-T-A-T-E. If anybody had been watching on his end, that would have effectively ended things for me right there.

As good fortune would have it, nobody had.

The care package that was stowed away was a simple black briefcase, leather, the combination lock on either side reset to triple-zero. Without bothering to open it, I pulled it from the locker and made my way downstairs, purchasing a *firmenniy* ticket on the Trans-Siberian Railway line to Vladivostok. I paid in cash, using most of my remaining rubles, without giving a name or anything that could be tracked.

Using the train was much slower than returning to Sheremetyevo and catching a one-way to Vladivostok, though it was worth it to maintain the anonymity. By this point the Bloks, if not a host of other people, were bound to know I was in-country. On paper, I had been in Moscow for only a couple of hours, meaning the odds of me headed elsewhere yet weren't good. Their guard would be down for the time being; they'd loosely monitor the airports, waiting for me to catch a plane back.

Halfway across Russia, I contacted Pally and asked him to book my alias a flight from Moscow to Kiev, set to board later in the day. I deliberately chose a city that was close enough to be believable, hoping that they might be lulled into thinking I caught a phony trail, was following it up in neighboring Ukraine.

With any luck, by that point I would be on the ground in Vladivostok and moving into position as the cover of night fast approached.

I waited six hours into my journey, long after the city lights of Moscow had faded, the snow-covered Urals whipping by outside my window, before finding a private sleeper stall. Until that time I remained in a public coach, watching every person who came and went, monitoring anybody whose gaze lingered, anyone who passed through more than once. Just twice did my radar pick up even the slightest hint of suspicion, each time confirming the target was not a threat.

Tucked away in my own space, I flipped each of the numbered combination codes to 4-5-1, the numerical correspondents to the acronym DEA. While not the most sophisticated system in the world, it worked efficiently for purposes such as this, when there was no call for passing along a combination, for putting anything into writing.

The silver clasps both flew open, and the top lifted back with the slight cracking sound of new leather prying upward. The matching scent came with it, the familiar smell of premium cowhide mixed with cold metal.

One look inside and I instinctively lowered the lid back into place, checking the door for a long moment, making sure nobody was about to enter. I sat waiting, my breath held, feeling a bit less apprehensive now that I knew what was inside the case just a few inches from my hand.

Outside, the world continued to move past, the foreground whipping by in fast succession, the peaks in the distance remaining stationary.

The terrain reminded me of Yellowstone in wintertime: everything shrouded in white, pine trees weighed down with large tufts of snow.

Raising the lid once more, I assessed what lay inside, a veritable cornucopia of needed items. If somehow the next twenty-four hours passed and I was still breathing, I would make it a point to repay X in any way I could, over and above helping him get free of his Russian exile.

Framing the top and bottom of the case were a pair of Heckler & Koch Mark 23 handguns, a noise suppressor screwed into the end of each. One at a time I raised them and checked the slide and the feed, noting by their weight that they were already loaded.

An extra pair of magazines sat beside both of them, twelve rounds each, giving me a total of forty-eight bullets. There was no way of knowing how many I might need, but it was a reasonably safe assurance that I would be lucky to even get that many shots off before meeting my end.

Besides, trying to carry more than one spare magazine each would just be cumbersome.

Beside the guns was a Garra II folding knife, a nod from X to our previous life together, a joke going back to our first days in training. With one hand, I snapped the weapon open and examined the curved blade, a serrated edge on the inside, a razor sharp hone on the outside. While I had often preferred the straight-ahead style of the Marine K-Bar, many in my class had assumed I preferred the Garra for its hawksbill blade.

At the moment, I was just happy to have anything at all.

I placed the knife down and picked up the boxy gray satellite phone beside it. I thumbed it on and scrolled through the directory, finding a single number programmed in. Assuming it to be his, I closed out of the phone book and rested the phone in my lap, then pulled out the last item in the case.

Lining the bottom of the package were two items of clothing, both double knit for warmth. The first was a simple black watch cap, a half-arc affair meant to cover the head and ears without coming down over the eyes. In my case it would also serve well in holding back my hair, keeping everything tucked away.

The second was a long-sleeved polypropylene shirt, also in black, tightly knit for warmth from the biting cold wind. It would serve me much better on the move than the dress shirt and jacket I'd been wearing for two days, offering me better mobility and decreased visibility.

"X, I owe you, friend," I muttered, taking the phone up from my lap.

The main line to the southwest headquarters was the same as it had been when I worked there five years before. Hutch had insisted that every field agent know it by memory, wanting it to be stored as few places as possible, despite the fact that it could be found using something as simple as a Google search. One at a time, I punched out the numbers, a small beeping sound resonating with each one, before bracing my back against the wall, my gaze aimed at the sliding door before me.

If anybody was coming inside, there was no way they were coming through the window. With my left leg propped on the bench seat I was sitting on and the briefcase open on my lap, I kept my right hand wrapped around the handle of one of the Mark 23s, and the other hand kept the phone pressed to my face.

Best guess, the local time was around two in the afternoon, making it somewhere between two and four in the morning in California, depending on my exact location. Just two weeks before I would have never dreamed of making a call any later than ten p.m., but now I dialed without thinking twice.

Something told me the person I was looking to contact would be awake anyway.

"Diaz," she snapped, not a single trace of sleepiness in her tone. She sounded annoyed, her official voice on. The fact that she was at her desk and answering the phone explained both.

"Hawk," I said, a simple one-word statement. If she was surrounded by anybody, she could cut me off, say I had the wrong number, or just hang up the phone. If not, we could talk.

There was a pause and a long sigh, followed by the moan of a door swinging closed, the latch catching and sealing it shut. The distinct sound of a lock being thrown also rang out, followed by her falling back into her chair.

"Where the hell have you been?" she asked, suddenly sounding much more worn down, exhausted even.

"I take it the raid didn't yield a damn thing?" I asked.

"Not really," she replied. "By the time our guys figured out a location and we got there, they had cleared out. We found a couple of safes standing empty, a few trash can fires still smoldering with ashes, but not a hell of a lot we could use."

I processed the information, which was much the same as I had expected. "So enough to indicate you had the right spot, not enough to implicate anybody who might have been there."

"Exactly," Diaz said. "We had two SEAL teams, a half-dozen agents from the office here, me, Hutch, all standing around looking at a bunch of nothing."

That, too, seemed to coincide exactly with what I had expected.

"So where are you now?" I asked.

"We seized the house and sent a tech crew through it. They've been there all day, that's actually why I'm still on now. I'm expecting a call from them at any time."

I adjusted my weight and settled in against the wall, keeping the case leveled on my lap, my fingers resting atop the trigger guard. "They finding anything?"

"Yes and no," she said. "Traces of cocaine, drug residue everywhere. DNA evidence coming out the ass. Looks like the place could be anything from a brothel to a drug runner's den, we just don't know yet."

"Shit," I muttered, shaking my head, the cold steel of the outer wall starting to pass through the suit coat and button-down I was wearing.

"We went back and shook Juarez down again today," Diaz said, "managed to get a couple more names out of him of distributors he didn't give up in the initial case. We're going to go after them first thing in the morning—but I have to be honest, at this point we don't have a lot. The Russians seemed to have vanished."

My eyes went glassy as I stared at the door in front of me, for a moment almost wishing it would open and one of the Bloks would be foolish enough to step inside. The tips of my fingers went white as I pressed down on the handle of the gun, aching to slide it free and unload the magazine inside it.

"So, where are you?" she asked again.

Every part of me wanted to tell her. She had earned the right to know, and, more important, she had earned my trust. At the same time, there was no way to be certain the line we were speaking on was clear. More than once our plans had been leaked to the opposition. Last night's fruitless raid was just one more example of that.

I was too close to allow something so foolish to derail me.

"I was in Russia this morning," I said, "but didn't find what I was looking for. I'm headed back to the airport now to catch a flight to Kiev."

Lying to her wasn't something I was fond of, or even proud of, but it was a necessary evil. It coincided with the fake ticket Pally had purchased for me just a short time before, and it would provide continuity if anybody was listening.

"Kiev?" she asked, obviously confused. "What the hell is in Kiev?"

"I'm told that's where the Krokodil is coming from," I said. "I'm almost to the airport now, I'll contact you whenever I know something more. Apologies for calling so late."

I could tell by the tone of her voice there were more questions she wanted to ask, but she picked up by my tone and my statement that the conversation was over. Very soon it would all make sense to her, but for the time being that was as much as I could divulge.

"No apologies," she said. "Keep me posted, and get your ass out of there if anything gets ugly. This isn't your fight anymore."

Her choice of words brought an ironic smile to my face. Despite the fact that I was no longer an active agent, this was more my fight than anybody else's on the planet. The Bloks and the Juarezes and whoever else might be affiliated had ensured that long ago. The fact that they sought me out years after the fact only served to reinforce it.

"Right," I said, my gaze hardening, my grip growing tighter on the phone in my hand. "I'll talk to you soon."

Chapter Thirty-Eight

The guard watching over the Tomb of the Unknown Soldier in America's Arlington National Cemetery was trained to act on a very precise schedule. He began by taking twenty-one paces across the front of the tomb. A rubber mat, replaced twice a year, was laid out on the ground to keep the continual foot traffic from wearing a trench in the polished white marble. There was a twenty-one-second pause before the guard would turn, take the same number of paces in the opposite direction, and pause again.

Years before, Sergey Blok had heard about this practice while watching a documentary on the Cold War. The program had been shot and edited by Americans, so the entire thing was little more than self-serving propaganda, but that lone piece of trivia had stuck with him.

It surfaced now as he paced back and forth in front of his desk, waiting for Pavel and Viktor to arrive. Almost a full day had passed since their midnight retreat from the compound in Baja, twenty-four long hours of him waiting, assuming the worst, hoping it wasn't as bad as feared.

Twenty-four hours for the animosity, the resentment of his nephew, to stew and grow.

At twenty minutes after the hour he spotted the 1938 Buick Town Car pull to a stop on the curb. His pacing ended halfway across the room, and he was drawn toward the window to watch from the second floor as both men piled out onto the sidewalk. The moment they were out of the car his driver sped away, his profile never once turning to face them, indicating the drive had been less than pleasant for all parties.

At first glance, Viktor looked disheveled, his steps uneven as he opened the front gate and headed toward the door. Behind him Pavel walked with both hands balled into fists, his standard-issue glower more deeply set than usual. He remained a couple of feet back from Viktor as they made their way forward. Sergey was almost able to visualize how much Pavel wanted to explode on his unwanted charge.

Sergey waited until they were out of view before taking a seat behind his desk and waiting for them. He had given Anya explicit directions to remain out of sight for the morning, telling his butler to escort their visitors up the moment they arrived. At best the conversation that was about to take place would be heated, at worst a complete donnybrook.

Given the circumstances, and what he'd just seen coming up the front walk, Sergey honestly couldn't tell which outcome would be preferable.

It took three full minutes for Pavel and Viktor to make their way up the stairs into his office, though the voice of Viktor long preceded them. Sergey could hear him stumbling around the house, bumping into items, his boots stomping against the hardwood floors. Repeatedly he berated the butler, calling for vodka and wine, demanding food after their journey. More than once Sergey wanted to jump up from his chair and go storming down the stairs after his nephew, but forced himself to remain in place. There was already enough bad word of mouth surrounding the Bloks out there, and he could ill afford to add to it by rumors of family infighting.

If something needed to be done, it would be done quietly, far away from any curious eyes or ears.

Pavel was the first to enter, knocking softly on the door to the office and waiting for permission from Sergey before pushing through. He walked in and stood to one side of the desk, every muscle in his body coiled, a mountain of pent-up rage, his entire being strung as tight as a guitar string.

"Good morning, sir," he said, his hands balled up and resting atop his thighs. He glanced down at Sergey just a moment before shifting his gaze to the wall above him, his jaw clenched.

A moment later Viktor spilled in, the smell of booze hanging around him like a cloud. A black dress shirt hung untucked from his skinny frame, a rumpled black trench coat over it. His hair was disheveled and his eyes bloodshot, and he looked to still be entrenched in a bender several days in the making.

"Uncle," he said, coming to a stop beside Pavel, and running both hands back over his scalp, attempting to force his hair down into some form of normality.

Sergey could feel contempt well within him as he stared at his nephew before shifting his attention to Pavel. From this point forward the young Blok was nothing more than a liability, a hazard to be hidden out of sight at all times, kept away from any serious business discussions. His handling of Baja the last few months had long had Sergey leaning in that direction, but his appearance this morning, his physical state, had sealed the decision.

"How was your trip?" Sergey asked.

Pavel pushed an angry breath out through his nose, a simple gesture meant to relay his displeasure, before nodding. "We arrived safely. Thank you for making the arrangements."

Reading between the lines, Sergey could surmise that Viktor had been a pain in the ass from the minute they left.

"Were there any problems?"

"No," Pavel said. "The arrangements were clean, our identities never questioned, in Mexico or in Hong Kong."

Sergey nodded. His question had been aimed more to let Pavel know it was okay to speak freely about Viktor, but knew his enormous employee would never do so, mindful always of the pecking order.

"What happened in Mexico?" he asked. Already he had received multiple reports on the incident, complete overviews covering everything from the evacuation to the apprehension by enforcement officials. He wasn't as much interested in what the men before him had to say as to see his nephew's reaction.

The politics of a family business meant that he couldn't simply pluck away a problem person like a weed and cast him aside so that the rest of the organization could grow. He had to set a trap, allow for the individual to do something foolish, to overstep boundaries, to do something that would cause the other family members to excuse the action.

His brother had been gone the better part of a decade, succumbing to cancer long before his time. In his stead his wife, Sergey's sister-in-law, controlled their interest in the organization. To simply do away with Viktor, no matter how warranted the action might be, would be a stroke of disrespect to both his sister-in-law and his brother's memory.

"When word came in that the DEA was coming," Pavel said, "we followed the protocol you laid out for us."

Beside him, Viktor raised a hand, taking an uneven step forward toward the desk. "What happened was the first time a little trouble showed up, we tucked our tails between our legs and ran away like cowards."

Sergey felt a flush of heat rise to his cheeks, noticed Pavel's fists grow a little tighter, but kept his attention on Viktor. "And how would you have handled the situation?"

"Like a man!" Viktor bellowed, stepping forward and pounding the side of his fist down on the desk. The combined sounds of the outburst rang through the office, setting Sergey back an inch, pulling Pavel closer, ready to pounce should the need arise.

Bitterness flowed into the back of Sergey's throat, the taste acerbic on his tongue, as he regained his bearings, staring back at Viktor. His mind shifted to the .38 revolver stowed in the top drawer of his desk, within easy reach, almost daring him to draw it and take aim. For just a brief moment he allowed himself to envision the sight of his blood-spattered nephew flying backward through the air, landing in a heap on the floor as the last little bit of air wheezed from his lungs.

"Are you saying I am not a man?" Sergey asked, letting the rage show in his voice.

Again Viktor pounded his fist down on the desk, the deep boom sounding out in the room. "I'm saying we should have fought! We built this business by taking what was ours, not running and hiding! Not asking for permission!"

Unable to stop himself, Sergey rose to his feet, pressing both fists down into the top of his desk, prickly heat running the length of his body beneath his maroon track suit, sweat threatening to burst through at any moment. His eyes receded into tiny beads of black, his head glistening beneath the overhead light.

"Listen right now, you little shit," he spat, "*we* didn't build a damn thing. *I* built this business from the ground up, forty-five years of toiling away, day after day, to make this what it is. You haven't done anything. If it was up to you, this whole thing would have gone down in some Wild West showdown last night."

"No, Uncle," Viktor said, leaning forward, his posture matching Sergey's, "my father built this into what it is. *He* was the driving force. Since his death, you've done nothing but tread water."

"Tread water? Are you an idiot?" Sergey spewed back at him, spittle hanging from his bottom lip, dripping onto the desktop beneath him. "Who do you think the architect of Krokodil has been? This stuff would have been on the streets years ago, but your father wouldn't hear of it."

Viktor's face twisted itself up into a mask of self-righteousness and rage. "No! That is not true. It was all his idea to begin with—it's just taken you this long to do anything with it."

"You want to call us cowards?" Sergey said, leaning forward farther, continuing the attack. "The only coward here was your father, replaced now by you."

There were no more words between them. In one swift movement Viktor snatched his right hand up from the desk and swung it across Sergey's face, his fingers connecting with cheek, the sound of skin slapping against skin ringing out in the room.

The blow stunned Sergey a moment, his body snapping back more from surprise than pain. He could feel the outline of Viktor's hand on his face, the spot tingling with each beat of his heart. His jaw dropped open as Viktor loomed before him, finger stretched out, pointing toward his chest.

This was the moment he'd been waiting for, the opportunity he had hoped might present itself since they first arrived. He wasn't expecting an actual physical assault, though that worked just as well as anything he could have imagined.

Rotating his head at the neck he turned to Pavel and nodded once, a short upward movement no more than an inch or two in length. A look of unbridled pleasure passed over the cross features of the enormous man, his right hand appearing beside his shoulder and driving itself forward, a quick, spring-loaded action practiced thousands of times over the years.

The shot caught Viktor just behind the temple, Pavel's massive fist covering most of his victim's head. Sergey watched as the light blinked out of Viktor's eyes, as his face went blank, as his entire body fell slack. Head and shoulders leading the way, his form was lifted into the air, hanging a long moment before collapsing onto the floor, contorted into a heap. There was no sound from him once he hit, no movement of any kind.

Sergey circled his desk and stared down at his nephew. His intentions were never to get physical with the young man, but Viktor himself had broken that barrier first. Even better, he had done it in front of a witness. Sergey could now bring his nephew home, stash him far away from the front lines, and there was nothing anybody could say against him.

He shifted attention up from the unmoving pile of black clothing, the smell of blood and vodka in the air. "I bet that felt good, didn't it?"

The corners of Pavel's mouth peeled back in a stilted smile that looked out of place on his face. "I have been waiting years to do that."

Chapter Thirty-Nine

All told, it took just over ten hours for the Trans-Siberian train to deliver me from Moscow to Vladivostok. The farther into my journey I got the less crowded the train became, and I spent the final two hours with just a fraction of the original crowd. Most riders got off at a small town not far from the big city, using the *firmenniy* as a form of modified commuter rail. Along the way we picked up a handful of strays here and there, but it was readily apparent even to me that the destination was a far less attractive place to be than the origin.

Ten minutes on the ground confirmed just that.

The smell of the sea filled my nostrils as I exited the train station, a dull, drab building made exclusively from gray stone. In the distance I could hear the sounds of ships in dock, see the flashing lights mounted on high, guiding vessels into port.

Using the cover of my private compartment, I had stripped out of my jacket and shirt, putting on the polypropylene shirt provided to me by X. Sized large, it was a bit snug in the shoulders and around the middle, a harsh reminder that I was no longer twenty-eight and the size he remembered.

Not wanting to stand out too much while still out in plain sight, I put the shirt and jacket back on. The three layers were warm almost to the point of discomfort. The ski cap I kept stowed away in a pocket, waiting until I was closer to my chosen target before sliding it on.

At such a late hour, the city seemed to be quieting down for the night, by far the most movement coming from the docks to the south. Bathed in halogen light by banks of overhead bulbs, the entire area was as bright as noon, and activity flourished.

After an initial glance, I kept my attention aimed away from it, careful to protect my night vision. With the shoulder bag over one arm and briefcase in hand, I walked five blocks from the train station, passing run-down storefronts and decrepit eateries, none with more than a few small clumps of people inside.

Those I did see were huddled tightly together, dressed in heavy clothes, their moods somber. Nobody seemed to even glance my way as I slid by, just another faceless stranger in the city.

I walked slowly, using the windshields of parked cars and the front glass of buildings to scan my tail. Content that nobody was following me, I flagged a taxi down and gave the driver an address five blocks from my first intended target, reciting the location Pally had given me a few hours before.

When I talked it through with Pally, we'd agreed that the residence would be the best place to start. There was no way Blok would be at the production site this time of night, and showing up there first would only alert him to my presence. The odds were overwhelmingly good he already knew I was in-country, or at least en route. The faux plane ticket to Kiev might have gotten him to let his guard down a bit, but that would work in my favor for only so long.

If I started with him, there was a chance, however slim, that I could get to the production site and raise hell before anybody could warn them to my presence. If I went to the warehouse first, there was no way somebody wouldn't tip him off beforehand. Doing so assured that he would either have an army waiting for me or disappear into the night, neither of which I was especially fond of.

I had the taxi drop me off near what appeared to be a family restaurant, making a series of grunts and emphatic gestures to grab the driver's attention and get him to slow. The man shook his head in complete disgust as I counted out the forty rubles for my fare, added another ten to the pile for him, and stepped out into the cold night air.

My foot had barely touched the sidewalk when he zoomed off, a flash of tires smoking and taillights blazing, making sure I knew he did not appreciate my presence or my business. I played the part of an innocent foreign rube until he was gone before turning a hard right and heading off in the opposite direction.

Not once in my life had I ever been to Vladivostok. I was depending entirely on the directions Pally had given me, telling me exactly where I should get out of a cab and how far I should travel to reach my destination. If any part of him wanted to do me in, this was his chance, by leading me into a certain trap with no way of knowing for certain that I was wrong about him. I could only bank on the fact that I had always done right by him and pray he would return the favor.

One block past the restaurant, the streetlights behind me faded, and a quiet neighborhood took its place. From what I could see through the darkness, the street was lined with older, stately homes, all constructed more than fifty years before, comprised mostly of brick and mortar. Their exteriors appeared strong and imposing, even more so by moonlight, with towering trees dotting their yards. A handful had lights visible through the front windows, a few more with the reflected images of television screens dancing off them.

Somewhere in the distance a dog barked, setting off two more in response. On the opposite side of the street an elderly woman shuffled along, her hands shoved into the pockets of her coat, her gaze aimed at the ground.

My heels clicked against the sidewalk beneath me as I gripped the handle of the briefcase in my right hand, rested my left along the strap of my bag. Relieved of most of its cargo, the case was considerably lighter than when I'd first picked it up.

Both of the Mark 23s were wedged along the small of my back, handles pointed out toward my hips, noise suppressors resting against my butt. It had made for an uncomfortable ride in the cab, sitting with ramrod posture, but it was worth it. Either one could be extracted in less than a second, already loaded and ready to be fired.

The Garra II was slid into the front pocket of my slacks on my right side, my stronger hand. The blade was still folded shut, most likely to be employed only in the event of an emergency. That left just the phone and the spare magazines packed tight against each other in the bottom of the briefcase to prevent sliding around and making costly noise.

One by one the houses filed by on my right, and my gaze flicked to the side at every third one to check the numbers. Four long blocks fell away as I walked, letting the feelings I had suppressed long ago come to the surface.

The first time I ever laid eyes on my wife was in a genetics class my junior year of college. I was in there out of basic student obligation, looking to fill a core requirement after my first three choices were already full. She was there as a premed student, taking the course as an elective, hoping it would be useful in her future career in medical research.

Far and away the most beautiful nerd I had ever seen.

Her name was Elizabeth Spence, and she hated me from the start. Some couples like to brag about how they knew the moment they met that they were going to spend the rest of their lives together. We liked to joke that if she'd had her way, we never would have even had a conversation, let alone a child.

It took me more than six months to get her to say anything to me that wasn't laced with arsenic, another three before she would even consider a date.

By graduation we were engaged. Three years later, we had a daughter named Alice.

Having had five years to dwell on it, there were a thousand things I did wrong along the way, a million more I would change if given the chance. I never would have gone into the Navy, would have told the DEA to stick it the minute they came sniffing around. Not once would I consider moving them to the southwest, leaving them alone for long stretches of time, nobody to protect them in a hostile environment.

Of course I couldn't change any of those things, and I'd had five long years, sixty months, two hundred and sixty weeks, to have to accept that. When most people make mistakes, they have to change jobs, move to a new city, at worst declare bankruptcy. My mistakes cost me my wife and daughter, the last two women I will ever love in this world.

The last of the numbers dwindled down on the buildings beside me, depositing me alongside a two-story brick home framed by a front porch extended between two wings stretching out to either side. Easily the largest house on the block, it commanded the lots to either side of it. A series of obvious additions had been made to it over the years, stretching the home to look like it included a dozen bedrooms and just as many other rooms serving various purposes.

A black wrought iron fence encompassed the grounds, a gate with a simple latch standing at the end of the front walk leading up to the door. Briefcase still in hand, I let myself in and strolled along it, noting two windows with lights on, both on the second floor.

The state of the place indicated a number of things right off, all working to my advantage. First, the lax security told me that Blok wasn't expecting me to show up at his home. Whether that meant he didn't believe I was in-country or just didn't think I knew where he was I couldn't be sure, but either way it was a fact that greatly played into my favor.

Second, it also told me that Pavel wasn't nearby. There was no way the famed brute could be on the grounds and let me get this close without doing something to stop me. Even if a trap was lying in wait on the other side of the door, I could have been carrying an IED in this briefcase right now to wipe out half the house. He would never allow that to happen.

Finally, it told me that Blok wasn't taking me seriously. He had lived in a state of false superiority for so long, he didn't fear the possibility of somebody walking up to his front door and doing to him exactly what he had done to me years before.

In all that time, the only thing that had kept me from being consumed with rage, from letting my thirst for vengeance overtake me, was the simple fact that I never had a face to aim it at. Even then, despite what I was working on at the moment, I had known the Juarezes weren't the ones who killed my family. If I had thought that for even a second, I would have wiped them all from the face of the earth five years earlier, prison be damned.

The whole situation, from the depravity of the actions to the public display it was done under, was too deplorable, even for people like them. The kind of people who would go after a man's family, who would murder his wife and daughter and stake their bodies out for the world to see, had to be nothing short of monsters.

For five long years I had lived not knowing who those monsters were, peering out into the darkness, wondering if they were lurking, suppressing my rage. Finally, I had a face, a name, a target for it. Someplace to aim everything I'd been carrying all that time.

I could feel it boiling within me, forcing its way to the surface. Despite the cold night air, sweat bathed my brow, soaked through the undershirt, drenched my button-down. My breath came in long, deep pulls, and my heart pounded in my ears. Every sound in the neighborhood found its way to me; each nerve in my body tingled with sensation.

On the edge of the front porch I deposited the briefcase and the shoulder bag, dropping both to the floor and drawing the Marks from my back. The grips on each one fit easily into my hands as I pulled them free, moonlight flashing off their polished steel barrels.

Yeah, I'd made mistakes, but nothing compared to what Blok had done. He had picked a fight with someone he wasn't equipped to handle, started something he couldn't finish.

His mistake wasn't in being a monster.

It was in creating one.

Chapter Forty

After ten months spent in the balmy, arid climate of Baja, it was a welcome respite to be back in Russia. The familiar November chill had set in, this year a little stronger than the previous few, frost already covering the ground just hours into the evening.

Still dressed in nothing more than a T-shirt, Pavel drew in a deep breath through his nose. The cold air cleared his nasal passages and filled his lungs, the taste bitter in his nostrils. Just the mere scent of it reminded him that he was home where he belonged, far from the warm ocean breezes and sandy beaches of Mexico.

Once more a smile crossed his face as he circled around to the opposite side of Blok's sedan and opened the door. Viktor's unconscious body had been leaning against it. Upon the door's release, his frame spilled out onto the ground, his shoulder taking the brunt of the fall, his forehead not far behind. A gash opened on his brow, and a tendril of blood ran down into his eyebrow as Pavel put one hand into his armpit and hefted him upright.

Dipping at the waist, he positioned Viktor's body over his shoulder and lifted him from the ground. Viktor's slight frame weighed almost nothing. Pavel slammed the car door shut and headed toward the front door as Viktor's arms and legs flopped on either side of him.

The punch had been glorious, a long time coming and even longer overdue. If Sergey had not been standing there, Pavel would have taken his time and really relished the shot, winding up for a haymaker that might very well have ended Viktor on the spot. As it were, the direct right had more than done its job, aided considerably by the alcohol flowing through Viktor's system.

After nearly twenty years in the business, the blow was more than just a punch to Pavel. It had been delivered on a direct order from Sergey, an order for him to strike a member of the family. For such a directive to be issued meant he was now considered on the level with everyone else, a sign of things to come.

What this meant for him moving forward he wasn't sure, but it had to be a good sign. In no way did he want to return to Mexico, but if ordered he would do so happily, taking over the network there, making sure Krokodil became the next big thing to seize America.

Pavel adjusted Viktor a tiny bit on his shoulder and jerked the front glass doors open, stepping by the heat blowing down in the buffer zone and passing on through the second set of double doors. Even at the late hour they remained open; the evening shift was on and the enterprise was operating in full swing.

Stopping just within the main door, Pavel rested his hands on his hips and took a look around. The last time he had been inside was almost a year earlier, when the process had been nothing more than Anatoly and a small group of scientists, all still working to perfect the product. Their lab had been just thirty feet square, a plastic bubble rising up out of the middle of the enormous space.

In the time since, things had expanded exponentially, with finished product now lining the west side of the building, raw materials in equal amounts standing on the opposite end. The once tiny research facility had quadrupled in size, and a team that looked to be a dozen strong moved about inside, their white suits giving them all the appearance of beekeepers at work.

Pressing his lips together tightly, Pavel nodded in approval. He passed one last gaze over the room, taking in what would soon be making its way to North America, before turning to the left and heading toward the corner. Around him he could hear the whine of forklifts speeding about, could smell their burnt rubber in the air.

His gait slow and easy, Pavel walked past a string of offices extended out from the wall. Many had glass fronts lining them, their doors standing open as he passed, most with their lights off. Inside was the standard office fare of desks and tables, one housing snack and soda machines, a card table for workers taking a break.

Pavel made his way by each of them to the far corner, toward a solid metal door surrounded on either side by concrete blocks painted white. He ignored any stares that fell on his back from the workers outside, entering the room and shutting the door behind him.

A single switch on the wall brought a candescent light fixture above to life, and a filmy yellow glow filled the space. Otherwise there was not a single thing in the room, its walls natural gray block, its floor polished concrete. The floor slanted inward from each side, culminating in a steel drain cap. Despite being clean and dry, the air inside was damp and smelled of mildew.

Tilting his torso to the side, Pavel let Viktor fall from his shoulder, and his body landed with a slap against the smooth floor.

The decision had been Sergey's, though Pavel had not fought him on it. Traditionally the room had been used for interrogations, occasionally to make an example of a wayward employee. In a previous life it had been used for storing harsh manufacturing chemicals, but the concrete walls worked just as well for muffling the screams of anybody inside.

Given the state Viktor was in, and what he had done, they stood in agreement that he was best served by a night or more in the room to think things through. While he was there, Sergey would consider the proper thing to do with him, even suggesting creating a new post for him somewhere in Siberia.

Pavel had thought more along the lines of the bottom of the Baltic Sea, though he kept the thought to himself.

The order had been to deliver Viktor to the storage room, but to do no further damage. As much as he wanted to drive his boot into Viktor's face, ribs, groin, he fought back the urge, leaving him lying on his side in the middle of the floor and turning the lights out as he went. His next destination was to be Kiev, and he would have ample opportunity to let out his rage once there.

He caught a few men quickly looking away as he emerged, and the rubberneckers hurried back to their work at the sight of him. The glower remained in place as he headed back toward the door, his phone vibrating against his hip halfway there.

It took a moment for his massive hands to fish the implement from his pants. He lifted the device to his face and responded without looking at the screen. Sergey was the only person who ever called him, so there was no question who it would be.

"Yeah, sir?" Pavel asked, pressing his left index finger into his free ear to block out the whine of tires on concrete behind him. Over the line he could hear heavy panting followed by the sound of a woman screaming. He couldn't be sure, but it sounded a lot like Anya, terror in her tone.

Extending his pace to great strides, Pavel covered the last of the floor to the door and pushed his way outside, and the silence of the night flooded in around him. He kept his finger jammed into his left ear and pressed the phone down hard with his right, straining for any sound on the opposite side.

"Yeah?" he repeated, adrenaline starting to course through him.

"Pavel," Sergey said between ragged gasps, his voice weak. "He's here."

Chapter Forty-One

Knock and announce. It was a maxim drilled into us when working with the DEA, meaning that before we ever entered any private home we were to knock three times and announce who we were prior to going inside. One of the most basic tenets of American law enforcement, not knocking and announcing our identities was right up there with failing to read a suspect their Miranda rights for the fastest ways to get a case thrown out of court.

The rules when working internationally were a bit different. Not entirely, but with many, many shades of gray. That was why from day one, if there was even the slightest chance that a perpetrator would ever end up in a United States courtroom, we were sure to knock and announce.

Working against five years of muscle memory, I blew through the front door of the Blok home without doing either. If someone wanted to nitpick, an argument could be made that I did both by driving the heel of my shoe through the wood pane alongside the doorknob, sending the front door hurtling backward, shards of wood spraying up around me.

I was not law enforcement, and there was no way in hell these people would ever make it to see a courtroom.

A Mark 23 held in either hand, I let the momentum of the kick carry me inside, my arms extended, my silenced weapons adding another ten inches to both. The door opened into a wide front foyer, hardwood flooring extending out in every direction. To my right was a sitting room that looked to be barely touched, the furniture resembling something found in the sixties. On the left was a formal dining room, table settings and a centerpiece all in place, the overhead lights off.

"Excuse me, sir, can I—" an older man in a smoking jacket and slacks asked, appearing from the middle hallway and walking toward me.

I cut him off midsentence; a pair of shots, one from each gun, stopped him midstride. A low flash of light barked out of each on command, the recoil minimal in my hands. One bullet struck him in the left half of his chest, the other tore a hole between his eyes. His body fell straight back where he stood, blood pooling behind his head.

Guns still stretched out in front of me, I stepped past his body, avoiding the widening sanguineous circle beneath him, and proceeded into the front hallway. The wood floor creaked slightly as I went. Long shadows moved over everything. Only a few lights were still on within the house.

The hallway ended in an expansive kitchen, a modernized affair with stainless steel appliances and a palatial refrigerator masked to look like cabinetry. A quick check found the place to be empty, the rich smells of food hanging in the air. Dinner was not far past.

I ignored the scent and continued moving through the house, every sense on high alert, my body rigid, moving one cautious step at a time. While my shots had been muffled, there was no way Blok hadn't heard me come through the front door. From the outside the only visible lights were on upstairs, meaning he was most likely holed up there, waiting for me to come to him.

So be it.

Sliding the gun in my left hand back into the waistband of my slacks, I grabbed a cast iron skillet from atop the cold stove top and carried it with me. Again I stepped over the remains of the butler lying in the hall, the front of his coat now slick and stained with dark blood, the circle beneath him thick and shiny.

One step at a time I ascended the staircase, my back to the wall, gun in one hand, pan in the other. I held the cast-iron cookware close to my head to help shield me from any gunfire, the thick metal more than capable of stopping most small-arms fire. An inch at a time I rose upward, pausing halfway up and listening.

Somewhere above me, the smallest creak of a floorboard sounded. My heartbeat evened out and my breathing receded to completely normal, my body tense but focused, feeding on the adrenaline I had starved it of all these years.

Hefting the pan in my left hand, I lowered it by my side and tossed it high, aiming for the middle of the top landing. I paused a split second before hurtling my body upward after it, the matte-black object hitting the second floor just before I did.

Four shots rang out in rapid succession as it got there, two of them striking iron, and yellow and orange sparks flashed in the darkness. They slammed into the pan from the right; the shooter was standing to that side, firing a handgun.

My mind managed to compute all that information as I leapt over the last few stairs and landed on my shoulder, gun trained out with my right hand, left cupping it for support. Without bothering to wait for suspect confirmation I squeezed off three quick shots, muzzle flashes igniting in front of me.

My target was a pudgy older man dressed in a maroon track suit; his shaved head made it almost impossible to decipher a definite age. The first shot whizzed past him, shattering the window at the end of the hallway. Glass exploded out into the night air, and a gust of cold wind rushed in behind it.

The second bullet struck him in the right shoulder, and his upper body twisted to the side. His gun jerked at an angle as he did so, squeezing off another round that took a chunk of plaster from the wall. Blood spurted from his wound, spraying against the hardwood floor, blending in with the dark red of his suit.

My third shot struck him in the thigh, pitching his body forward at the waist. A throaty moan slid from him as he doubled over and pressed his free hand against the wound. Blood bubbled up between his fingers, pulsing forward in bright red stripes, spilling between his digits, and streaking the shiny floor beneath him.

Artery shot.

Once more he fired an errant round into the wall before retreating into the room on his right, dragging his leg behind him, moving slowly. A trail of blood smeared the floor as he went.

Leaving the cast-iron skillet where it lay, I pulled myself to a standing position and drew the second Mark from my waistband. If anybody else was in the house that could fire a weapon, the odds were they would have already shown themselves, long before letting the old man himself take two direct hits.

Many times before, I had heard the expression that someone sick with bloodlust was seeing red. Around me, the hallway downstairs, the floor in front of me, were both painted red. The metallic smell of blood hung in the air.

Even still, what I saw wasn't red. It was black. Making Sergey Blok bleed was not enough, would never be enough, not for me or the memory of my family.

He would feel my pain, and he would die, just as they had.

I reached the door he had passed through in just a few quick seconds. The trail of blood beside me was even heavier than I thought, thick spatters dotting the floor. With a quick breath I spun out on the floor, both guns in front of me, my knees sliding across the slick boards.

Standing across from me was a woman in her sixties, a pink housecoat on over flannel pajamas, knit stockings on her feet. She stood ten feet back from the door, her husband's gun held in both hands in front of her.

The moment I appeared around the base of the door the gun flashed twice, two harsh barks in quick succession. She wasn't ready for me to be so low to the floor, both shots whizzing by above me.

My first shot caught her square in the chest. The beginning of a scream was cut off halfway through, the air wheezing out of her. The gun fell from her hands as she wobbled in place, clutching her chest, the light blinking out of her eyes.

Taking my feet I kept one gun pointed in her direction and stepped into the room, my left hand aimed out wide.

Seated behind an expansive desk was a man whom I presumed to be Sergey, his dumpy form slumped into a rolling chair. His right hand rested atop the desk, his fingers slick with blood, trying to operate a .38 revolver. In his left was a wadded-up roll of cloth he pressed into his thigh, most of it soaked through with blood.

He stared at me with defiance in his eyes, the life ebbing from him just as surely as it was his wife. Given the gaping hole through his femoral, I gave him no more than thirty seconds before he was done, too.

"Blok," I said, stepping forward, malevolence dripping from the word.

"Tate," he responded, the same tone in his response.

The fact that he used my given name proved just how little he knew about me. Nobody ever called me Tate, not even the teachers I had in school or my parents growing up. To this man, I was never an adversary, not somebody worthy of respect or fear.

I was nothing more than a potential roadblock, something to be mowed down on his way to getting what he wanted.

"So you know who I am?" I asked.

He stared at me through narrowed eyes, sweat dotting his brow, breaths coming in shallow rasps. A small nod was his response, no words crossing his lips.

Without looking away from him, I fired three times into his wife, the rounds hitting her center mass, tossing her body against the wall before it slid to the floor, bloody streaks behind her.

"Then you know you never should have killed my wife and daughter," I hissed, twisting both arms around to face forward, guns aimed at his chest.

Across from me Blok stared at the bloody remains of his wife, his face a mixture of agony and contempt.

After a long moment he moved his gaze back up to me, a murderous roar sliding out from him. Propping his weight against his bad leg he pushed himself to a standing position, trying to hurtle himself forward at me, his hands pawing for the gun on the desk.

Firing each gun in succession I put a half-dozen rounds into him, starting at his chest and placing the last one right in the middle of his bald head. It entered at an angle, tearing a short trench through the skin before exiting the top of his scalp, slamming into the wall behind him.

His body hung suspended in the air, weightless, motionless, for a long second before falling backward, depositing itself in the chair. His momentum pushed it back several inches across the floor before it came to a stop.

The house was now silent and, except for me, lifeless.

Chapter Forty-Two

Even though Blok and his wife were both dead, I knew they were only the tip of the spear. Somewhere out there was Pavel, along with Viktor and who knew how many others. Those two for certain knew who I was, the rest would probably figure it out eventually.

I decided to help them along, just in case.

I left the Bloks upstairs in the office, their blood striping the floors and walls. There was no need to arrange their bodies in any particular manner, no point in exerting the effort to put them on display. In an hour or so, it wouldn't matter anyway.

Keeping both guns in hand, I made my way back down through the house, not bothering to mask my noise. Anybody even close to the place would have heard the shots fired from Sergey and his wife, would see the front door sagging open. If they were brave enough to venture inside for a look, they would see the butler lying in the middle hallway, his unblinking eyes staring up at the ceiling.

Stepping over him, I made my way back into the kitchen and dug through the cupboards below the counter, coming up with a gallon jug of cooking oil and a bag of flour. I returned the Mark 23s to the small of my back and ditched the jacket, sliding it down over my shoulder and leaving it on the kitchen floor.

The button-down shirt I stripped off as well, twisting it into an elongated bundle, the finished product looking like a homemade cigarette two feet in length. I jammed the tail end of it under the grate on the stove and turned the heat on high. A blue-hot flame sparked to life beneath it. A few moments later the material caught, the smell of burnt cotton filling the space.

Bright orange flames licked upward behind me as I started with the oil, dribbling some on the bottom of the shirt, splashing the remainder around the kitchen. As more of the shirt burned, the light grew stronger, illuminating the walls around me. Photographs of Blok and his family stared down as I deposited the last of the oil throughout the kitchen, leaving the empty jug on the floor by my jacket.

Grabbing up the flour in one hand I trailed an uneven path of the flammable white powder behind me, sprinkling it down the front hallway, tossing a thin layer on the butler, throwing large handfuls into the parlor and dining room to either side.

In my wake, the oil caught with a thunderous whoosh, heat and light both kicking up fast. Flour hung in the air like white smoke, mixing with the real thing now funneling out of the kitchen, and visibility was dropping by the second. The mixed scents filled my nostrils as I opened the front door and stepped outside, bits of white dotting my slacks and black compression shirt. My skin shone with perspiration, the end result of the extra clothes, adrenaline, fire.

The front door still stood gaping wide as I stepped out into the night, found my briefcase still resting where I'd left it just minutes before. Already my mind was moving on to the next step, knowing that time was limited before the fire was called in and authorities found the scene. With luck the blaze would be burning strong enough by then to keep everybody back, the police having to wait until at least morning before pilfering through and finding the charred remains of three people inside.

Armed with only a rough outline of the streets nearby, I needed to put as much space between myself and the house as possible. The scent of smoke lingering on me was too strong to allow for public transportation, my only hope to catch another cab in a public area, allow it to carry me to my next stop.

Briefcase in hand, I made it three steps down the path before I saw it, my pace slowing to an abrupt halt. My supercharged system somehow managed to push out a bit more adrenaline, my heart rate once more rising. In a slow, exaggerated movement, I raised the briefcase to shoulder height beside me and released it, the black leather valise landing silently in the grass.

Standing before me, his hulking figure just inches inside the gate, blocking my exit, was Pavel. Behind him a black sedan sat idling on the curb, its lights off, a puff of exhaust rising from the tailpipe.

"Hawk," he said, his voice a deep rumble that sounded more like a growl.

As I had suspected all along, he was the one in the organization to be reckoned with. The fact that he knew and employed my real name proved he had done his homework. His role was as an enforcer for the Bloks, one he took quite seriously. Under different circumstances I would consider him a worthy adversary.

Those times were long in the past, though.

"Pavel," I said, letting him see the silenced Mark 23 in my right hand.

Behind me I could sense the fire was catching on, tearing its way through the house. The sound of wood snapping carried out into the night, hungry flames devouring the bait I left for them, expanding into the rest of the home. Smoke began to pour out, the smell strong, acrid. Shadows and disparate colors danced across the front lawn, bathing everything in multiple hues.

Pavel motioned with his chin toward the house. "Sergey? Anya?"

"And the butler, too," I said, nodding.

His mouth twisted into a sneer, his eyebrows lowering a fraction of an inch, bunching together above the bridge of his nose. "He was shit. They were family."

"So were my wife and daughter," I replied.

I had no interest in standing on the front lawn having an epic back-and-forth with him. As much as this man needed to die, I had no interest in becoming a martyr in doing so. The clock was ticking, and the Russian police weren't far away.

Sensing my train of thought, Pavel reached behind him and removed a handgun from the small of his back. He dangled it in front of him before tossing it into the yard, then reached back again and pulled out a pair of Russian shashkas, the curved blades almost two feet in length. He swung them back and forth across his wide body, the muscles in his arm reacting to the movement like corded steel, the striations obvious in his forearms, before tossing one my way. It skidded across the concrete with a spark, coming to a stop just inches from my toes.

"Why don't you put down that gun and we settle this like men?" he asked, his mouth and eyes both twisting up in a look that bordered on glee.

Even on my best day, physically I was no match for this man. In most situations, my training was enough to carry me through. Ninety-eight percent of the people I encountered were used to relying on natural acumen, their size, strength, to get them through. When pitted against such opponents, I was almost assured victory.

In a case like this, though, where both men were similarly trained, poised, physical attributes made the difference. Not who connected the most punches, but who did the most damage while doing so. In that regard, it was obvious Pavel was without equal.

What he didn't realize, though, was I had no intention of a fair fight.

I didn't say a word, just raised my weapon and fired twice, one to each of his knees. The firelight behind me muted out the muzzle flashes as I stepped forward toward him, guns extended. He wavered in place for just a moment before his bulk became too much to support, his knees folding in on themselves. He fell straight forward onto them, slamming down onto the concrete, the sound of bone splintering reaching my ears as he hit hard.

Even if I were to walk away and not look back, he would never be right again. The damage to his joints was too great, his size too immense, to ever allow them to recover. From where I stood I could see the lower halves of his legs jutting out at odd angles, blood seeping through his pants and onto the concrete.

To his credit he never made a sound, masking the pain he was in as he stared up at me, malevolence on his face. "Coward," he spat at me, watching me grow closer, weapon in hand, the second shashka still lying where he tossed it.

I put a third shot into his right wrist without responding, one final bark of the gun that twisted his body to the side, bright red blood coursing onto his pale skin. His hand flopped open on impact, useless, as the shashka fell from it, blade clattering against the ground. For a moment he started to reach across his body with his left hand before abandoning the idea, accepting his fate.

There were no illusions on my part. This wasn't part of some elaborate scene I had planned out in my head, flying across the world, dealing retribution to those that deserved it. My scheme was never to be facing down the man who killed my family and best him in a hand-to-hand duel, with a burning building providing the backdrop.

People who thought real life worked that way watched too many movies. My reason for coming, my *only* reason for coming, was for blood. Years of trying to suppress what had happened had done nothing to quell the hatred inside of me. It had eaten me up every day, kept me from falling asleep, forced me to hide in the mountains, ashamed of what had happened, afraid of what I would become if I ever allowed myself to confront those feelings.

No more. Never again would I avoid the bathroom mirror in the morning or fear going to bed at night. For five years I had hidden, fearful of what I'd become. In doing so, I had grown ashamed of what I became. I had never sought this out, had never wanted Lita to show up on my doorstep and solicit my services, but she had and now here I was.

I was going to finish it.

"I tell you what a coward is," I said, sliding the shashka away from him with the toe of my shoe, gun trained on him the entire time. "A coward is someone who sneaks out into the desert and kills a woman and a little girl in cold blood. A coward is someone that is so afraid of a man he's never met, he'll target his family."

I tucked the gun into the small of my back alongside its companion and hefted the sword from the ground, holding its gleaming steel blade up so the burning Blok home danced across it. Beside me I could hear Pavel muttering, his words thick and low, monosyllabic swears spit out in Russian.

Something deep within told me he hadn't given my family the benefit of a few last words. I'd be damned if I afforded them to him.

"You wanted to fight like men, you should have found me five years ago," I said, whipping the blade across me, the honed edge of it finding the base of his skull, tearing through it without opposition.

Chapter Forty-Three

The lo mein noodles were a little chewy, the chunks of carrot and broccoli a bit like rubber. In the bottom of the carton, pools of sauce had congealed into gelatinous blobs, clinging to pieces of chicken, coating the sides of the paper container.

The late lunch was less than ideal for Mia Diaz, the only thing she could find after ten minutes of rummaging through the break room that wasn't clearly labeled with somebody else's name. Given that the office was over twenty miles from the closest Chinese restaurant, the origin of the carton or the date it arrived were both mysteries, neither of which she was especially keen on deciphering at the moment.

Her time at the office had started more than two full days ago. The first night had been spent organizing and conducting a raid that proved to be an exercise in securing a vacant home. The second was spent manning her desk, waiting for lab analyses, hoping for something concrete to come back that she could use to pin down the Bloks.

In the time since, she had burned through both changes of clothes she kept on hand and even gone against her usual self-imposed rule to stay far away from the community cots, catching a total of four hours in the preceding two days. She was now to the point in her body cycle where every flat surface presented itself as a satisfactory place to stretch out for a nap, every food item that wasn't marked toxic seemed fine for consumption.

Diaz had just forked a hefty clump of noodles into her mouth, slurping up the uneven ends of them, as the fast-becoming-familiar scent of herbal tea greeted her nostrils. Even in her near delirium, shoveling down week-old Chinese food, the scent turned her stomach, bringing a bit of moisture to her eyes.

"I wondered what that smell was," Hutch said in greeting, pushing himself inside the door and coming to a stop, his shoulder leaning against the frame. He peered over at the carton and said, "Szechuan Garden, never heard of it. New around here?"

Diaz held up a finger for him to pause and chomped down on the mouthful with vigorous aplomb, swallowing everything half chewed. It caught in her windpipe and landed in her stomach with a mighty splat, a small burp rolling up and out of her in reaction. She covered her mouth with a fist and waited until her stomach settled before lowering her fork and leaning back in her chair.

"Oh, excuse me," she said. "I actually have no idea. I saw the carton in the fridge and claimed it as my own."

"Ah," Hutch said, rocking his head back in understanding, raising his mug to his lips. "The spoils of war."

A smirk shoved the left half of Diaz's mouth up, her head tilting back with it. "Something like that. And I hardly think a man who walks around drinking that swill has the right to be commenting on smells."

"Touché," Hutch said, raising his eyebrows. "Anything new coming in from the tech guys?"

"No," Diaz replied. "Lots of residue, lots of fingerprints, but nothing substantial enough to make a compelling case yet."

"That's what I figured," Hutch said, nodding. "That place was clean by the time we got there the other night."

Diaz nodded, a sick feeling rising in her stomach. His assessment, his word choice, both fit perfectly. The place was clean by the time they had arrived, almost too much so. The scene had practically been scrubbed in anticipation of their arrival.

Across from her, a forlorn smile crossed Hutch's face as he looked down at the mug with a face that bordered on longing. "Yes, I will miss this when I'm gone. I've tried having some shipped into D.C., but it just isn't the same."

Fingers laced atop her stomach, Diaz raised her eyebrows at him. "Going somewhere?"

Hutch kept his attention down on his mug a long moment before looking up, his eyes widening just a bit. "Yeah, I was just stopping by to let you know. The word has come down from on high. It seems things are slowing down here, so my presence has been requested back in the capital."

Diaz nodded, the information clicking with what she'd been wondering for the better part of a day now. While the case was certainly far-reaching, it wasn't anything over and above a handful of other things the DEA was working on at various times. While he did have some personal background involved, it seemed unusual for a ranking bureaucrat to spend so much time in the field.

"The only reason I've stayed this long was hoping Hawk would turn up," Hutch said. "This began as a bit of a personal favor to him, after all."

There was momentary pause, Diaz getting the impression it was her turn to interject. Unsure what to add, she simply said, "Yeah, he didn't really seem like the kind to up and disappear like that."

"Ha!" Hutch said, shaking his head, his face mirthful, as if her comment was a joke. "Not counting those five years he spent in the mountains, you mean?"

A forced smile came to Diaz's face. Having heard the breadth of Hawk's story, she had a hard time thinking of his time alone in Montana as disappearing, but fought down the urge to say just that.

"Yeah, besides that, obviously."

"Nobody knows whereabouts he come from and it don't seem to matter much. He was a young man and ghostly stories about the tall hills didn't scare him none," Hutch waxed, his attention aimed on the opposite wall.

The words themselves made no sense to Diaz, though she sensed it was another movie quote she wasn't meant to understand. She made no attempt to feign knowing, instead sitting quietly, her stolen lunch on the desk before her, watching Hutch stare off at nothing.

After a moment he snapped himself awake, shook his head, and looked back to her. "I don't suppose you've heard from him, have you?"

Diaz met his gaze for a long moment before twisting her head from side to side, her expression neutral. "Not since he told me we had things under control and walked out of the base two nights ago."

The two sat in silence nearly a full minute, neither emoting anything at all, before Hutch drew in a deep breath. "Well, he'll turn up somewhere eventually again, I suppose." He took in the last of his tea and lowered the mug to his side, a few stray droplets dripping to the floor by his feet. "Anyway, it was a pleasure working with you again, Diaz. Hope to see you soon."

He stepped forward and extended a hand across the desk, which Diaz stood and met.

"You too, sir. I look forward to it."

Chapter Forty-Four

Nabbing the sedan from Pavel was a stroke of pure luck. By the time I dispatched the brute, I was certain the clock was running low. Most of the lower level of the house was already awash in flames. Once I collected the briefcase and climbed into the idling car there weren't yet sirens in the distance or flashing lights refracting off the clouds above, but I was reasonably certain they weren't far off.

Even in the quietest of neighborhoods, people will let things go only so far. They might not react to hearing some strange noises, especially if they were at all familiar with who the Bloks really were, but there was no way they would sit on the sidelines and let a house fire consume them as well.

Somebody had made the call, of that much I was certain.

Having the getaway ride sitting on the corner, keys in the ignition, engine already warm and idling, made things much easier. Being in a country where the steering wheel was on the left and people drove on the right side of the road helped, too; my only jobs were to toss the briefcase and shoulder bag onto the passenger seat, turn the thermostat from cold to cool, and drive off into the night.

I made a point to get off their street as fast as possible, then work my way back to a major thoroughfare and put a wide chunk of ground between us.

After the confrontation with Pavel, I had to force my nerves to remain even. There was no way I was going to draw them back all the way to calm, not with every ending in my body on fire, my heartbeat hammering along at an absurd pace.

No less than a handful of thoughts fought for the top position in my mind, each as powerful as the others around it. The first, and most obvious, was the fact that I had just dispatched the men responsible for the deaths of my family. It had been a long time coming, a journey addled by fear and uncertainty, but in the end it had been easier than anticipated. I'd escaped without much more than some scratches, showing up in the middle of the night, taking them where they least expected it, finding them where they felt the most secure.

I might not have been proud of the things I'd done, but I certainly wasn't ashamed, either. It wasn't a fight I had started, but had made sure to damn well finish.

The second thing that I had to keep reminding myself was that I was now driving in a car registered to none other than Sergey Blok. Should the police notice it missing, or somebody put out a search for it thinking he might not have been home when the fire started, I was in trouble. Dressed in black, spotted with flour, streaked with Pavel's blood, there was no scenario in which I wouldn't be hauled straight into lockup and never heard from again. I had to put distance between myself and the fire, but I also had to get to my next location.

The final thing, the part I needed to remind myself of more than any other, was the fact that I wasn't done yet. As much as I wanted to pound on the steering wheel, turn up the radio, raise my head toward the heavens and scream until my throat was hoarse, I couldn't. I needed to keep a level head.

I needed to remember that I wasn't finished until Blok's life's work was annihilated, just the same as he had done to mine.

Reaching across the middle console, I twisted the combination locks on the case to matching 4-5-1s and flipped open the top. The few items inside had jostled themselves around a bit in the previous hour, but everything appeared intact, ready to play their part.

The first item to come out was the phone, my left hand draped over the steering wheel, my right working the controls on the device. While intermittently switching my attention between the road and the mobile, I pulled up the one stored number inside and pressed Send.

"It's late," X said, his voice more annoyed than tired.

I ignored the statement completely. Instead I rattled off the second address Pally had given me from memory, going slow enough he could record it, fast enough not to insult his intelligence.

X remained silent until I was done before asking, "Okay, what's there?"

"Your ticket out of Russia," I said, skimping over the details because at the moment I had none. Given everything Pally had told me about the financial transactions originating there and the dimensions of the former manufacturing warehouse, I was more than certain it was the production hub for the drug that was about to enter North America.

Even if the Krokodil itself wasn't made there, it could be easily inferred that something inside would tell them where to find it.

"Yeah?" X asked, the annoyance gone, a twinge of excitement creeping in.

"Give me thirty minutes to clear the scene," I said, "then it's all yours. All I ask is when you become a rock star with the administration, you give some credit to SAC Mia Diaz in California."

"Mia Diaz," X sounded out slowly, no doubt recording the name alongside the address.

"You both helped me when you didn't have to. Thank you."

This time it was his turn to ignore a statement, brushing it aside without acknowledgment. "I'll see you soon, all right?"

"See you soon," I responded, flipping the phone shut and tossing it into the open briefcase beside me.

Squeezing the wheel with both hands, I followed the road I was on back through town, headed toward the warehouse. I let the scene at Blok's fade from memory, the familiar anger buried within rising to the surface, ready to do what I must to finish the job.

Taking up the two Mark 23s from the seat beside me I laid them across my thighs, popping the half-used magazines and changing them out for fresh. Combined, that gave me twenty-four bullets, plus the knife in my pocket, to take on whatever waited inside.

I would think it more than enough firepower for a manufacturing facility in the middle of the night, but if not, at least I had taken care of the ones that mattered before meeting my end.

Recalling the directions Pally had drilled into me, aided by hours on the train to recite them over and over again, I pulled off the main road onto a darkened side street demarcated by a series of Russian characters starting with a *K* and ending in *Y*. I followed it for almost a mile, watching as a small residential clump slid by behind me and the land to either side opened up, trees and houses giving way to barren concrete lots.

The warehouse I was looking for was positioned at the very end of the road, the only structure with any lights on. Just a single overhead lamp was visible in the parking lot outside, a smattering of vehicles parked beneath it. Most of the enormous building was shrouded in darkness, but fluorescent bulbs were apparent through a row of frosted glass encasing the top.

Again my breathing and heart rate leveled out as I set my gaze on the building, following the road as it wound toward it, pulling to a stop just beyond the reach of the overhead lights. I killed the front lamps on the car and left the engine idling, assessing the situation before me.

From where I sat, the only clear point of entry was a set of glass double doors positioned directly in the middle of the building. In total the expansive structure looked to stretch a few hundred yards long. Massive shipping doors on either end were pulled shut, looking like they had not been used in some time.

The windows along the top of the building were almost thirty feet off the ground, too high for entry under optimal conditions, which I was far from. I was armed, but otherwise I had nothing of real use, no cavalry coming for another twenty-eight minutes. My goal was to be long gone before they arrived, bypassing any extended awkward questioning, letting X and Diaz take the credit from afar.

Three days ago I had been granted Special Consultant status, though my guess was that had since been rescinded.

Without seeing the back side of the building, it was a fairly reasonable guess that my best, and probably only, real point of gaining access was the set of doors staring back at me, just over two hundred yards away. In an ideal world I would have been able to gain entry from a point that provided me some modicum of cover, allowing me to scope out what I was walking into.

If the last years had taught me anything, though, there was no such thing as an ideal world.

One at a time I moved the guns from my thighs to the briefcase, wedging them in place. Squeezing the wheel tight in both hands, I rolled my wrists back and forth twice. Bits of leather shaved off, dotting the front of my pants.

I paused just long enough for one last deep breath before dropping the gear shift into drive, my foot slamming the accelerator toward the floor.

Chapter Forty-Five

The nose of the sedan burst through the first set of double doors, their metal casings twisting away over the front of the car and shearing back along the sides. Shards of glass cascaded around the vehicle as if raining down on the roof, coating the front windshield. I could hear them pinging against the steel body, bouncing off the gleaming black paint, flying out behind me in a misshapen rooster tail.

A moment later the nose slammed into a second set of doors, the barrier flying backward, tearing away whole and sliding across the floor, the jagged metal of their hinges screeching against the concrete. I was unprepared for the second blast, and my head slammed forward against the wheel, my own knuckle catching me just above the left eye. Stars erupted in front of my vision as warmth dripped down over my face, the salty, metallic taste of blood seeping between my lips.

Halfway into the room I regained my bearings and slammed on the brakes. The tires squealed as I came to a stop, and the smell of burned rubber trailed behind me. I grabbed up the guns from the seat beside me and stepped out, weapons raised at shoulder height, my head swiveling from to side.

On either end of the enormous space I could see boxes and drums of what I assumed to be pre- and post-product, both sides stacked high, row after row aligned with neat precision. If my hunch was right, it would be more than enough to get X any post he wanted, keep the streets of California safer for at least a little longer.

In front of me, heavy plastic sheeting hung from the ceiling, the same sort of makeshift sterile environment I'd seen many times before. On the opposite side of it I could see lab equipment and conveyor belts, two handfuls of people in white protective gear all staring back at me, none of them moving.

Surprise was on my side. It was time to move.

I had no compassion for these people; no offering them quarter, no standing guard over them until backup arrived. These people, the product they created, were the reason my family was dead. It was the reason countless others had had their lives ruined, through fallen loved ones and harsh addictions. Even if these people weren't the ones pulling the trigger, they were what called for men like Pavel.

It was an ugly, vicious system, one they were all guilty of participating in. If I let a single one of them walk away, they would be back on the street within a year, if not sooner. That same vile substance that was stacked high beside me would find its way to some other city, would be the cause of some other law enforcement agent's downfall.

The mere thought of it brought bile to the back of my throat, the same familiar rage surfacing within me.

Heavy or not, the plastic sheeting was no match for the .45-caliber bullets my guns spat, one after another in rapid succession. I started with four rounds from each. Five people fell to the floor in order, red blotches blooming over their white suits. On impact each one melted to the floor, the others standing in complete shock at what was happening, watching without moving.

I picked off each of the people standing directly in front of me before stepping forward, a jagged string of bullet holes scattered several feet wide across the plastic. Shoving the gun from my right hand into the back of my pants, I slid the Garra out and popped the blade release, swiping a vicious slash, connecting the bullet holes in an uneven line.

The sheeting fell to the floor, the material slapping against the concrete as it landed in a heap. For the first time people inside began to scurry away from me, the protective covers on their shoes making them slip and fall, a tangle of shapeless white bodies trying in vain to flee.

Using my left hand, I began firing again, bullets striping the opposite side of the space. Men writhed in midair, their bodies jerking in ugly spasms, their arms flailing above their heads.

I jammed the knife in my right hand into a finished block of Krokodil waiting on the conveyor belt to be loaded, leaving the handle sticking up at a ninety-degree angle, and pulled the second gun out again.

A small piece of me was almost disappointed by the fact that not one of the men inside stood their ground. Nobody drew a weapon and tried to return fire, or even attempted to throw a chunk of their precious product at me in an effort to slow me down. Instead they all filed toward the back corner, trying to free themselves of their plastic prison, their sterile attire making it impossible for them to gain purchase and move away fast enough.

By the time I reached the far end of the homemade lab, a litany of bodies lay in my wake. Blood spatter coated the polished concrete floor, dripping from open wounds, seeping into the powder piled everywhere.

Leaving the bodies untouched I passed through the flaps comprising a narrow doorway at the back end of the space. A dull throbbing settled in behind my left eye, a trickle of blood continuing to drip down my face. I could feel the adrenaline ebbing within me, knowing I needed to finish the job and move on fast.

A series of black skid marks striped the floor outside the plastic, the telltale signs of forklifts at work. Swinging my gaze in a wide arc I spotted two of them parked side by side in the corner, silent, no operators nearby.

My arms hung at a forty-five-degree angle from my shoulders, the barrels of the guns pointed at the floor, their elongated noses extending almost to my knees. The thumping in my head grew in intensity as my heart rate increased; my shoulders bunched up tightly as I walked heel-to-toe, watching for any sign of movement.

There was not a single sound as I walked back the length of the lab, past dozens of yards of clear plastic, past my own makeshift door, which was now an uneven, gaping hole. One quick glance inside told me that nobody had survived the first purge. Their bodies remained where they'd fallen, their positions as misshapen as the moment they'd been hit.

Sweat bathed my skin beneath the heavy knit shirt and slacks, and a sheen of moisture was visible on the backs of my hands. Droplets worked their way down my forehead and mixed with the blood as I inched forward. The taste of salt was heavy on my lips, stinging my eyes.

I ignored each of these things. My attention settled instead on a string of offices embedded in the left half of the warehouse, opposite of the direction I had taken after crashing through the front door. Added as an afterthought to the larger structure, they were no more than eight or nine feet tall, an even, flat ceiling extended across the length of them.

Glass windows lined the entire expanse; blinds had been left open along most of them, doors gaping as well. In my mind I thought back to the transactions Pally had tracked across the globe, most likely originating in these rooms, actions performed by pencil pushers in shirtsleeves working nine to five, now long gone for the day.

To most of the offices I gave no more than a passing acknowledgment. The probability of anybody being inside them was negligible, more likely nonexistent. Illicit drug trade or not, a warehouse is a warehouse. The white-collar workers go home at quitting time, but the real muscle of the operation is on hand all night long.

Bypassing the dark and shuttered windows, I set my course for the dull glow of neon red extending from the only door with a light on in the place. It showed itself by protruding an uneven trapezoid out into the warehouse; its sides were formed by the edges of the door, and its bottom extended outward before fading away at some indeterminate point.

I'd been on enough worksites the world over to know the telltale indicators of a soda machine when I saw one. Judging by the forklifts sitting idle on the opposite side of the building, their operators had either cut out a side door or were hunkered down inside this room. If they were gone, I didn't have the time or the inclination to chase them around their home city in the dark. If not, they were soon to meet the same end as their coworkers.

Raising the guns from hanging at an angle to almost parallel to the floor, I circled wide toward the break room door and entered directly through it, my silhouette framed by the doorway. There was no point in trying to hide myself or slide in around the side. If anybody was waiting inside with a weapon, they would have opened fire by now.

Weapons raised, I entered to find a rectangular room a little longer than it was wide. A soda machine rested against the back wall, a vending machine stocked with candies and chips beside it. Counters extended out on either side, various odds and ends strewn about.

Plastic silverware, napkins, condiment packets.

The remainder of the room was filled with round tables with silver bases, each surrounded by brown plastic chairs with slits in the backs. The room was empty.

A sigh passed over my lips as my guns dipped a bit lower. I turned and walked back out into the warehouse, then stopped just past the edge of the room, watching. Nothing throughout the entire space moved; the competing scents of fertilizer, sawdust, ammonia in the air, and a hint of blood laced in around the edges.

Curling my arms toward the base of my spine, I began to stow my weapons when a low sound drew my attention to the left. Even, persistent, barely audible but muffled. Keeping the Mark 23s at the ready,

I crouched into a shooter's stance and inched toward the noise, which grew stronger as I went.

It took less than a minute to find the source, a metal door in the far corner of the cavernous room. Painted white, it was set even, with concrete blocks on either side of it colored the same hue. A heavy metal padlock clasped the door shut. Its surface vibrated just slightly, in tune with the banging on the opposite side.

The sound was too loud, too steady, to be caused by anything random. The room looked like a basic storage shed, but something falling over inside would not make the banging noise that now met my ears. Whatever is was was alive, and not pleased with its situation.

For the briefest of moments, I considered leaving whoever was behind the door trapped inside. X and the sweeper team would find them soon enough, having someone alive and breathing they could lean on for information. Depending on how they worked them, a veritable bastion of useful intel could be gleaned.

The more pragmatic, realistic side of me pushed it away just as fast. What was more likely was the guy wouldn't say a word, or if he did, it would be complete shit. They would talk fast, end up demanding immunity, live a nice long time on American taxpayer dollars.

I had no interest in sustaining a man responsible for the death of my family for even a day, let alone the rest of my life.

Bringing the guns together in front of me, I fired a single round from each, sheering the U-ring in the lock off just above the base. The square chunk of steel fell to the floor, smacking to the concrete and leaving a small indentation on impact before tumbling to the side. The top half teetered in place for a moment before falling down behind it, ringing hollow and thin against the floor.

Inside, the banging stopped as the door handle turned, slowly, evenly. When it had gone as far as it could, it stopped. The world was in slow motion as I kept my guns trained ahead of me. Then the door opened.

The first thing out of the room was a plume of stench, urine, sweat, and booze. It passed over me, barely registering with my adrenaline-heightened senses, and was swallowed up by the chilly warehouse.

Behind it followed Viktor Blok.

His hair and face were disheveled, the recognizable visage of a man on the back end of a three-day bender. His clothing, all black, made from silks and cashmere, hung from his lank form, swinging from side to side as he walked forward.

"About damn—" he started before lifting his gaze to see the barrels of twin Mark 23s aimed his way. His eyes and mouth formed congruent circles, and his focus changed from the guns to me.

"You," he said simply, as realization set in, followed quickly by unadulterated fear.

"Me," I replied, squeezing both triggers at once.

PART V

Chapter Forty-Six

The moment I walked out of the warehouse in Vladivostok, my chief concern became invisibility. No longer was I concerned with the Bloks, or the Juarezes, or any other cartel on the planet. In that instant my chief worry became an enemy far more sinister, with a reach that extended beyond anything I'd yet encountered.

The only thing out of X's care package I took with me was the phone, leaving behind the weapons for him to dispose of as he saw fit. There were ways I probably could have gotten rid of them, but on the off chance they were ever found and tied back to what had happened, it might ignite a fiery investigation. That wouldn't do for me, or for DEA interests in Russia, so I left them behind, trusting they would be swept clean, taken care of the way they preferred.

Shoulder bag looped over one arm, I found my way back into town and made it to the train station, catching a return train back across country departing in two hours' time. Using the station bathroom, I cleaned up my face as best I could and pulled on the watch cap, making sure the black wool covered the gash and most of the residual bruising. I wiped away as much of the blood and debris from myself as I could before my ride out of there arrived, finding a private compartment and commandeering it for myself.

Using the strap on my shoulder bag, I tied the compartment door shut and stretched my body out across one of the benches, my legs doubled up, my feet resting against the wall. Folding my arms across my chest, I let the gentle sway of the train lull me into a half sleep, the hours sliding by as I came down off an adrenaline high.

For the first time in a week, I allowed my guard to drop just the tiniest bit. I rested knowing there was nobody left to come after me, not a soul alive who knew where to find me even if they wanted to. I was a ghost, a nameless passenger on a train, a cash fare that could be anybody going anywhere.

The first gray streaks of dawn began to stripe the sky, shining down on the snow-covered peaks to the north, before I stirred from my position. Leaving the tie on the doorknob in place, I made a single call to Pally, asking him to get me home.

The rest I left to him.

He was nothing short of a genius.

The train deposited me near Sheremetyevo a few hours short of noon, providing me plenty of time to catch a cab out to the terminal. By that point Pally had arranged four different itineraries for me, two under my actual name and two under my old alias. Each of the possible routes departed within an hour of each other, piecing together random trips circumventing the globe, all depositing me back on American soil late the next day.

Using the last of my rubles I purchased a plain black T-shirt from an airport gift shop and a red hooded sweatshirt, letters stretched vertically down the left side of it in support of a sports team I had never heard of. Opting to keep the watch cap, I deposited my polypropylene gear in a bathroom stall and checked in for my flight, choosing an option that sent me through Berlin, London, and finally landed in New York City.

Upon arriving at LaGuardia International, I caught a shuttle to a rental car counter and took out a Dodge Charger on my alias's ID.

That was six days ago.

Not even two weeks had passed since the last time I sat on Hutch's porch, though a great deal had changed. The last of the fall leaves had fallen from the trees, their orange-and-gold tones now turned to brown, and were piled along the curbs, ready to be sacked up and hauled away. In their stead were barren branches, gray fingers clawing against a slate-colored sky, rattling with every gust of breeze.

The temperature outside had dropped another ten degrees, forcing the casual outdoorsmen inside for the winter, leaving only a handful of hard-core types to troll the streets alone, bundled in wool and flannel. None of them seemed to notice me as I sat and waited, the toes of my shoes pushing the swing back and forth a few inches at a time, my hands balled into the pockets of my coat, a small red cooler on the ground by my feet.

A year ago at this time I was back in Montana, putting the last touches on things before winter set in. Firewood to be stacked, a freezer to be filled, plumbing to be checked over for breaks in the line.

Now here I sat, swinging on a porch outside of Washington, D.C., every last one of those chores still needing to be tended to. If I didn't get to them soon, there was little chance I would make it through the winter unscathed, though that was a concern that didn't seem to bother me.

No longer was it so imperative for me to remain out of sight, hiding until the last possible minute from the world before emerging, doing just enough to make a living before going back into hibernation for the winter. In the past week a great many of the demons I had carried with me for so long had departed, drifting away in the night, my eyes opening to a world that seemed clearer, lighter, than the one I'd known before.

I had only one last item I needed to tend to before I could truly be at ease, and it was of far greater importance than any amount of firewood would ever be.

At half past six, a pair of headlights made their way down the street, just as they had a few weeks before. Once again they paused by the street at seeing my rental sitting there. Then the car eased into the driveway and stopped halfway down it, the headlights casting a bright glow over the front of the house and illuminating my profile.

There was no attempt on my part to hide my face, nor did I make any effort to turn and stare at him, to wave and let him know it was me and everything was okay. After a moment the lights blinked out and the engine turned off; the car's hot inner workings hissed in the cold night air, and an occasional pop was audible. I remained seated where I was as Hutch opened the door and stepped out, his wingtip shoes clicking against the sidewalk.

He'd added an overcoat to the ensemble he wore before, a long beige number with the collar flipped up around his neck that ended just past his ears. He trudged forward with his hands shoved into the pockets and stopped at the foot of the stairs, taking me in.

"You've done well to keep so much hair, when so many's after it."

A smile crept across my features as he took the stairs one at a time and walked forward, sliding down into the chair beside me.

"Please tell me that cooler doesn't have the same thing in it you brought me last time."

A snort jerked my head backward as I stared out at the silent neighborhood, remembering the desiccating hands of Mateo Perez and Lita Haney I'd showed up with last time. Even after everything that had happened I still didn't know her real name, doubted I ever would, not that it mattered any longer. She, like everyone she was affiliated with, was a distant memory.

"No," I said, turning my head back and forth, "this one is a celebration."

Bending at the waist, I lifted the lid of the cooler and extracted a bottle of Johnnie Walker Blue from it, holding it up to him and giving it a shake. "This is the good stuff, isn't that what you told me?"

Cold Fire

His eyes crinkled around the edges as his lips curled up into a smile, seeing the bottle in my hands. "That it is."

I handed it across to him bottom first, the glass cool to the touch. "Please, do the honors."

Accepting it from me, he twisted the cap off and took a long pull, smacking his lips with pleasure. He held it out at arm's length and examined the label in admiration before taking another swig.

"Thank you," he said, finishing the drink with a deep breath. "Damn, that is smooth."

"Better than that herbal tea you were choking down last time I saw you?" I asked.

"Ha!" Hutch coughed out. "The reason I drink that shit is so I *can* have a pull on this every now and again."

I matched the laugh, a short, staccato sound, my gaze still aimed in the distance. "I bet. You know what I don't understand, though?"

"What's that?" Hutch asked, taking one more drink before passing the bottle my way.

"Why the fuck you had to give them my family."

All traces of mirth, or friendship, or even acquaintanceship, were gone from my voice. I turned so he could look me full in the face, stare at me as he attempted to answer the question.

Hutch's mouth dropped open as he shifted to look back at me, the color receding from his features. He kept the bottle extended my way a long moment before lowering it to the ground, the glass bottom sounding hollow against the floor board.

The fingers of my right hand curled around the grip of the derringer tucked away in the pocket of my coat, barrel aimed his way, poised to go off should he try anything. No indication of anything crossed my face as I sat and stared at him, waiting for him to try to formulate a response.

"The first time I arrived here, you weren't the least bit surprised to see me," I said. "At the time, I bought your little story about keeping tabs on us, but little things kept creeping in, things that taken together didn't seem to add up."

My voice remained even as I stared across at him, careful not to draw any attention from the neighbors.

"The first was this house, the sudden taste in expensive whisky, things consistent with a marked increase in liquid cash. You're a lifer, suckling at the government teat since you were twenty-five years old. You've done well, but not finer-things-in-life well."

Across from me Hutch's face took on an ashen appearance. A small sound slid from his throat, a tiny twitch flickered in the skin near his right eye, but otherwise he sat unmoving.

"The second was your decision to go to West Yellowstone to see Pavel. You weren't there to check on things for me, you were there to make sure whoever was there wasn't spilling their guts. Once you arrived and saw who it was, you knew things were safe, caught the very next plane down to California."

Anger, bitterness, resentment started to tickle the back of my throat as I spoke, almost daring my former mentor to do or say something that would allow me to squeeze the trigger.

"After that, things really started to pile up. How did Lita happen to know when Mateo left witness protection? Where to find me? That he might come looking for my help?"

Unable to respond, Hutch shifted his attention back to the street. He kept his hands folded, his fingers laced, hanging between his thighs, pointed down at the ground.

"Once we were on the ground, they were always a step ahead of us. They knew where Carlos was, about the safe house. Everything."

My voice rose just a little bit, my body's natural reaction to the anger, the feeling of betrayal, within me. My left hand squeezed into a ball so tight my fingers ached. The index finger on my right hand caressed the trigger of the derringer, wanting, needing, to pull it.

"You know what really did it for me, though?" I paused a moment to see if he would venture a response. When none came, I continued on. "When Diaz told me about you bringing in the Juarezes. Just months after my house was torched and I walked away, suddenly these guys come and turn themselves over to you? Cut a deal, go state's evidence?

"We had enough on the books to bury every last person in that network. Instead, you tossed Manny in minimum security, accepted a couple low-level pushers in exchange, and let the majority of the crew stay in place."

My gaze hardened, I stared at him a long moment before turning my head to face forward, looking down the length of the porch. "I admit it took a long time for me to put it together, but once I did, I felt like an idiot that it hadn't happened sooner.

"You were the only one with access to where Mateo and Carlos were being held in witness protection. You knew where the safe house was, because Manny gave it to you when he came in.

"That's why I knew not to bother going down to Baja. There was no way anything of value was going to be left behind. You had too much lead time to warn them. Instead, I went off script on you, showed up in Russia, caught them all with their pants down."

Again I paused, waiting to see if there was anything he wanted to say to refute me, any explanation he could offer for all of it. No words passed his lips, though, in denial or defense. Instead he sat staring out, his features pale, looking much, much older than the man who had walked up ten minutes before.

"You know the part I can't for the life of me figure out, though? The part that I've wrestled with every day since leaving Russia? Why the hell did you have to give them my family? Elizabeth loved you, Alice adored you. Was this house, those paintings on the wall in there, really worth all that?"

My voice was raised to just below a shout, my face strained as I tried to keep myself rooted in place.

The last five years had been time spent battling my own emotions. Most of that period was spent trying to suppress them, believing I had nowhere in particular to aim the rage, keeping it locked away for fear it might consume me.

Two weeks ago that changed. The blind evil that haunted my dreams became real; it developed a face, a name. I had someplace to aim my ire, and I did so. I let it drive me forward, doing the very things I had always feared I might, and feeling all the better for it.

Now that those things were out of the way, I had only one last emotion left to deal with. While the triggerman and the puppet master had both been cruel monsters so far from home, the lynchpin to all of it, the man that made it possible, was the one sitting right beside me. He had taken and abused my respect, the trust of my family, and betrayed them for his own personal gain.

If I had anything left inside me, any form of emotion after carrying so much rage for so long, I would have turned my disgust inward. I would have aimed it at myself, thinking that I allowed myself to be duped, that even after all this time I had come to him when things went awry, thinking he was on my side.

There was no point in that now, though. A heavy burden had finally been lifted from my shoulders, and there was no need to replace it with something that could never be cured.

Five more minutes and it would all be over. Nothing would ever bring back my family, but at least their memory could be at ease.

"*Was it worth the trouble?*" Hutch asked me, his voice thick, the words coming out distorted. I watched as his eyes glazed over and his tongue slid out over his bottom lip, saliva glistening off his chin.

I leaned forward and put the bottle of whisky back into the cooler, flipping it closed and standing. Hutch tried to track my movements as

I went, but his weakening form wouldn't allow it. Pale blue ebbed into his face, his body going rigid as he swayed in place, throat constricting, fighting for air.

"*What trouble?*" I asked, leaving him in place on the porch, the lights on the Charger flashing twice as I unlocked it and climbed inside.

Chapter Forty-Seven

A subset of the Department of Justice, the Drug Enforcement Administration was headquartered in a squat, boxy building along the Potomac River, its mailing address residing on Army Navy Drive in Arlington, Virginia. On the east wing of the sprawling Department of Justice campus, it had easy access to all DOJ buildings and infrastructure, along with clear sight lines to the Pentagon, the National Mall, even the White House if looking from a high enough floor.

From the outside, the building looked like a multilayered cake that had been cut in half. Each floor was drab brown with a thick white divider. Windows were used only sparingly, a stark contrast to the newer glass structures that seemed to dominate the city.

Despite the winter chill biting the air, the icy wind whipping up off the river flowing nearby, Richard Rogan, director of the administration, had called a ceremony for the front steps of the building. Over his solid black suit with red tie, he wore a wool overcoat that came almost to his feet, a red scarf around his neck, black leather gloves on his hands. His meticulously parted hair refused to move even as blustery winds pushed into his face, and the cold made his cheeks grow pink.

Well back from the proceedings, I leaned against a tree, watching the events unfold. My position wouldn't quite be described as hiding, though I had no interest in stepping forward to partake in the events either. There were too many people around from a past life, the director included, whom I had no intention of ever speaking to again. My presence was to make sure one last thing was taken care before I drifted back into a better version of the life I had a month before, one with far less baggage attached, no dark storm cloud following my every move.

Already dressed for Montana in jeans, a fleece vest, and a heavy canvas jacket, I kept one shoulder pressed into the tree, oblivious to the weather, even as it pushed my hair across my forehead. By the same time next week it would be thirty degrees colder where I was, if not more.

The wind whistling by served to make just enough noise to keep me from deciphering what the director was saying. His voice was muffled and distorted as it sounded out from the speakers set up to either side of him. With each puff of wind, the speakers swayed in place, threatening to keel over. Feedback kicked through the microphone and out over the crowd.

By the third such incident I could tell from his body language that he was ready to wrap things up; he stepped away from the podium and turned to his right, shaking the hands of X, then Diaz. Both accepted the handshakes with straight faces and terse nods, being forced to endure stolid words about jobs well done, making their country proud—the sorts of things all directors said when cameras were rolling.

The crowd clapped politely as he returned to the podium and made a few closing remarks. My hands never left the deep pockets of my coat as I watched and waited.

Three minutes later the ceremony was over. Rogan and the other higher-ups from the administration stayed just long enough for a couple of quick photos, awkward postures and forced smiles all around, before retreating inside. The crowd, consisting mostly of media personnel, remained just a moment longer with the stars of the hour before drifting away as well, heading toward the parking lot as their deadlines loomed.

I watched as the janitorial staff went to work on the setup, breaking down chairs and clearing away the speakers. With collars flipped up and shoulders hunched against the wind, they worked quietly and efficiently, not once paying any attention to the solitary person who came down the front steps and made her way to me.

Diaz looked a little more tired than the last time I had seen her. The cold had sapped most of the color from her face, belying dark circles under each eye. Her mane of curls was pulled back in a harsh ponytail, and her face was void of makeup.

If not for the smile on her face, she would have looked absolutely miserable.

"Weren't even going to say hi?" she asked as she approached, hands buried halfway up her forearms into the pockets of her heavy black overcoat, her body drawn in on itself in an attempt to keep warm.

A wry smile crossed my lips as I shook my head and said, "Didn't want to interrupt you during your big day. Figured you'd get a second for little old me at some point."

"Little old you," she repeated, shaking her head. She turned her body sideways so the wind was at her back and stamped her feet, rocking back and forth. "Could have at least clapped, you know."

A quick, sharp laugh passed over my lips, a bit of white extending in front of me. "I'm here, aren't I?"

"That you are," Diaz said, raising her eyebrows and nodding. "Something tells me you won't be this time tomorrow when they add Hutch's name to the Wall of Honor in there."

The Wall of Honor, an award bestowed on all agents who died in the line of duty, a list now over thirty people in length. The last thing I wanted when leaving his house was to make a martyr of the man. He had tainted his own legacy beyond even being included as a footnote in the DEA history.

How anybody could have found him hunched over in a chair on his front porch and thought to construe that as death in the line of duty was beyond me.

I guess that was the kind of perk that came with being a ranking official.

"Can't," I said, opting to comment as little as possible on the topic. There was a tiny shred of me that figured Diaz already knew what had transpired, both in the desert and here in D.C. An even larger shred told me she would never act on either. "Need to get on the road, get things ready for winter."

"Ah, yes," Diaz said, giving me a knowing look that meant both she recognized me ducking the topic and would conspire with my return-to-Montana narrative. "The cabin in the woods, back to roughing it, all that."

Again the corners of my mouth curled up. Once upon a time, she would have made for a great partner. She had a quiet confidence and a lack of bullshit that I could have worked with for sure. "Yeah, all that."

"*The Rocky Mountains is the marrow of the world.*"

A deep smirk pushed out of my nose, tilting my head backward. "You finally watched the movie."

"I did," she confirmed. "You're no Robert Redford, but I could see the resemblance, I guess."

My lips widened even farther, my teeth peeking out through the smile. It was the same line my mother had used on me a hundred times before, every time my father alluded to the origin of my name.

"How about you? What's next?"

Turning at the hip, Diaz motioned toward the headquarters, extending an elbow without removing her hand from its pocket. "They offered us both positions here. Supervisory roles, promise of fast tracks to the top. They didn't say as much, but I think the idea of a black guy and a Hispanic woman practically had the PR people salivating."

Another low chuckle slid out from me, nodding in agreement. I would have never thought to frame it quite that way, but I couldn't disagree with her, either. "Congratulations."

"Naw," she replied, shaking her head, drawing the word out several seconds long. "This place isn't for me. I gave them a list of things I needed back in Cali, told them where to send my raise."

"I'll be damned," I said, though her words didn't surprise me. Once, right before moving to California, I too had been offered a position in D.C. Having gone to undergrad nearby I had no problem with the city, but the thought of working in that bastion of bureaucracy was enough to make my skin crawl. "X?"

"Jumped at it," Diaz said. "Asked me to say thank you if I saw you and to let you know you're more than even. Said he'd be in touch once you got settled."

That, too, wasn't a surprise. If somebody were to ever sit down and analyze our trade, I'm sure a winner could be determined, though neither one of us ever would. He went out on a limb for me in a time of need; I made sure he was rewarded for his efforts. Had the situation been flipped, I'd like to think it would have still played out the same way.

I slid my gaze from the building to Diaz. Her face was taking on a ghostly pallor. "So back to the desert for you," I said.

"Back to the desert," she said, "where it's not so damn cold."

This time I managed to bite back a laugh, shaking my head. "I would say you're welcome to visit in Montana at any time, but if you think *this* is cold . . ."

She smiled without showing her teeth, her lips pulled into a tight line. "Just the same as I would say you're welcome back in California at any time. I can always find room for a good consultant."

I matched the thin smile, both of us acknowledging the offers without comment. At some point, perhaps, one of us would pick up the phone and make good on them. Perhaps not.

With a tiny nod I moved forward and wrapped one arm around her shoulders, pulling her close, her cold cheek pressed against mine. Her hands slid around my back and she returned the embrace a long moment before releasing, both of us taking a step back.

"Thank you," I said. There was so much more I could have added, defining every last thing I was thankful for, from her offer to all she had done in the preceding weeks. I didn't, though, knowing, fearing, I would leave something out, and the situation deserved better.

"Thank you," she echoed, following my lead, making no attempt to define it.

One step at a time we drifted away from each other until eventually we both turned, putting our backs to one another, already moving on toward our next destinations.

The sun was high in the sky, a golden orb sitting directly overhead and casting a bright yellow glow over everything it touched. The grass alongside the road seemed radiant, bathed in its hue; the river in the distance reflected it as it danced along the rocks beneath it. After weeks in the desert, twenty long days of staring at nothing but varying shades of sand, the entire world seemed amplified, like a movie with just the right amount of color saturation.

The skin of my forearms was deep chestnut brown as I draped them over the steering wheel. The hairs along them were sun-bleached blond, standing in stark contrast to the skin beneath.

My truck rumbled over the highway as I drove along, leaning forward, willing us to go faster, for my destination to somehow move itself closer. On the seat beside me sat my discarded shirt and tie, a blue blazer long since stripped off and stuffed in my duffel, which was stowed in the truck bed. Atop the rumpled pile of clothes beside me was my faded holster and service weapon, the leather sweat-stained and cracking, beginning to give off a pungent scent.

Wearing only a tank top and slacks, I let the warm southern California air wash over me, cocoon around me. It felt pleasant without being too hot. It swirled inside the cab of the truck, drowning out the radio, filling my senses. On it danced the scents of jasmine and lavender, as the spring rains awakened the desert community and brought out the foliage in full force.

Two miles west of the turnoff for Tecate I hooked a right, turning south onto an unmarked road, the narrow lane wide enough for just a single car at a time. Wild grasses and shrubs hugged the drive tightly on either side, their bright green standing in contrast to the gray asphalt, their tops swaying in the breeze. My tires found the grooves worn into the roadway by years of use, the engine pushing a little harder than necessary, the road stretched out in a straight line in front of me.

The Gonzalez farm slid past on my left, a series of low-slung buildings all standing quietly, sun reflecting off their roofs. A pair of thick and waddling horses grazed in the paddock out front, their tails swatting flies in a constant circular motion. Neither one looked up as I passed.

A mile farther down the Rhodes spread came into view, a central farmhouse with white construction and a red roof standing two stories high. The smell of hay and livestock passed over my nostrils as I drove by. I glanced over at the pristinely kept front lawn, the fountain beside the driveway that spouted water in a wide fan almost ten feet high.

Nervousness, excitement, apprehension welled in the pit of my stomach as I crested a hill and my final stop came into view.

Tucked away in the corner of a small valley, a two-story farmhouse sat warm and inviting, its light exterior standing out against the dark green background. Behind it flowed an offshoot of the Tecate River, a lazy, rambling finger that framed the house on two sides, providing all the water that was needed, keeping things cool in the summer.

My heart hammered away in my chest as I pulled off to the left without bothering to use the blinker. The only other car that ever ventured this far down was already sitting beside the house. Bits of gravel kicked up from my tires, pinging against the undercarriage of the truck. A plume of dust rose behind me as I slid to a stop and stepped out.

The moment my boots touched the ground, the front door of the house swung open, long and easy, its springs groaning as it traveled in a complete half arc and reached the wall behind it. The familiar clomping of boots on hardwood rang out, one at a time, in no particular hurry, as my wife stepped out onto the porch.

Her hand-stitched brown leather boots stopped midcalf, giving way to toned legs and a yellow sundress; its hem, starting mid-thigh, was ruffled a bit by the breeze. Her honey-blond hair swung down around her shoulders, framing a heart-shaped face with clear blue eyes and high cheekbones.

She stopped on the edge of the porch, one hand resting on the railing, her right foot crossed over her left. A mischievous smile flirted with her lips as she stared down at me, a sparkling light flashed from her eyes.

Given the time of day, I knew Alice was down for her nap, tucked away upstairs, curled up with her favorite stuffed bunny. In an hour or two I would take the stairs three at a time to wake her, join her in bed, and demand to know every last detail since I'd left.

For the time being though, it was just me and Elizabeth.

The grass of the front lawn was soft underfoot as I walked across it and stopped just short of the front steps, staring up at her. I'd pictured her in my mind every moment since I'd been gone, but it was nothing compared with seeing her in the flesh, an expectant look on her face, feeling the air crackle between us.

"Damn, it's good to see you," I whispered, letting her hear every bit of feeling I had for her, cramming it all into just six words.

She stared down at me a long time before tilting her head to the side, her hair drifting out across the exposed skin of her upper arm. "What took you so long?"

There was no good way to answer that question, no way for me to ever explain all that had transpired since we last saw each other, so I didn't even try.

"Just got held up for a while, had to go hunt some Krokodils."

"Did you get them?" she asked, a look of complete understanding on her face.

"Yeah," I whispered, adding a small nod for emphasis.

"Yeah," she repeated, extending a hand out toward me.

One step at a time I rose to the porch and accepted her hand, her soft skin sliding against my palm, our fingers intertwining. Without a word we passed together through the front door of the house, the world around us succumbing to darkness.

The sweet, sweet darkness of peaceful slumber.

ABOUT THE AUTHOR

Dustin Stevens is the author of *The Zoo Crew* series, *Quarterback, Be My Eyes, Scars and Stars, Just a Game, 21 Hours, Liberation Day,* and *Catastrophic.* He is also the author of several short stories appearing in various magazines and anthologies, and is an award-winning screenwriter.

He currently resides in Honolulu, Hawaii.

Made in the USA
Middletown, DE
10 July 2022

68964425R00189